MAKE ME LOSE

Bayshore #1

Ember Leigh

Published by Ember Leigh, 2019

EmberLeighAuthor@gmail.com

Cover art: Amanda Walker PA & Designs

Editing: Elisabeth R. Nelson

Proofreading: Victoria Miller

Hear the playlist: http://bit.ly/MakeMeLosePlaylist

MAKE ME LOSE

ABOUT 'MAKE ME LOSE'

Grayson Daly and I aren't just rivals. We're enemies.

Born minutes apart on the same day in the same hospital, our parents thought this meant we were somehow destined to be together. We knew we were just destined to *beat* each other.

Competition boiled over until junior year, when the cold war turned into an unexpected peace offering. Maybe my hormones allowed me to notice his broad shoulders, stormy gray-blue eyes, and soccer star's chiseled frame. But after I fell for him...he stomped all over my heart.

Ten years later, I'm at the top of the realty game in Bayshore and Grayson is just a distant memory. Until he shows up from NYC, his ego bigger than a skyscraper, and asks me to sell the house he recently inherited.

It's easy to say no. Even though I want to climb him like the jungle gyms we used to dangle from in strong arm battles.

But I forgot that Gray doesn't take no for an answer. And that he isn't content unless he's defeating me.

He butts into my evenings on the boat. Ropes me into water skiing battles. Even shows up at the bar and creates a scene when I'm scouting a date to the upcoming Bicentennial Ball.

It's almost like he's gunning to win *me*.

But if he wins, that means I lose.

And I'm not ready to cede victory just yet.

DEDICATION

This book is dedicated to the FunCoast and all the wild and wonderful summers spent on the Lake Erie shores.

CHAPTER ONE

HAZEL

"All I'm saying is, you can't take your dad."

It's a shame my best friend, London, can't see me rolling my eyes. She would have laughed so hard she shot her beverage of choice out of her nose. But truth is, I'm alone in my spacious lakefront office. It's ten a.m. I've finished my coffee and am already itching for another. And only I can feel how hard my eyeballs are shooting into the backs of their sockets.

"Yeah. Got it. And you know what?" I counter, reaching for my empty coffee mug. The emptiness I find is depressing, but not depressing enough to make another trip to the cute coffee shop around the corner, The Daily Grind. "I'm not taking my father to the Bicentennial Ball. Never planned on it."

London is an asshole. But I love her, so I keep her around. Also, she knows me better than anyone on Earth. We went to high school together here in Bayshore, but that's not where we really connected. The magic for us happened in college, when we went to the Ohio

State University. Back before we knew what the hell we were doing. Back before we knew how fucking awesome we'd turn out.

Awesome and chronically single.

"Hazel, I know you love your dad," London says. "I love your dad. But you need to find a date. A real date. And he needs to be hot. Like, *your level* hot."

I heave a sigh, as though it will help anything. London is making the trip home for the Bicentennial Ball and renting a room at the boutique hotel a few blocks from my office because she fully plans on hooking up with some overlooked hottie from our collective past.

Me, on the other hand? I live in Bayshore permanently. Which means I have my own comfy king bed on my own quiet, tree-lined street, and a very intimate knowledge of how many un-overlooked hotties remain here. And the numbers are depressing.

Like, *Tinder has stopped loading any matches*-style depressing.

"I think you forget what our hometown is like," I remind her, tapping a pen against various points of the edge of my desk. My gaze drifts to the windows lining the northern wall of the office. Briggs Bay glitters a tealish-blue a block away. A motorboat cuts through the water, leaving a frothy, white-topped wake in its path. Even though I'm in air-conditioned comfort, I can feel the humid bite in the late-morning air simply from staring at the lake.

It's a feeling I've come to love.

Like practically everything about Bayshore. Except for its startling lack of single men my age, that is.

"Oh, no," she says ruefully. "I remember." She doesn't come back much, like a lot of our graduating class. The ones who stayed, I see regularly, given the fact that damn near everyone in this county uses me for their real estate needs. That means I've got my thumb on the pulse of who's who, who's married, and who's gone downhill in Bayshore.

And now that my graduating class is nearing the end of our twenties, the number of people who didn't casually go downhill but slid there on a super-greased sled would surprise you.

"What about the Daly brothers?" London asks, which forces another sigh from my lips.

Of course. The Daly brothers. The perpetually handsome bachelors who used to strut around this town like a flock of virile geese: loud in how handsome they all are, slightly dangerous in that they will probably come chasing you down during a quiet lunch at the park and break your heart. Not that geese regularly break hearts, but that's beside the point.

I'm probably bitter. Still. It's only been ten years, but part of me hasn't quite forgiven Grayson Daly for his virile-goose antics. Aside from Grayson, I love the Daly family. I grew up with those guys. And despite the fact that one of their boys came out an asshole, I really do love Grayson's mom. It's not their fault that Gray is an arrogant jerk. Actually, scratch that—their intense, ladder-climbing dad probably had something to do with Grayson turning out like he did. They got four other good boys, so statistically, one of them had to go bad.

"Two of them live out of state," I said, frowning as I attempted to reengage with my computer. A few people wander past my floor-to-ceiling windows overlooking Water Street. They're holding maps, marking them as some of the thousands of tourists who populate this town in high season. "Dominic lives in the Cleveland area, I think. And the youngest two are still around. I see Maverick from time to time. He's usually high."

London snorted. "Well, those two are a little young for my tastes."

My frown deepens. I don't like talking about tastes when it comes to the Daly brothers. For a brief, psychotic period of my life, I was in love with Grayson Daly. And then he shit all over my trust. We graduated, and after a few other character shaping activities, here I am. The most successful real estate agent for my age in the entire state of Ohio, dressed to kill on the daily.

"I'll go on Craigslist," I say. "I'll put up an ad. Seeking Super-Hot Date for two-hundredth Birthday of Bayshore. Must be willing to pose for endless pictures and buy all my champagne and appear on my Instagram as a doting partner."

"There we go," London encourages.

"Great. You know, you just agreed with my idea to solicit a date on Craigslist. This means I've hit rock bottom." I'm grinning as I give her shit. My ten-minute goof-off window is ending. These scheduled breaks to call friends and family keep me alive in my fast-paced realty business. I work damn near eighty hours a week most weeks. I love my job, though, what I've created. It's not a burden. It's my dream life. Living in my hometown, my cozy house two blocks from Briggs Bay and, a little further, the expansive, choppy waters of Lake Erie.

"I wouldn't call your dating life *rock bottom*," London says. "More like...pitiful."

I snort. Even better. But she's not wrong. The little bells on the front door of my office jingle, signaling a newcomer. I've had my four-inch glossy black heels propped on the edge of my desk, a form-fitting skirt hiking up a little too far for professional comfort. I sit up straight, glancing at the new arrival.

He's gotta be about six foot two. Broad shoulders, a build that falls somewhere between football and soccer star. Stormy blue eyes that cut right through me from across the gallery.

My throat immediately seizes. I jerk my gaze away, lest this man realize that I know who he is.

The man who we were talking about only moments before. As though this conversation had summoned him from the pits of Hell.

Grayson Freakin' Daly.

"You there?" London asks.

I force my voice to sound normal. I keep my gaze on my computer, as though I'm the busiest, most important, most unaffected person in the world at this moment. "I really appreciate your call. I think that our collaboration will be extremely lucrative. Thank you, George Clooney, for your interest in Hazel Homes." I slam the phone down on the receiver, my heart pounding.

That's the other thing about Grayson.

He and I, we've had this killer competitive streak since the day we were born.

And apparently, that was summoned from the pits of Hell along with Grayson.

I swing my gaze his way, batting my eyes, popping on the brightest smile I can muster. "Hello there! How can I help you?" My heart is pounding so quickly I might pass out. I have no idea how to handle this. All I know is that my old responses are popping out of the deepest depths of my being like no time has passed at all. The responses that push me to win, to beat Grayson, to be better than he is.

And apparently, the best path forward is acting like I've never seen this handsome devil before.

Grayson cocks a smirk, the type that takes me right back to that psychotic period when I fell in love with him for three months. Except now he's older, more refined. He's got on a medium-gray suit that sits halfway between Billionaire Chic and Vogue model. Alligator shoes that come to a point. He stuffs his hands in his pockets as he begins an intolerable saunter toward me.

"You're really going to act like you don't know who I am?"

The gruff bass of his voice sends heat straight to my pussy. I blink demurely for a few moments, feigning my best confused face. I squint at him. I let it draw out. Maybe too long.

"Hazel," he says. "Cut the crap."

His commanding tone irritates me so much that I do exactly as he says. I set my lips in a thin line. "Oh, jeez. Yes, Grayson Daly. It can only be you." I avoid his gaze as I set to work reorganizing my desk. Anything to avoid looking at his impossibly handsome frame, his dark hair clipped short on the sides but longer on top, allowing one delectable finger wave to emerge. "Sorry, I didn't recognize you." I can't help myself. The words fly out. "You got old."

He cocks his head to the side, an expression like *oh, come on* creasing his face. "I'm ten minutes older than you, so I assume you feel the same way about yourself."

Ugh. He always threw that *ten minutes older than you* crap in my face growing up. Like it allowed him to ultimately win. Well not anymore. I'm taking my ten extra minutes of youthfulness and running with it.

"I'm as perky and bright as they come," I say, tossing him a plasticized smile. "A veritable fountain of youth." As I face him down, I try to see myself in my mind's eye. Hoping my fire-engine red lipstick isn't smeared. It never is, but on the day that Grayson shows up, you can never be too sure. I thank the gods above that I got my eyebrows done earlier this week. I would have prepped more, had I known Grayson was going to saunter into my office as if he was auditioning for the role of Unaffected Businessman. But I'll have to work with what I've got. "Now, how may I help you, sir?"

An annoyed burst of air rushes past his lips. Treating him like I don't know him, don't care about him—this is my new plan of attack.

"Thought you might be able to help me sell a house." He works his jaw back and forth as his gaze skates around my office. The walls are bright white with gothic black frames dotting the feature wall where my awards, certificates and licenses are displayed. I'm not one for bright colors. Give me all the shades of black, purple, and gray, and I'm a happy camper. I would live inside houndstooth if I could.

"I won't be needing it, since you couldn't pay me a million dollars to live in Bayshore."

I grit my teeth. I know what *his* attack plan is now. And it's high-grade annoying.

"Ah. That's right. Who would want to live in the Midwest's number one beach town? Quality of life must be something that doesn't appeal to you," I shoot back, starting to write an e-mail. Just for something to occupy my hands. There's nothing in the *To* field. I'm typing gibberish.

"Populations above one hundred thousand appeal to me," Grayson says, pulling out the armchair facing my desk. He clears his throat, then makes a big display of sitting down. A waft of his cologne reaches me. It's husky and earthy and probably expensive as hell. Like Gucci meets lumberjack. "Broadway appeals to me. Diverse restaurants appeal to me. More than one movie theater appeals to me."

He must live in a big city. Probably New York. But that's fine. He doesn't know that people are leaving big cities in droves to come to places like Bayshore. He doesn't know how much I'm cleaning up on the recent shift to the smaller towns, smaller lives movement.

"Arrogance has always appealed to you as well," I say, smiling his way without looking at him. "It's actually one of your strongest suits." The word makes me glance at the suit he's wearing. Big mistake. The e-mail I'm writing now says "skkskkkksksskk sk fuck you."

He flashes a humorless smile. His knee is bouncing. "So will you sell this house for me or not?"

"No."

"My grandmother passed away," he said, the edge going out of his voice. His gaze moves to the floor. *Shit.* Didn't see that one coming. "This was her house."

"Is that supposed to change my mind?"

"Sort of."

Silence thuds between us, and I hazard another glance at him. Those stormy eyes of his haven't changed, not even a little bit. His nearly black brows are drawn together. Like he's pleading silently. Or begging. Not that Grayson would ever beg.

Still, the quiet between us dissolves some of my defenses. Grayson is a fox, more than when we were in high school and he ended up being voted the prom king. He's got that look about him that makes women wilt with wanting him. And hell, I'm the same way. Even though I hate him. If he were one-fifth less of an asshole, I'd be all over him.

And if I didn't care about upholding this decades-long competition, I'd abandon my morals and jump his bones now.

But no. I've got something to prove.

"I'm sorry for your loss. Why are you selling the house?" I sniff. I'm trying to walk that fine line between bitchy and consoling. His grandmother did nothing wrong. I knew her—she'd been a lovely lady. Grayson's mom herself had come to tell me the news a few days ago, which signaled the start of the pit in my stomach, just *knowing* that Gray might be returning to Bayshore.

Even though part of me was certain—or perhaps simply hopeful—that he wouldn't come back for his grandmother's funeral.

Looks like I was wrong.

"I already told you. Nobody could pay me enough money to stay in this sluggish, uninteresting town." The evil glint returns. I'm done being soft with him.

"Our sluggish, uninteresting populace can't wait to be rid of you," I assure him. "And you're going to need to find somebody else to sell your house. Somehow, with the approximately three hundred people that you think live here, I've managed to make millions." It's a slight exaggeration. I've *grossed* millions. He doesn't need to know that. "Which means I don't need your money. Have a good day."

He doesn't move, though I think I catch a trace of panic in him. Or maybe I want it to be that way.

"You're the only realtor in town," Gray counters.

"Not true. There's a very capable though vastly underutilized real estate agency down the street," I remind him. It's Cabanas Real Estate, run by the Cabana family. They're nice people, but I already know why Grayson can't go there. The Dalys and the Cabanas have been at each other's throats for nigh on twenty-five years. What started as boat-dock neighbor friendliness turned into a cheating scandal turned into active resentment. There's a *Romeo and Juliet*-style feud simmering between these families. God help any Daly son that goes after a Cabana girl.

"Hazel," he says, as though reminding me of my name will help his case. I send him a pretty smile instead. "Come on."

"Not sure what you want me to do. All clients are at my discretion." I lean forward, grabbing my elbows, pushing up my already-pushed-up breasts. Just to give him a luscious glimpse of cleavage. I don't know if he ever thinks about me anymore or if he's wondered what I became since he jilted me right before senior prom.

But in case he has thought about me, in case he's ever wondered what became of nerdy little Hazel, the girl he set out to make miserable, to beat in every way possible?

Well, here's his answer.

Hazel wins.

CHAPTER TWO

GRAYSON

It would be wrong to say I've hated Bayshore my entire life.

Rather, my disdain for my hometown was a slowly simmering stew. It started with a few inputs—long, boring winters, frustration as a teen with the lack of things to do—and then once I hit my late teens, it thickened into something more. A true, richly layered distaste.

But you know what *has* lasted my entire life?

Competition with Hazel.

I storm out of her office, opening the door as forcefully as I can. The bells jingle wildly, like Santa's sleigh crashing into a house, and I don't spare another glance as I head for my car. I should have known better than to even try with that woman. I'd done it as a favor to my mother, who just lost *her* mother—my grandmother, sweet little Grammy Ethel. I should be doing anything I can for my mom right now.

And I tried. Even agreeing to set foot in Hazel Homes took a lot of internal pep-talking. Hazel and I don't have the best history. Its equal parts idyllic childhood mixed with the fiercest brand of competition most people have never heard of. The second she opened her mouth, I knew she was back to her old ways. Trying to *win* against me.

It's not our fault, really. We had the bad luck of being born on the same day, so all of our newborn pictures have each other in them. As a result, people thought this meant we'd get married, which the general populace of Bayshore made sure to tell us to our faces all the damn time.

But Hazel and I have something you might call a problem with authority. One thing in common, at least. So all of the encouragement to be together backfired and bred something entirely different. Entirely *opposite,* actually.

I thought ten years apart might have allowed things to cool.

But with Hazel, there's no cooling allowed. She kicks me right back up to a boil with one glance.

In every way possible.

I yank open my car door and slump inside, heaving a sigh. I take a moment in the cool, leather-scented air to remember who the fuck I am and what this is all about. I can't get Hazel's heels out of my head. The image of her feet propped on her desk, cream silk legs on display, vixen red lips parting as she laid eyes on me...fuck. Made me want to rip those heels off her and toss them across the room. Tell her we could spend some time catching up on the past ten years.

My cock is throbbing. Not a good sign. I haven't gotten laid in a long time, so it's understandable. It's a totally normal reaction to seeing an attractive woman. My eyes can't be blamed for still finding Hazel attractive and sending the message to my dick that the collective unit of Grayson would like to bang her. It doesn't mean anything. It's just science.

I work my jaw back and forth as I dig my phone out of my pocket. I brush my cock. Now I'm fully hard. Thinking about Hazel is not a good plan. I would fuck her brains out if she'd let me, I'll be honest. The nerdy Hazel I fell for in high school has turned into a woman I wasn't prepared to behold today. I didn't know what to expect.

My mom warned me she'd blossomed, but she'd failed to mention that she'd turned into a rose bush. Gorgeous, sweetly scented, bursting with beauty, and prickly as fuck. I'm probably bleeding somewhere right now.

"Mom?" I can't keep the irritation out of my voice once she picks up. "Just stopped in to see Hazel."

"How did it go? What does she think of the house?"

I pinch my eyes shut. I've been in town for less than twenty-four hours. There are a helluva lot of details to see to when someone passes. "Uh, didn't go too well. She flat out refused to sell the house for me. Looks like I'm going to have to go elsewhere."

My mom tuts, and then comes a long, murmuring train of, "Ohh no, no, no. That won't do."

"Sorry, Mom." I look out the windshield at the long shoreline road stretching ahead of me. Summer in Bayshore is almost in full swing, but some lilac bushes lining the road still have their blooms. This is the best time of year to be here. Even in my quest to move on, move out, and make all the money in the world, I never could deny how magical Bayshore was in the summer. "I'll sell it on my own or something. I'll figure it out."

"Honey, you will have Hazel sell that house," my mom says, her voice oddly stern. "Make no bones about it."

"Make no—" I stop myself, drawing a slow breath. "Mom. She said no. It's her discretion. She said it herself."

"Go back there and talk to her."

"She'll probably stab me in the eye with her evil heels," I say. Except the heels aren't evil. The heels are perfectly fine. *Too* fine.

"It's a risk you need to take," Mom says. "The alternatives are not alternatives." The cryptic statement makes sense to me. The other main agency in town is owned by the Cabana family, and they're still on Mom and Dad's shit list from something that happened in the 80s.

I start my car, mulling over my options. I'm quiet so long my mom snaps, "Gray? Do you hear me?"

I grit my teeth. And like I always do when backed into a corner by my loyalty and devotion, I murmur, "Yes, Mother."

"Let's go see the house now. I'll meet you there."

Her idea leaves no room for question. She's been wanting to go through the house with me. My newest possession. It's weird, to think that now I suddenly own property in Bayshore. It's a little absurd, really. If it weren't for Mom and Dad, I'd never come around here. As it is, I barely do. There are a few reasons why. But mostly, it's a place I've left in the dust. And in life, there's no time for going backward or getting smaller. There's only room for better. For higher. For more.

Bayshore just isn't big enough for my ambitions.

My mind wanders to Hazel as I drive past the boat basin. The sky is that color of blue that seems cartoonish. Like the only source was from an artist's palate. A few sailboats are slipping out of the docks, and the lake looks calm, almost serene.

The early summer breeze filling my car is intoxicating. It reminds me of so many things. Lazy mornings at my grandma's house, playing hide and seek with my brothers while she hung laundry in the backyard. It reminds me of staring out at the brilliant day while Mrs. Larchmere finished up her lecture on Chaucer in English class junior year.

It reminds me of that blissful period when Hazel and I called a truce at the end of junior year. How we'd play fierce bouts of tennis, pushing each other hard, only to dissolve into secretive, juicy make out sessions in the corner of the court.

I push the nostalgia away once I get to my grandma's old house. Clarity and compartmentalization are my friend now. I've got a lot of emotions to beat back, and hell if I'm going to let sentimentality win so early in my visit home.

My mom is grinning at me as I pull into the driveway, wearing cat eye sunglasses with a light shawl billowing out behind her as she holds out her arms before I've parked the car. Like she's already hugging me in her mind. I can't help but smile as I get out of the car and wrap her in a big hug.

"You just saw me this morning," I remind her.

"I know, honey," she murmurs, patting my back. "I know."

I don't come around enough. I get it. We both look at grandma's old house. She and Grandpa originally lived in Maine, then moved this way because of Grandpa's job with the railroad. They'd started in this little house, then bought a bigger, second one for their growing family. And honestly, I don't get why Grammy left me the most sentimental part of her history. The place where it all started.

"I haven't been here in *years*," I mutter, stuffing my hands in my pockets. Mom leads the way up to the front door over the small, uneven, brick path. Untended daisies grow in thick clusters along the side. Bushes are overgrown onto the path and look better fit for the outside of a haunted house. The place needs a lot of work, but despite the hint of abandonment, it's really cute.

Yet all I can think of is how a place like this would fetch *millions* in the New York City market. If I could somehow teleport this property to Brooklyn or the Rockaways and sell in *that* market, hell, I'd be well on my way to investing myself toward billionaire status. There's a little start-up I'm ready to invest in. A social media site that looks promising, like Facebook without all the privacy issues and guilt. I want to be an early investor, because I've made it my mission to be the richest Daly by age thirty. And this investment *will* pay off.

I'm just a little short on the initial money. And the funds from selling this house will go directly to that start-up.

Floorboards creak as we start a slow, nostalgic stroll through the house. There's no furniture, and most everything is dusty. It smells like some combination of childhood and neglect inside, pure moth balls and sunbaked wood. Mom alternates between thoughtful sighs and clucking her tongue. The walk down memory lane is noisy.

"It still looks great," I say once we've made it to the master bedroom upstairs. It's about a thousand square feet, which to me, after a decade in NYC, feels like a mansion. I peer out the bay window, which overlooks the tiny front yard and the narrow street leading toward the water. The bay sparkles teal and choppy; my skin itches wanting to head to the beach. Aside from all the sad stuff coming up, I need to treat this visit like a vacation. Which means getting in the water, ASAP.

"You should really consider keeping it," Mom says, her gaze drifting out toward the bay. You can barely see the wall of rocks separating the bay from where it opens into Lake Erie. Head north on the water, and you'll make it to Canada. As a young boy, I used to think it was close enough to swim to. My older brother, Dominic, dared me to try once, and I did. I about died that day, and he only laughed as I went to the ER. One of many reasons we've barely spoken throughout the years.

Once we hit high school and started thinking about the future, Dom turned into a mega dick. Even worse than when we were younger. And sure, a lot of it had to do with Dad. The way he always pushed us to aim high bred a fierce competition between us all, but worst of all between Connor, Dom, and me.

And that just widened the chasm between me and my brothers. Made me even more determined to fly the coop and show Dom and

Connor that I could be the best. Show Dad that I wouldn't just be successful, I'd be *more* successful than he was as the CEO of the Bayshore Hospital. Which meant that New York was the only fit place for me, and six was the minimum number of zeroes I planned to have trailing my bank account by age thirty.

"I have no reason to keep it." I scan the neighbors' houses from this vantage point, what I can see of them through the trees, at least. Most of the houses in this neighborhood were built in the 1930s, but the neighborhood has since become a vacation-rental hot spot. The bay sits a block away. The sandy beach is a two-minute walk from me right now. It's impossible to find a better place in Ohio.

"You have plenty of reasons to," Mom insists, folding her arms. Here we go. "First of all, it would be nice to see you more than once every other year."

"We video chat all the time."

"And your brothers? Do any of you realize anymore that you have siblings?"

I stay silent, searching the neighborhood for something of interest to change the subject. I don't need to confirm what she already knows—that I barely talk to most of my brothers. I'm ashamed of it, though I don't really know why. Dom and I never got along, so not talking to him isn't a big deal. Connor and I text a lot, and we've met up a couple times on work trips. But the others?

My gaze is snagged by a lady in a black pencil skirt and high heels. Gleaming, chestnut brown hair is pulled back into a low bun. My gut cinches.

"Oh, hell," I mutter, leaning forward to confirm. It's Hazel. It *has* to be Hazel. I'd recognize those creamy calves from any distance. I'm momentarily mesmerized by the sashaying of her ass.

"Look! It's Hazel." Mom sounds way too pleased.

"Yeah. What's she doing here?"

"She's on her break." Mom sends me an annoying grin. "She drives home, has lunch, and then walks the block every day on her break."

"In those heels?" I ask, which was dumb. My gaze goes straight to them. I scowl, as though this might help convince my heart rate to resume a normal speed.

"Our Hazel is the star of the neighborhood." Mom's voice is wispy now, like Hazel has gone on to Hollywood, or perhaps the Great Beyond. "The star of Bayshore, actually."

"Why? All she does is sell houses." I can't look away from her retreating figure. She hangs a right onto the road hugging the shore, and in just a few seconds I lose sight of her. I blink a few times. The fog lifts. I can think again. "It's not that difficult. I could go get my realtor's license tomorrow and do the same thing. And probably sell more than she does."

My mom laughs and shakes her head.

"I'm serious," I insist.

"Then do it!" Mom counters. "It'll keep you around here."

I grunt, turning away from the window. "I can't. It would be too easy."

"Always competing," Mom says quietly. And she's not wrong. "Though maybe the two of you at each other's throats your entire lives made you who you are today. You, my big city boy, and Hazel, the small-town queen."

"If Hazel gets the title of queen, then I should be the king."

"You'd have to marry her to get that title," Mom says, squeezing my arm.

I let out a sarcastic, *"Ha ha."* Marriage is something I'd like to dabble in someday, but not now, and *never* with someone like Hazel. No matter how perky those ass cheeks are, no matter how bad I want to run my fingertips up the porcelain arc of her calves, Hazel is out of the question.

"She would sooner spear me with her ten-inch heel than let me get down on one knee in front of her." Again, very dumb. More thoughts about those heels. But I barrel on. "I don't know what it is about this city that thinks Hazel and I are long-lost soul mates, but I'm pretty sure we've been proving to you all for approximately twenty-eight years how wrong you all are."

Mom smiles wistfully, wandering toward the hallway, totally ignoring me. "Did you see the billboard on your way into town? On Route 2?"

I follow her out of the master bedroom. Our footsteps thud down the stairs as I try to place what she's talking about. "There's about three hundred billboards within city limits, Mom."

"*Hazel's* billboard," she says, and then my gut cinches and I remember. *Fuck.* Yeah, I did see it. Saw it a little too well. Hazel's trademark figure, leaning ass-to-siding against a cute little cottage. In big bold letters, the ad says, "Ask Hazel." That's it. Sexy woman hinting at real estate. I didn't put two and two together until I saw her in her office earlier.

The woman's branding game is fire. And I sorta love it.

"Yep," I admit glumly. *Ask Hazel.* Of course she was the number one real estate agent in the area. Bachelors probably clamored to sell houses they didn't own. Putting Dad's old house up for sale while he was taking a shower. Convincing Uncle Jack to go halfsies on selling a duplex only to buy it right back. I could see men doing crazy things for a chance to be near that barbed-wire bombshell. "Didn't really stand out to me. Was kind of...cryptic, honestly."

"Don't be a smart-ass," Mom warns.

"I'm not being a smart-ass," I lie. "It was confusing. 'Ask Hazel.' About what? About how much my vacation rental is going to languish in the long Ohio winter? About what a fat cut she's taking of my house sale simply because she knows how to wear red lipstick?"

Mom sighs, long and drawn out.

"You're being a little mean," Mom says gently, patting my back as we wind through the 70s-styled kitchen. Golden rod, burnt orange, and checkered floors galore. It needs a facelift badly. Hopefully it won't hurt the resale value.

"Just honest," I say, but she's right. I'm being mean. Old habits die hard. "Besides, she was pretty mean to me today when I asked her to sell the house." Mean and sexy and a huge turn-on. "So let's call it even."

"There's never been an 'even' with you two. Or with you and Dom," Mom murmurs, lowering her sunglasses as she steps through the front door and into the brilliant, mid-day sun. Smiling back at me, she holds out her hand, beckoning me to join her, as she did throughout my childhood. "Now, let's go have some lunch with your father and your brothers. I have you all in one place, and I intend to force my five boys to like each other for as long as I can."

Mom starts the slow walk back to her house, which is one block down. Which means Hazel is probably within shouting distance. I'd ask where she lives, but I don't want to bring her up again. Or look curious. Or worse yet, hopeful.

But it's not hard to figure out. If Hazel's walking the neighborhood on her lunch break, she probably lives somewhere close. Which means that, for my visit home, I'll need to be extra careful.

Avoiding Hazel is the priority. If I come face to face with her again, who knows what could happen. One of two things is sure to come out: competition or unrestrained lust.

And God help me if it's the latter.

CHAPTER THREE

HAZEL

I wish I could say that it was business as usual at Hazel Homes the following day, but it wasn't. Far from it.

Every time the front door jingled with a new arrival, my skin prickled. Hoping it was Grayson. Wishing for another chance to be around that man.

And the idiocy of that makes me even madder. Why does he get to be the one to light my fire like that? Still, after all these years? Wasn't the high school heartbreak enough? The decades-long competition that had turned us into bitter and driven adults?

Grayson fills my head like cement fills a hole. Hardening into an unmovable, unshakeable presence. I thought by age twenty-eight, I'd be a little more resilient. A little more headstrong, and I don't know, *sane*. But no. Grayson Daly shows up and reduces me to a quivering, wanting, teenage puddle again.

Except this time, I've got leverage. This time, I can throw it back just as hard, if not harder. Maybe the past is done for him, but I haven't forgotten what an asshole he was to me senior year. It was ten years ago, sure, but it speaks volumes about his character. And that character clearly hasn't changed. All sexiness aside, I only deal with kind, level-headed, smart men. Which instantly disqualifies Grayson.

I take a few Saturday morning appointments to show houses, per usual, but leave my afternoon and evening free for the express purpose of hitting the lake. I need the time to unwind. To jostle loose the sticky feelers that Grayson left behind like some sort of obscure jungle newt.

It's still early in the summer, so we've only been out a few times. But when I go out on the lake, it's usually with my Bayshore crew. A few old friends from high school, all of them single and married to their jobs like I am, and then a couple new friends, Bayshore transplants who came because of the newly developed tech sector in the area. London would be here if she still lived close. I tend to send her teasing snaps of me in the sparkling sun, backed by Lake Erie, with the hearts filter on blast.

"Tubes or nah?" My high school buddy, Luke, doesn't bother greeting me. He's standing at the edge of the dock, barefoot, holding up two huge vinyl inner tubes for my appraisal.

I assess them, tossing my purse into the back of the Sea Ray. We're still waiting on Anthony and Callie, two more friends from high school, and Bryce, a new arrival to the community who's a fun drinking buddy and might be my only shot at taking a date to the ball.

"I wanna ski," I decide, slipping my sandals off at the dock. I step into the boat, gathering my balance as the boat rocks with some incoming chop.

Luke grunts and nods. "Yeah. It's a skiing day."

The boat is Luke's, but we all chip in for gas and snacks, so it's sort of a communal boat. I'd never take it out without Luke, but still, there's a certain sense of ownership between all of us. We buy it Christmas presents. It's part of our Bayshore family.

Anthony and Callie show up next, wearing grins and sunglasses, lake ready. Anthony gives us all high-fives. Callie slips onto the seat next to me, curling up like a cat.

"I'm hungover," she moans. "I'm too old for this shit."

"Hangovers in your late twenties are the worst," Anthony confirms, stepping onto the boat. It rocks with the weight of his six-foot-two frame. He's got a backward ballcap on, mostly to hide the fact that his hairline is receding.

"That's why I try to avoid them," I say, pinching her sides. Somehow, she's already tan even though we've had approximately two weeks of weather nice enough to take your clothes off.

"Anthony took me to this mixer at the Cleveland Art Museum," she says, kicking at Anthony as he walks past. He cackles in return. The two of them are sort of on-again, off-again. They both have demanding jobs, so I think they're always looking for outlets and not commitments. I can relate to that. An outlet is sounding mighty fine these days.

"What up, fam?" As if on cue, Bryce shows up, fist bumping Luke and Anthony as he makes his way onto the boat. He drops his backpack at the back with the others, and stands there, beaming at me. "Hey, Hazel."

"Hey, Bryce." He's made it plain that he wants to hook up. And honestly, I've tried. He's not a bad looking guy. Think a distant cousin of Nick Jonas. We had a drunken weekend night a few weeks ago that led to heavy petting. I wasn't feeling sex, so he went home, and we haven't talked about it since. The amount of time that's gone by without any acknowledgement of our failed hookup leads to a mathematical compounding of embarrassment. I think this is why we took calculus in high school—to understand the quantum levels of embarrassment possible in social interactions.

And people think I've got my shit together.

I can't even ghost correctly.

Luke flips on the exhaust blower. It hums as everyone settles into place. As usual, I've got the purse full of healthy snacks. Anthony always brings beer. Callie usually covers the junk food. Bryce and Anthony sit at the back of the boat, arms stretched across the ledge. The sun lights them up like Abercrombie models. For a second, I wonder if maybe I should be with Bryce because he's available and it's easy.

I don't know what I'm looking for. I just know that Bryce isn't it.

But maybe he should be.

Luke starts the engine, and the boat rumbles to life. He's got a big boat—enough to sleep all of us in the cabin and then some. As he's pulling out of the slip, a Jet Ski zooms up toward the public load-in area. Luke slows the boat, lifting his glasses to peer at the Jet Ski. I think he's about to shout at the driver. Luke likes to get rowdy.

"Are you fucking kidding me?" he shouts. But there's laughter in his voice. This isn't because somebody pissed him off. Luke howls, lowering his glasses and reversing the boat so quickly it jolts.

"I can't *believe* this!" he shouts, turning the wheel. He's heading for the load-in area. "It's motherfucking Grayson Daly!"

My stomach pitches to my toes, and I turn in my seat, searching out the offender. Anthony is standing and grinning, shielding his eyes against the sun as he waves to his old high school buddy. Callie groans, feebly turning her gaze toward the bay.

And then I see him.

Grayson is bent down by the dock cleat, roping off the Jet Ski. His calves flex, legs sprinkled with dark hair. My belly clenches into an iron fist as I tell myself that I am *not* sexually attracted to him anymore. Nope. Definitely do not care about the biceps bulging as he waves at us, or the sexy gruffness in his voice as he hollers back at his old high school buddies.

Grayson and Luke ran in the same group. Anthony was in a different circle but was friendly with everyone. Luke idles closer, his smile ear to ear.

"Get the hell out of here," he says. "What are you doing in these parts?"

Grayson rests his hands on his hips, looking every inch the lakeside hottie. His life vest is sleek black, somehow chic, and matches his black and white swim trunks. "Back in town for a little bit. My grandma just passed."

Luke swears, and Anthony shakes his head. "I'm sorry to hear that, man."

"Trying to enjoy the lake while I can though, you know?" Grayson flashes a winning smile, one that nearly cripples me.

"For sure. Dude, you gotta come out with us. What're you doing right now?"

I shrink lower in my seat. *Please don't see me.* If he sees me here, he might back out. Even though I want that. I definitely would rather he stay away. Like all the way back to New York.

"Nothing, bro. I'm all yours."

Luke whoops, and Anthony pumps his fist. Bryce lifts a brow, waiting for the introduction. Callie twirls her index finger limply through the air.

"Great," I hiss in Callie's direction. "Way to ruin our Saturday."

She laughs weakly. "Oh, that's right! You hate Gray!"

Luke sends me a confused look as he clambers back into the driver's seat to steer the boat closer to the dock. "What's that?"

"Remember?" Callie sits up, color returning to her face. "Hazel versus Gray. May the best color win!" She's reciting the stupid phrase our friends used to taunt me with. Nobody really ever understood the rivalry. They thought it was fun and games, which it wasn't—it was life or death.

Luke snorts as he maneuvers closer to the dock. By this time, we're probably within hearing range, and I hate it. "That's right. Twins separated at birth."

"We're not twins," I mutter.

Thankfully, I'm wearing dark sunglasses so I can spy on Gray as we pull up to the dockside. His gaze is on me—sizzling there, breaking skin—and I'm embarrassed. This is stupid. It's been ten years since high school and we're still known for this stupid rivalry. Haven't we grown up yet? Can't we move on?

Callie perks up a bit as we idle closer. She leans in. "Damn, Grayson got *hot*."

That's the truth. Water is dripping from his life jacket down his legs, swim trunks plastered to rock hard thighs, dribbling down the granite curve of his calf. I jerk my gaze away before I can see his feet. I always loved his feet. There was something sturdy and manly about them, which is stupid, so I'm not going to look.

He comes onto the boat. Anthony hops up and they give each other a bro hug, followed by Luke. I hear them introduce Bryce, who offers his hand. Grayson is the tallest of the four of them. Also the hottest. And definitely the biggest ego. Then his gaze swings our way.

Callie sits up a little. "Hey, Gray! Long time no see."

"How's it going, Cal?" He heads our way, and I freeze. I don't know how to be in this context with him. As if the angry outburst from two days ago hadn't happened. I look everywhere but at him.

"Callie, we should let him sit here so he can talk with Luke," I say quietly, sending a forced smile toward Gray. This is the adult Hazel shining now. The one who knows how to confront her childhood rival and take the higher path. I stand, scooping up my purse and towel. I head toward the small staircase leading to the bench seats on the bow. "Callie?"

"Oh, yeah." She hops to life, following me. Grayson sits in the seat we evacuated, at the driver's left side. I make the mistake of looking behind me as I climb up the stairs, and Gray's gaze is waiting for me. He wets his bottom lip, scruff on his jawline that wasn't there when he showed up at my office two days ago. My pussy clenches.

Yeah. This is awkward.

Callie collapses onto the vinyl bench next to me, draping her head back against the cushion. "Oof. That staircase was rough."

"Do you need water or something?" I paw through my bag. The boat lurches to life, and Luke begins turning us around, headed out toward the bay. "You know, choosing a boating day for your hangover-related activity was probably not wise."

"Yeah, but I needed to get out of the house," she moaned, tossing her arm over her eyes. "Anthony and I had fun, that's for sure. I'm just not used to drinking like I did in college. And last night definitely ended in beer pong."

I snicker, my gaze drifting back toward Gray as I hand over a bottle of water and a bottle of ibuprofen. He's leaning across the aisle to talk to Luke as he accelerates slowly, the wind picking up, mussing up their hair a little. Soon the boat is humming and we're out of the No Wake zone, picking up speed heading toward Lake Erie.

I have my chestnut hair pulled back into a messy bun, made messier by the wind assaulting us. The sun feels so good that I have to strip down to my bathing suit. I carefully remove my boatneck dress, tuck it into my purse, and then lay out on the bench. Keeping Grayson right in my line of vision as I rest my head on the edge of the cushion.

He doesn't look my way for a long time. I would know, I'm staring at him like a creep. But for some reason, it's important to me to make him want me. To make him see what he threw away.

It's ridiculous. I'm the first to admit this. But there's no greater motivator than being unexpectedly reunited with my first love—the only man to ever officially *spurn* me. His being hotter than hell is an extra challenge. His hating on Bayshore is the third layer to this really bizarre cake. If I can crack all three of these things—make him want me, reject him, all the while being in Bayshore—it seems like there's some sort of prize waiting for me.

Something better than an orgasm, maybe.

No, scratch that. Orgasms are the best. But this sense of satisfaction, if I can obtain it, promises to be a close runner-up.

I keep an eye on him as I strategically arrange my limbs. First up: tossing my arm over my head, dangling like any lithe model would in a *Glamour* shoot. Then: one knee bent, slightly tilted, showcasing some ass. Never mind that I'm blindingly white. Followed by: slightly propped on elbows, looking around with pouty lips, like wondering *where the hell is that champagne I ordered?*

Callie breaks into my secret operation. "Hazel, are you okay?"

I flop back onto the bench. "Yeah, why?"

"You're rolling around like you're about to be sick."

I deflate, letting both my knees slide to the bench. I stare up at the perfect cerulean sky. Not a cloud to be seen. "Just trying to get comfortable."

"Maybe *I'm* about to be sick," she moans.

I sit up quickly, looking back at her. "Cal, are you serious? Stick your head over the side. I'll tell Luke to slow down."

She doesn't say anything for a moment, then holds up a palm. She swallows and shakes her head. "No. I'm fine. It passed."

I lift my glasses to peer at her, then make the mistake of looking toward Grayson while my lenses are up.

We lock eyes. His stormy blues have turned into an F4 tornado—it'll fuck up the barn, but won't whisk away the family—and I'm trapped in the crosswinds.

There's so much in that gaze. Questions. Curiosity. Lust. Except I can't tell what's real and what's imagined. Or how much I'm projecting because I'm still an eighteen-year-old girl at heart, eager to prove herself against her lifelong rival.

I lower my sunglasses, lie back down. As I do so, Bryce cuts a path from the back of the boat up to the bow. He grips the handrails as he snakes his way toward me. Sits right next to me, smiling down at me like I'm the only person he's ever wanted to see in the world.

I smile back up at him.

Not because he's the only one I want to see.

Because he's the only one that Gray can see me with.

CHAPTER FOUR

GRAYSON

The lake has always been my safe haven. Fighting with my brothers? Go to the lake. Need a secret place to neck with your high school girlfriend of the moment? Let's go to the lake. Wanna show off your great bod while checking out all the gorgeous curves of your former rival-turned-love-interest?

Yeah. Get to the fucking lake.

And this time it feels like a big breath of fresh air—because it literally is—except my whole body is wound tight, a coil ready to snap. I can barely unclench my fists. It gets better when I sink back into the seat, my back toward the bow. I take a few deep breaths, hands relaxing. The pretty blue sky lulls me into peacefulness. This is more like it. Weird how relaxation correlates with Hazel being out of sight.

"Yo, buddy, hand me a beer?" Luke shouts over the sound of the wind.

I nod and reach for the cooler. In my steps to pass it off to him, my gaze swings toward Hazel. Sitting on the bow like a pin-up model, swatting at Bryce's shoulder. Her toothy smile is a punch to the gut. I forget to unclench my hand and Luke has to rip the beer from my grip.

He laughs. "Damn, boy!"

I slap him on the shoulder, easing back into my seat. I lean over the aisle separating us. "She with that guy?"

I don't elaborate or clarify. Because I don't want to. I hate that I'm even asking. If I offer no details, it's like I'm not asking.

"Hazel?" he shouts.

My skin crawls. I want to choke him so that he'll keep it quiet. I jerk my head into a nod.

"I don't think so," Luke says, all his hair flopping to the right side as he executes a sharp turn. On the bow, Hazel giggles and falls right into Bryce's lap. He looks delighted. What an asshole. I look away, focusing on the receding sandy shores behind us. There aren't a lot of boats out today, and the chop isn't so bad. I decide in that moment I'm going to absolutely kick Bryce's ass in skiing.

"Let's start here." I point toward one of the famous coves on the shoreline. It's quiet and tree-shrouded, perfect for the first pull of the day.

Luke clucks his tongue. "You're readin' my mind, bro!"

The boat slows, and the hum of the motor dies down. On the bow, Callie groans and rolls onto her side. Hazel sits up, the creamy skin of her belly crinkling. I can't look away from the mauve triangle of stretchy fabric covering her pussy or the apple tops of her breasts spilling from her bikini top. Fuck. This was a bad idea after all.

"It's so nice out here," Hazel coos, snuggling into Bryce's out-stretched arm. He grins down at her.

"I'm gonna take a quick dive," I say, unbuckling my life vest. I drop it to the seat and launch myself off the side of the boat, cannonball-style. The splash reverberates around me. When I surface, I whoop with laughter. That felt damn good. Cleansing somehow.

"You wanna go first?" Luke comes to the side of the boat, holding my life vest.

"Sure, why not? Better set the standard early," I crack, swimming toward the side of the boat.

From the bow, Hazel snorts. "Oh please."

I ignore her. I'm not going to give her what she wants, which is a reaction. Every inch of my skin can feel her wanting me to notice her. And I refuse. Instead, I swim to the back of the boat, haul myself up on the deck, and strap my life vest back on.

"Two or one?" Luke asks, when Anthony starts getting ropes untangled.

"Two," I say. "It's been a while."

Anthony cues up the water skis while I ease into the lake again. He hands me each ski one at a time, pre-soaped so I can wiggle my foot into the rubbery opening. Then he tosses the rope out to me. I'm wobbling in the water, trying to get the hang of these things again. Huge, bulky, unwieldy weights strapped to my feet.

Luke whistles, giving me a thumbs up in the mirror. There's a whole secret language to waterskiing, like catchers on a baseball diamond. Anthony is the spotter on the back bench to watch if I wipeout or need anything. It's pretty clear that Hazel plans to critique my performance, based on how she sits up at attention once I yell, "Hit it!"

Luke speeds off, and the tension turns the rope to stone. I hang on for dear life, counseling myself on all the things I once knew like the back of my hand: don't push the tips together, keep my knees slightly bent, unfurl like a birthing moth. Once I pop up, the exhilaration of the sport comes rushing back. This is a piece of cake. And damn, it feels good to be out on the water.

The sun beats down on me, turning the lake surface into a choppy water prism, warming the life vest as Luke takes wide, looping turns. I zigzag across the tall waves behind the boat, even catching some air. I forgot how good an exercise this is for the upper body. Each time I cross the wake, I shout with laughter. I signal for more speed.

I end up going for a full seven minutes. We're damn near ten miles from Bayshore. I eventually let go of the rope and sink down into the turquoise water. A great first run. And plenty impressive to any amateur, which I just know Bryce is. When I resurface, I paddle toward the boat, arm crooked over the two skis. When I'm back in the boat, dripping water and grinning, I ask, "Who's next?

Hazel stands, heading toward me, fire in her eyes like always. "Me. Now that amateur hour is over, it's time to let the real pros have a shot."

I fight back a smile. "Amateur hour? I'd love to see an amateur with a seven-minute unbroken run like I had."

"Amateurs use two skis," she says with a tight grin, ripping off her sunglasses. She jerks her chin toward Anthony. "Get the slalom."

These are fighting words. Competition licks through my veins, no matter how badly I want to remain neutral. I can't not take the bait. It's like telling a dog to suddenly stop sniffing other dog's asses. We've been doing this since we were born. It's in our DNA.

"Yeah, get the slalom, Anthony." I call over my shoulder. "Once Hazel wipes out in thirty seconds, I'll show her what a real slalom skier looks like."

"Ha!" Her sarcastic laugh slices through the air. "Like you would know. You get lucky on two skis after ten years and think you're suddenly an expert. Where do I sign up for Grayson's master class?"

Bryce has come down to the back of the boat, curiosity on his face as Hazel and I spar. Callie, too, has pulled herself into something resembling sitting up, hair mussed as she tunes in.

"I forgot how entertaining this was," Anthony mumbles to himself.

"Is he bothering you?" Bryce asks directly to Hazel.

Oh, great. Knight in shining armor over here. I roll my eyes. How do we explain it? We can't. There's no explanation for how we revert to competitive children.

"Permanently," Hazel says.

"These two sorta have..." Luke pauses, a laugh escaping him. "Dude, how do I say it?"

"Bitter rivalry, I think is the term," Anthony opines.

I want to say *she started it* so badly, but that only makes things worse. But seriously. She did start it. She started it today, and in her office, and right before prom. Hazel is *the* shit-starter.

"Unresolved daddy issues?" I offer, but that's definitely not the case. Hazel and her dad are close—always have been, since her mother passed during childbirth.

"You should talk," Hazel grumbles as she snaps her life jacket on. And she's right. Between the two of us, *I'm* the one with the asshole dad. The bright purple vest juts out from her chest, which forces my gaze down the sturdy slopes of her thighs, down to her cute little feet, toenails painted the deepest shade of purple. My gaze fastens on the cantaloupe curve of her ass—an ass I was once lucky to squeeze.

Hazel has gotten better with age, and her appearance today is a stark contrast to the immaculate pinup girl I found at her office. Don't get me wrong—both Hazels are hot as fuck. But out here on the boat, she looks more like the Hazel I once knew. Full, soft lips, without a trace of lipstick or gloss. Wisps of her cinnamon hair flying free around her face, escaped from the confines of her messy bun. Those gold-flecked, mossy green eyes that still make my chest hurt whenever she looks my way for too long.

In a different world—a different dimension, maybe—we would have tied the knot after high school. We would have fallen so deep in love that they put up a goddamn plaque for us in the Bayshore pavilion that said *From Bitter Rivals to Sweetest Lovers.* We'd have kids by now, probably the estimated 2.5, and live somewhere active but bigger, like Cincinnati or, hell, Philly.

But instead, this is where we are. Still shooting death rays out of our eyes. There's no sweet ending to this story. Just more rancor.

Hazel sits on the back deck and wiggles her feet into the rubbery openings of the slalom ski. Then she pushes off and slips into the water. Anthony tosses the rope. I take my place by the driver's seat. My buddy Bryce joins me a moment later.

"We like to pick at each other," I offer after a moment, as though he needs to know more about what exists between Hazel and me. "She likes it, I promise."

He sends me a weird side glance, and I can tell I'm not doing a good job of convincing him. Whatever. He's a moony-eyed douche. Hazel could do way better. I work my jaw back and forth, knee bouncing as Luke idles out into the lake a little, lining Hazel up with the center of the boat. Slalom skiing *is* harder, and a much better work out.

"The water isn't really good for slalom skiing today," I tell Luke as he struggles to keep her centered with the back of the boat. It's too choppy. Slalom skiing is best on the quiet waters of the bay in the early morning, right after dawn, when the water looks like glass. "We should pull her in."

"You think?" Luke casts a doubtful look through the rearview mirror.

"Anthony, you should pull her in," I shout to the back of the boat. "It's too choppy—she'll get hurt."

Hazel must have heard me, because my worry is followed by a very succinct "Fuck you, city boy!"

I grimace and sit back in my seat. Looking at Bryce, I say, "She's a peach, isn't she?"

A moment later, Hazel shouts, "Hit it!" and Luke takes off, accelerating hard to help the slalom ski take flight. Hazel emerges from the water in a huge spray, both graceful and bad ass, and all I can do is take it in. I'd record the spectacle if I were bolder. But I'm not—so I try to keep my jaw from hitting the floor.

Hazel is all grin and powerful thighs as she cuts back and forth across the wake, leaning back to cut some huge sprays, sometimes so far it looks like she's about to lie down on the lake surface. She's really good—I'll admit that. But I'll never admit how much I've been fantasizing about having those thighs wrapped around me since I've been back.

I look over. Bryce is grinning like a fool, sending out the occasional thumbs up. Desperate, much? Luke would have told me if there was a thing there, but I need to be sure. I lean over to him.

"You know, Hazel probably seems like a catch and all, but..." I pause, wondering if I have the balls to go through with this. It's necessary, I remind myself. "Truth is, she's a lesbian."

Bryce snorts, not looking particularly bothered. "Oh, yeah? Even better then."

Fuck. What will it take to get him to give up the chase? "Well, you should probably know—" My brain's gears are whirring like the gears in Willy Wonka's Chocolate Factory. "—she's actually got like, a problem. *Down there.*"

Bryce sends me a disbelieving look. "A problem?"

The wind whips through my hair as I look out at the lake, forcing solemnity into my voice. "Yeah. She's got this...*rash*...that covers her entire pubic area. Doctors still don't know what causes it. Or if it's contagious."

Bryce's expression turns from disbelief to cockiness, and I think I may have shit on my own parade.

"Didn't see any rash the last time I was down there," he delivers coolly.

Fuck. Well, that backfired. So much for *not with Bryce.* I mask my irritation by crossing my arms and searching the lake distractedly. "It comes and goes." I sniff. "Just thought you should know. Between men."

So that clears that up. Hazel is off limits—not like she was ever within my reach to begin with—and I should shut the hell up and move along.

But it's impossible to rip my eyes off Hazel.

It was all through high school, and it's worse now.

And if anything, our history roaring back to life has brought more than competition along with it. Now, I'm remembering how hard I fell for Hazel back in the day.

Good thing I'm older now. Wiser.

And too smart to let that happen a second time.

CHAPTER FIVE

HAZEL

I finish my award-winning slalom run and return to general fanfare on the boat. Except for Grayson, of course. God help him if he ever has a wife and children who look for approval because they won't get it from that one. Any kid he raises will probably turn into a major league maniac.

Bryce sweeps toward me and wraps me in a hug once I shuck my life vest, which is weird. He's never been so touchy-feely in public. Hell, we're not even dating. Usually he keeps his advances to text messages and drunken outings, so this is new.

"Hard to top that one," Bryce says.

"Give it thirty seconds and you'll see." Grayson heads to the back of the boat, snatching up his life vest.

"Oh, come on," Luke says, turning in his seat. "We can't go back and forth all day seeing who beats who. I wanna get my ass in the water too."

"You're right. Let's settle it now. I win." I beam up at him, all teeth, eyes pinched shut.

"You would never accept such a cheap victory," he accuses me.

Callie has dragged herself down to the seat next to the driver, looking slightly more alive. "Do tandem!"

All heads turn to her like God has spoken truth from the heavens. It really is genius. And perhaps the only way to truly see who comes out on top.

"Done." Grayson jabs his finger into the air. "Tandem it is. And if I win, you'll be my real estate agent and sell my grandma's house."

I squint at Grayson. "Now, that's not fair. I just had a long run, and that shit is hard."

"So you concede?"

It's pure bait. Of course I won't. I huff and stomp back to my life vest, snatching it up, jabbing the buckles together. "Get the ropes ready, Anthony."

Grayson looks *too* pleased with himself as he suits up, and I force myself not to check out the sculpted lines of his abs or the rolling hills of his biceps. But it's hard not to notice him. To absorb him, to get drunk on him. Masculinity and adrenaline and power roll off him in waves. It's always been like that with him. He energizes, simply from being close. I'm glad to see that, at least, hasn't changed. Even though he's pushing us into a pointless battle I can't help but participate in.

We both step onto the back deck, shooting daggers at each other. Standing barefoot next to him, I realize how much height he has on me. My head about comes up to his collar bone, if we're being generous. When he turns to receive the wide slalom ski, I'm reminded of the breadth of his shoulders. How wide and sturdy and manly he is. I swallow, jerking my gaze to Anthony, forcing myself to focus on his totally safe and neutral backwards OSU ballcap. He hands me the ski.

I sit on the back deck next to Grayson. Water laps at the edges of the deck, tickling the bottoms of my thighs through the wooden slats, as we shove our feet into the slaloms.

"It must be truly tiring to be such a sore loser," I mutter as I shove my dominant foot into the front hole. My other foot goes in, and I reach for the rope. "And weaseling your realty needs into a waterskiing competition? Pathetic."

In lieu of a response, Grayson shoves me by the shoulder. I topple face-first, the look of shock on my face probably the last thing he sees before I disappear underwater.

I surface a moment later, spitting water, and flip him the bird. "Not cool."

Grayson is laughing, real belly laughs, which take the edge off my anger. I've always loved hearing his laughter, and his smile is fit for a magazine ad. The man could make money off his looks. Just probably not as much money as whatever he's doing now. He pushes into the water and takes a few strokes away from the boat.

"You two ready?" Luke asks, turning the engine back on once we've floated far enough away from the boat.

"Yep," I confirm, wrapping my hands around the handle. I can't wait to show Grayson what a needless ass he is. "Though he loses an automatic ten points for pushing me into the water."

"I didn't need those ten points anyway," Grayson shouts.

Everyone settles into place on the boat, and nervousness licks through me. Shit, the tension is real. And it's *high*. Even though this means nothing, it also means *everything*. He sends me a darkly mischievous look. How is Grayson so good at doing this? Making mountains out of molehills everywhere he goes?

"Hit it!" I cry out when I feel ready, and Grayson echoes the same. The boat surges forward, a roar of engine and excitement. Energy zips through me, completely eradicating whatever soreness remained from my last run. We both surge up and out of the water, emerging from the spray like gods. The ropes are of different lengths and tied off to a pole at the back of the boat, so we can crisscross without running into each other. I look over at him. He looks over at me.

And then he swerves. Cutting his ski into the water away from me, sending a plume of spray up into my face. I sputter and mimic him, swinging out wide to the port side of the boat. Waves crash toward us, the whitecaps making my stomach bottom out. I hang tight and ride it out. The lake is too damn choppy to be slalom skiing right now. I was lucky to get my good run in.

Luke steers us toward an alcove where the water is slightly calmer. Grayson cuts hard back toward the center, and I instinctively do the same. We soar past each other, and I will my spray to cover him and submerge him entirely. It doesn't, of course.

I'm not a two-hundred-pound man with a four-hundred-pound ego, so my spray is naturally lesser. This isn't rationalization, it's a fact. It can't be held against me. Except Grayson seems to spread his spray like a peacock fanning its feathers. Probably because he has the rope closer to the boat and knows that his spray hits my face each time.

We crisscross a few times. My arms are tired already, but Grayson shows no signs of slowing. Callie is cheering from the middle of the boat. At least our rivalry helped cure her hangover. Grayson swoops toward the center and I veer to do the same. Except when he's barreling past me, my vision goes watery and white as he passes, and my ski goes *THUNK*.

Everything happens in a blur. The rope slingshots out of my hands; I'm flying along with it. My ski is left behind somewhere. I don't have time to scream before I hit the water in a painful, awkward splash.

Somersaults underwater yank my bathing suit bottoms down to my knees. I must have hit a huge piece of driftwood—nothing else could send me flying like that. Thank God I have the life vest—I kick a few times before breaking through the water in a sputtering, gasping mess.

I expect Grayson to be on board the boat collecting his trophy for superiority, thanking his fans who've always supported him in his quest to outdo me, but instead I find him a few strokes away from me. His face is creased with concern.

"Hazel!" he shouts gruffly. "Are you okay?"

That's real concern in his voice. I'm too shaken to bite back. "I...I don't know."

He swears and swims faster. In my periphery, I see Luke swinging the boat out wide, circling back to us. The ropes drag behind the boat. Gray reaches me and grabs me by the lapels of the life vest.

"What the hell happened?"

He's inches away from me, and I can't do anything but stare up into his stormy blues. His walnut brown hair is plastered to his forehead, and the lake water chops at our sides.

"I don't know," I whisper. I can't look away from him. Fuck, this would almost be romantic if pain weren't shooting through my left hip. Somehow, I've lost my voice a little too.

"Did my ski hit you?" he demands, his gaze skating across my face.

I shake my head.

"Are you hurt? Like your legs?" He reaches underwater and his hand brushes my bare hip. I suck at my teeth, remembering my bottoms are hovering at my knees.

"Hang on." I poke my tongue out as I try to reach my bottoms. I can't get past the life vest. They slip lower in my struggles, all the way down to my ankles. "Shit. My swimsuit bottoms..."

Gray's gaze slides to the surface of the water.

"Don't look!"

"I can't see anything." He watches me struggle for a moment. The boat is nearing, and Luke and Anthony are shouting out to us. "Do you need help?"

A frustrated sigh escapes me. My side hurts, and this sucks. *"Yes."*

"Bring your legs up to the surface," he instructs.

"I'm trying," I grumble, keeping my crotch piked low. Waves from Luke's boat reach us, and one smacks me in the side of my head. My toes poke out of the water a moment later, and he stills me by the ankles. His gaze finds mine, and I see all sorts of confusing things there. Heat, for starters. And question marks tinged with sensuality. Then he tugs the mauve stretchy bottoms of my swimsuit up my calves, over my knees.

Once I can reach them, I snag them and finish pulling them up. I swallow. My pussy is throbbing with the slightest hint of wishing those hands could keep moving upward.

"Are you sure you're okay?"

If I didn't know him better, I'd think he cared. But he doesn't. Because this is Grayson Daly we're talking about. Something snaps back into place and I find my tongue again.

"I'd be a lot better if your quest to physically outdo me didn't result in stupid shit like this," I snap. Luke idles close now. Bryce and Anthony are shouting out to us, asking if I'm okay.

"I think I'm fine," I call out weakly, mustering a smile. Grayson hops on to the deck and then squats down, offering a hand. I catch his big, manly hand and he helps ease me onto the platform.

Pain shoots through my hip, and I wince.

"That doesn't look good at all," Callie announces.

"Damn, what did you do to her?" Bryce demands.

"Nothing," Grayson says, squatting behind me, almost protectively. I take deep breaths, watching the water churn in the lake. To me, in a lower voice, he says, "Do you want to try to stand?"

I swipe the loose strands from my face and nod. His bicep bulges as he helps lift and steady me. My gaze falls to his swim trunks, which are plastered to his junk in a very revealing way. I snap my gaze up, guiltily. God, this man is too attractive. And he's being one percent nice to me, which is already giving my body the all clear to start *reacting*. This isn't cool.

If he treated me like this on the daily, I'd lose it. I'd fall for him without a second thought.

Just like the first time.

"I think we should call it a day," Luke says, worry in his voice.

"No, you guys." I wave off his suggestion. "I might be done for the day, but that doesn't mean you have to be."

"But you should take care of your leg," Callie insists.

"So drop me off," I suggest. "Then you guys can keep boating. We were just getting started. There's no use wasting this day because some asshole tried to drown me."

Grayson clears his throat. "This asshole didn't try to *drown* you—"

Ah, so he doesn't deny that he's an asshole.

"I actually think I hit some driftwood," I hurry to add. I feel my cheeks heating up, and I'm not entirely sure why. The about-face feels revealing. Like I'm calling a truce, which I'm definitely not.

Grayson helps haul me onto the back bench seat of the boat, and Luke gets the boat in motion. We navigate toward the two lost skis and haul them inside. We're heading back toward the docks at a good clip, wind rushing through our hair and everyone quiet in the loud hum of the engine. I let my head fall back and close my eyes, the sun warming my face.

Trying to ignore the fact that Grayson is still at my side. Heat pours off him like a nuclear reactor. And if he's not careful, he's gonna push me into meltdown mode.

Luke pulls up to the docks, and before I can open my eyes, Callie is packing her things.

"I'll take her back to the house, guys," she says.

"No," Grayson says, an authority in his tone that I haven't ever heard before. Maybe this is his Wall Street voice. "I'll take her back, Cal. She needs help walking."

Callie deflates a little as her gaze falls to my propped leg. "Oh right."

"I'll take her back." Bryce steps forward. "We can hang out afterward. I'll make you tomato soup."

I smirk. The thought is nice, but Bryce is clearly unaware of the fact that tomato soup makes me want to puke. Grayson must remember this detail because he says, "No. You're too weak. And Hazel doesn't like tomato soup."

I roll my lips inward to stave off the giggles.

"And what about me?" Anthony asks, a grin on his face. I can tell he just wants to see what Grayson will shoot him down with.

"You're the spotter," Grayson says. "They need you to watch them all ski."

"All right, I think Gray's got it," Anthony cedes a moment later.

CHAPTER SIX

GRAYSON

If you asked me what the driving motivation of being kind to Hazel included, I'd have two answers.

Being honest? I feel like a jerk. Because she's right—our competition led to her getting hurt.

Being a wise-ass? I want those thighs wrapped around me. *Now.*

Something snapped when I saw her hit the water like that. It reminded me that the rivalry is only fun if she's part of it. And she can't be part of it if she breaks her damn neck.

"Callie, hand me that bag," I instruct once I've helped Hazel onto the dock. Callie hands over the purse. Then I offer my back to Hazel. "Get on, cowgirl."

Hazel sighs softly. "Seriously, this is not necessary. Let me call my dad."

"But you live in this neighborhood," I remind her. "You're gonna make your dad drive all the way across the city when I can get you to your front door in minutes?"

"My grandma is closer," she says.

"Yeah, but she's ninety. I'll have to carry both of you on my back."

Callie snickers as Luke idles away from the dock. The four of them wave, and Bryce is frowning, which means I've done my job.

"Fine," Hazel grumbles. I hoist her onto my back. Her legs slide like hot silk around my hips. I grip her thighs, vision going spotty for a moment. Her breasts brush my back; her breath hits the shell of my ear. And with her so close to me, the scent of her fills my senses. Clementines and freesia. It's intoxicating, like she's captured the essence of femininity *and* summer in one.

"You good?"

"Yep." Her voice sounds pinched. Maybe she's thinking about how it would feel if I spun her around, hoisting her to face me. No, that's probably just *me* thinking about that.

She starts snickering.

"What's so funny?"

"You are such a piece of work."

I snort. "At least you didn't say crap."

Another giggle, her breath coming out in short puffs at my ear as I start the piggyback ride toward our neighborhood. The warmth of her wrapped around me pushes lust and a lot more through my veins. A heavy cloud descends, the type to chase out rationale and logic in search of that one, precious prize.

And what do you know? I got her thighs wrapped around me today after all.

"Grayson," she says huskily, or maybe that's my imagination since her mouth is an inch from my ear. Either way, my cock pricks to attention. "You don't even have shoes on."

"Yeah, I sorta forgot them on the boat." I pause, hoisting her again. She squeaks, which is too cute. I'm beginning to forget how t o *be* around Hazel. Having her on me has erased all the careful lines we've drawn for the duration of our lives. I should follow with snark, but I can't.

"Better hope Bryce doesn't throw them in the lake," she cracks.

I fight a smile. "Aw, my buddy Bryce? Now why would he do that?"

"Please," Hazel says, but her voice is devoid of that edge. The razor that can cut deep if she lobs it right. "He's probably ready to report you for harassment."

I scoff. "Harassment? He should have been around sophomore year." That was truly the apex of our competition. She even tried to join the men's tennis team, just to show me she could beat me in the matches. "This is nothing."

We're passing my grandmother's house, the one I recently inherited. I'm not going to bring up that she's on the hook for selling it now. I'll need to finesse my way into that one.

"Oh, hello there, Hazel!" A neighbor steps out of her house as we go by. Mrs. Thomas. She's been on this street for ages. She's probably eighty by now. "And Grayson?"

We both wave. "Hi, Mrs. Thomas."

"Good to see you back in town, Grayson. When's the wedding?" Of course, she's talking about *us*. The perfect couple that never was.

"Mrs. Thomas—" Hazel begins.

"This woman wouldn't marry me even if I carried her on my back to her house when she was injured!" I said, my voice full of that 90s-sitcom good-naturedness.

"She'd be silly to turn you down!" Mrs. Thomas agrees while shuffling to the mailbox. Hazel lets out the fakest laugh of all time.

"Real funny," she hisses once we're out of earshot.

"Was I wrong?" I ask, and Hazel doesn't respond. Because I'm not wrong. "We both know you'd never marry someone who could whoop your ass in everything."

A sharp laugh erupts from her, but it's genuine, not snarky.

"I would never marry someone who was hellbent on whooping my ass in everything," she counters. Again, this would be a good time for *you started it*, but I hold my tongue.

"Where the hell do you live?" We're coming up on my mom's house now.

"Next block over. Hang a left up here."

"So close to my parents," I murmur, keeping an eye on my parents' front door. My skin tingles, and I can sense it—my mom is about to walk out the door. The door creaks open as we approach. "Oh God—"

"Hazel!" Mom's voice pierces the air, and she waves like she's seeing a celebrity. "Now what is going on here?" She's using her I-know-what's-really-happening voice, and I shake my head.

"Hazel hurt herself skiing," I explain, walking faster. The bottoms of my feet are sore from all this hot concrete sidewalk action, but hell if I'll let that slow me down.

"Your son injured me," Hazel adds.

Mom tuts, shaking her head. "Back at it, I see."

"Wouldn't be a trip home without it." I hoist Hazel. She squeaks again, which makes my heart race, just as my brother, Weston, pokes his head out.

"Gray?"

I huff. I don't have time for all this shit. "Kinda in a hurry, guys. I'll be home soon."

I cross the street to make my point. Hazel is laughing softly in my ear again.

"Can't a man walk down the street in peace?"

"This street is the definition of peaceful," she points out.

"I don't remember the last time I walked down my street in Brooklyn and had anybody even acknowledge me."

Hazel hums low. The sound she makes when she's really thinking about what you said. It makes something nervous flutter through my limbs. "Must be why you came in so keyed up. Desperate to be noticed."

"I don't need to do much to be noticed," I shoot back. "Not like some people and their billboards."

"Is that a dig on me?" she asks. "That's my business, asshole. Listen, put me down right here. I can walk."

I squeeze her legs against me tighter and keep walking. I don't know where this is going, but I don't want it to end. And that's more confusing than anything.

"Your billboard looks great, by the way." Maybe that'll soften the blow.

She relaxes against me but sounds suspicious when she says, "Thanks."

I turn the corner. Green bushes line the sidewalk, a privacy hedge, and tall oak and maple trees tower above us. The waves crashing on the shore are distant now. A weed whacker hums from somewhere in the neighborhood.

I look up at the sky, barely visible through the branches and leaves of the trees.

This isn't so bad. Not at all.

"It's right here," Hazel says, pointing. There's a cute little century home, painted slate gray with a gable over the front door. Petunias and ferns and rose bushes line the brick walkway to the front door. Wrought iron lamp fixtures jut out from the house, lending it a gothic feel. It's cute as hell...and totally Hazel. I'd be able to pick it out as hers from the lamps alone.

"Wow." The awe slips out of me, but I'm not as keen to mask it anymore. Something shifted between us while she was piggyback-ing. Maybe she feels it too. "This is the best house on the block."

"Yeah, I know a thing or two about curb appeal," she says with a sigh. "You can drop me off here."

"You need to be on a couch or something."

"Here is fine," she says, swatting my shoulder.

"Hazel, I'm seeing this through." I step up to her door, hoisting her one last time. "You know I can't see our friends again and tell them I tucked and rolled once we got to your house."

She grumbles but fishes a key out of her purse. I bend so she can reach the lock. The door swings open, revealing a spacious, two-story great room. Dark wood floors are intermittently covered with slate gray rugs and low, comfy-looking couches. I step inside, craning my neck to look around. A staircase curves up to the second floor. Everything is as immaculate as a showroom, yet somehow distinctly lived in.

"Damn," I murmur.

"What?"

I jerk my gaze off the collection of ceramic owls sitting on little ledges on the walls. Of course Hazel would have owls everywhere. "I thought a realtor like you would have a mansion."

Her muscles go rigid around me. "Okay, insulting me outside in the regular world is one thing, but in my own house? Forget it. Put me down. It's time for you to leave."

I dig my fingers into the backs of her thighs, and some of the fight goes out of her. I wait a moment before I respond. "That's not what I meant."

"Then what did you mean?"

I head to the couch and slowly come to my knees so she can slide off. Once I'm gazing back into those mossy green eyes, I can barely remember what we're talking about.

"Grayson?" she asks.

I jerk my gaze off her to the shaggy gray rug beneath my knees. It's not shaggy like the 70s—it's shaggy like the expensive section at Target. "I meant that most real estate agents are completely sta-tus-obsessed and would have some elaborate McMansion, devoid of personality." I look around again, finding warmth and hominess in every corner. "This is the best home I've seen in a long time. In New York, in my circle, everyone's got a swanky place, but there's no personality in them."

Hazel seems to have softened a little. Her lips curl up at the edges. "Hm. Yeah. I see that a lot. Like the stock photo version of a nice home."

"Exactly," I say, pushing my palm over the edge of her couch, dangerously close to her knee. She crosses her ankles as she settles back into the cushions. My fingertips brush her skin, and I meet her gaze again.

Just to see if she's on the same page as I am.

To see if she feels even a fraction of this sexual tension.

"This place looks like you," I add.

"You haven't seen past my living room," she says with a laugh.

"Should I give myself a guided tour?" I ask.

"Be sure to pick up the headphones by the door, so you can get the audio accompaniment," she cracks. A laugh bursts out of me, and for a moment this *feeling* pulses between us. The best feeling in the world. Two people genuinely enjoying each other, digging the moment. It's been a long time since I've felt that with someone. Even longer since it's been Hazel.

And damn, if the way she's looking at me right now isn't making every inch of my body come to attention. Electricity snaps between us; the air grows taut. I trail my fingers over her kneecap, then trace that sensitive hollow behind. Her breath hitches.

So the unshakeable Hazel can be shaken by Gray, even ten years later.

"What are you trying to do?" she asks, a lazy tone to her voice. Like she's caught somewhere between a dream and distraction.

My heart hammers as my gaze drifts up the sun-kissed expanse of her thigh. Fingertips sizzling from the contact, I trace a slow, invisible pattern over her knee.

I want to be honest with her. I'm trying to fucking kiss her. To reduce this tension in my chest by a fraction. To see if she'll let me spend the rest of the evening at her side, getting lost in the past as much as the present.

"You know what I'm trying to do," I say, enjoying the goosepimples blossoming beneath my touch. She's never been good at fully convincing me she doesn't like me. Hazel talks a good game, but I know her weaknesses. The area behind her kneecap might as well be an earlobe. I swipe my middle finger over that dip again, watching as her nostrils flare.

"Taking advantage of the woman you mortally wounded out on the lake?" She lifts a brow, but her gaze is on my hand. Willing it to continue?

"Mortally wounded," I scoff and move my hand away from her. My skin protests the decision. And apparently she does, too. She moves her knee closer to me. My gaze snags on that scrap of fabric covering her pussy—that sweet heat I'd been lucky enough to know once upon a time—and I wonder what's going on in there right now. Is she wet from wanting me? Is she throbbing, wanting things to move further?

The ball's in my court right now. I don't know what to do with so much power. I wonder if she realizes that she lost. The evidence is her prickled skin. Her flushed chest. Her green eyes boring a hole through me.

"There's nothing wrong with being nice to my new realtor," I say. It's a struggle to hide the evil grin that wants to overtake my face, but I manage.

"Grayson Daly," she says, "You did not win that skiing competition. It was undecided due to participant injury."

I drag my thumb along the side of her thigh, heading for her knee. She rolls her lips inward.

"It would mean a lot to my mom," I whisper, then send her my best puppy face. "She's really upset ever since Connor brought Kinsley Cabana back from California."

Hazel sits up sharply, brows knitting together. "What did you say?"

"It's pretty tense at the house." I love how interested she is in this information. And most people who grew up with us would be. Kinsley Cabana is practically the Juliet Capulet to Connor's Romeo Montague. Except they're not sixteen—they're in their mid-twenties and consenting adults. Even if my parents and Kinsley's parents would rather die than have their offspring *mating*.

"Connor brought back...*Kinsley?*" She's practically shouting. "How—?"

"They both live in San Diego," I explain, "and apparently started dating out there. But I don't know. The whole thing smells fishy to me."

Hazel is gaping at me.

"They're staying at the house together. I see them every morning, eating oatmeal like a pair of octogenarians."

"I can't believe this," she whispers.

"Come on. Help my mom stave off heartbreak. Make my dad slightly more tolerable. Be my realtor."

Hazel's head drops to the cushion behind her, and she scowls. "Fine. But you need to leave."

Frustration and doubt crash through me. I'm ninety-nine percent sure she wants to pursue this as much as I do, but that one percent of doubt is a vast ocean. Maybe that's not sexual tension I'm smelling; maybe this is real-life exasperation.

Maybe I've been trapped in my own New York work bubble so long I've forgotten what it's like to engage in consensual flirting. Even with a thorn bush like Hazel.

Walk out of here. Walk out of here now. It's dangerous being this close to her, and I need to leave before I really do something stupid. Like ask her if I can push my fingers under those pretty purple bathing suit bottoms. My cock twitches just thinking about it.

"Great." I squeeze her ankle before I come to my feet. She looks panicked, but only for a second. "We can talk more about it at your office on Monday. Feels really good to have you on board."

She sighs, crossing her legs.

"You good here?" I prop my hands on my hips, scanning the room. "Or do you need more help tending your loser wounds?"

And then Hazel cocks her head at me, eyes shrinking to slits.

But I see the things she's trying to hide the most.

Like the start of a smile on those pretty lips.

CHAPTER SEVEN

HAZEL

I'm not going to admit how many times I came on Saturday and Sunday, imagining Grayson while my vibrator worked overtime.

It would be embarrassing. I should add, though, that it was the best weekend I've spent by myself in a long time.

His electric touch has always been dangerous, but when he touches my sweet spot? Forget it. I don't know how he made it out of my house with his dick intact. I was a breath away from claiming it for my own. It's been too damn long—I'm the first to admit that—but with the gorgeous wall of Grayson tempting me like that, practically demanding action from me?

I may be bitter and jaded, but I'm still all woman.

And honestly, I'm not mad that he plans to come in today. I'm refining my approach now. He wants to take this into sexual territory, then I can play his game. I'll lift my boobs so high they touch my chin. My heels will double as pole barn beams. I am about to be

every man's fantasy, and I can't wait for him to see me and not have me
.

I'm humming to myself as I prepare myself for my workday. I wake up at the crack of dawn because I thrive in the morning hours and I love watching the sunrise. I get testy if I miss one—it sets the wrong tone for the day.

Once I'm suited up—ruffly, lowcut blouse, form-fitting skirt, glossy black heels—and at the office, I work and watch the clock in equal measure. Wondering when he'll finally strut in. Whether or not he'll bring his hand to the back of my knee and turn my body into an aching pool of desire.

I squeeze my thighs together. I get a few calls early, and an unexpected visit from the newspaper delivery lady. Hours tick by.

And then finally—blessedly—he arrives. I spot him as he's parking across the street in a shiny black VW, the type of car you don't see in these parts too often. I go rigid as he steps out, sunglasses on, his tall, wide frame covered in a sexy black-on-black suit.

I whip my attention back to my computer. I can feel him approaching inside my bones. He's getting closer. Closer. Yes. Come into the office, Grayson! I am lassoing him in my mind's eye.

Except the bells never jingle with his arrival. I look up, glancing down the long line of windows. No Grayson. Not out front, trapped in conversation with our very chatty mailman who has trapped everyone in the middle of a big hurry. Not down the sidewalk of Water Street, which hugs my office. He's gone. Freaking *gone*.

I push to standing and head to the window to further inspect what I can see of downtown. It would be wrong to go outside and start searching for him, but I *want* to.

Sighing, I pace the far wall of my office. This is the sign I needed—I'm going crazy. This needs to stop. Immediately.

I jump when the bell jingles. I whip around. Grayson stands in the doorway, blowing on an open cup of coffee.

"Oh," I say, unnerved that my legs threaten to completely give way. Like they're made of Jell-O. Like they are traitorous limbs that need to be removed, lest they be associated with Grayson Daly.

"Morning," he says, breezing toward me. He sets a second coffee cup—with a lid—on the desk without a word. He sinks into the seat facing my desk. I swallow hard, but my mouth has gone dry. I can't tell if this is a Trojan horse or a peace offering. Either one is unacceptable.

"Why are you dressed like that?" I go through some mail on the top of my desk. I don't look at him. Strictly speaking, it's not *wise* to. One glance at him in the doorway and he'd robbed me of my vital energy. He's like a vampire, but without the sinking teeth. His gaze alone cuts deeper than any fangs and drains important energy better than any Dracula ever could.

He clears his throat, and that's when I notice. Something's off about him. He sets his coffee down, something haunted in his gaze. "Funeral's later."

I bite at the inside of my cheek. "Shit. Sorry, Gray."

He shrugs. "Is something wrong with the way I'm dressed?"

"No, no." I lean against the edge of my desk, frowning. "It's perfect for a funeral."

"So what's your excuse for how you're dressed?"

I blink, slowly turning to face him. I cannot believe he said that. Or that he returned the same tone I used with him.

"Do you have a problem with the way I'm dressed?"

His heated gaze skates over me. The tension spikes between us. I think I have proof that my evil plan is working. I decide to test it further. To gather evidence. For science.

"I'm wearing a simple, plain skirt," I say, crossing my arms right under my boobs. His jaw flexes. "A very normal, conservative shirt."

"Conservative," he repeats.

I cross my legs, grateful that my skirt was already riding high, and now half my damn thigh is exposed. I perch on the edge of my desk, daring him to admit that I look good. "I would call this look professional chic." I kick up a leg, turning my foot around to admire the heel. "Do you like my shoes?"

He sighs tersely, shifting in his seat. "Look a little high for someone recovering from a water ski crash. Though I think I've seen them at the dollar store before."

A laugh rockets out of me. Probably not the reaction he expected. "Okay, pal. Insult my designer shoes. I'm so offended. Do you want me to start talking shit about your German car out there? Is that the next step in this?"

"Insult my brand-new car and there will be consequences," he says, a sexy edge to his voice.

"Don't talk about my clothes then."

"Fine."

I pop to my feet. "Fine." I come around to the back of the desk, feeling both frustrated and resolved. I want more of him; I just don't know how to get it. I think the solution has something to do with that frustratingly nice appendage between his legs. "Let's get a move on. I have a one o'clock appointment that I can't miss."

Grayson sits up, rummaging in his inside jacket pocket. He pulls out his phone and answers a call. His face turns stony, and all the air in the room goes taut.

"Do I need to remind you," he begins, a testy edge to his voice I haven't heard before, "that I'm on vacation?" I try not to appear too interested as he takes the call, stacking folders that don't need attention.

"No," he snaps after a long period of silence. "You handle it. And if you call me again today, I'll cut your pay."

Grayson pockets the phone a moment later, glancing up at me. "What?" he asks.

"Wow. I didn't know you could be even *more* unpleasant than you already are."

He stands up, adjusting the cuffs of his suit. "It would be nice to have employees who could respect the one day of the year that I need to be unavailable."

The sentiment behind his words softens me slightly. He's in mourning, which makes his assholiness even assholier. "Aren't you on vacation?"

"Vacation means something else in New York. It means I'm working, just not physically present." Grayson runs a hand through his hair, tension straining at his jaw. Whatever his job is over there, he doesn't love it.

I'm not sure what to say. If he were anybody else, I'd try to console him. Learn more about his life. Maybe find ways to make it better, like a hug or offering a shoulder. But I can't treat Grayson like any old person. He's my enemy. I must be alert.

"Find a job you love and you won't work a day in your life," I say, heading toward the door. It's unhelpful and I know it. He follows behind me, and I lock up the office. It's a beautiful, sunny spring day. A breeze lifts my hair, bringing the tip of my long ponytail over my shoulder.

"Yeah, yeah," he grumbles, shoving his hands in his pockets.

"Meet you there?" I ask, jerking my chin toward his car across the street.

"I'm driving."

I glance down the street where my American-made car is waiting for me. Honestly, his car is sexier. I'd love to check out the interior. "You sure you can tolerate having me in that confined space for five minutes?"

He pulls out his keys and unlocks the door. The VW beeps softly in response. "I think I can manage."

My heels click over the asphalt of the road as we head to his car. Grayson slides into the driver's seat, and I come around to the other side. I'm already squeezing my thighs together. This is my weakness—a sexy man with a sexy car. Add in that suit, and I'm a goner. I should have insisted I drive separately.

Inside, the car is immaculate. A well-kept car is an insane turn-on. The engine roars to life, and I can tell he's got a non-standard engine under the hood. I roll my lips inward, the backs of my thighs loving the feel of the soft leather.

"Nice car," I mutter, reaching for the seatbelt. "You drive this in New York?"

He jerks his head to say *no* as he backs out of the spot and pulls into the street. "She spends most of her time in the parking garage. I get her out mostly to take road trips."

"Hmm." I keep my hands in my lap, though really I want to touch every inch of the interior. The inside even smells like him. Like if a cedar tree and a cologne bottle had a baby. My head is swirling by the time we pull up to his grandma's house.

I go into Realtor mode as soon as the car shuts off. Curb appeal stands out first. The front yard is a disaster. Landscaping totally weeded over. The front step up to the dilapidated porch is broken, cement pieces crumbled off to the side. Grayson leads the way to the front door and pushes inside.

The house is empty, and it's obvious it's sat that way for a long time. Cobwebs have gathered in the corners of the ceiling. The natural light is great, but the whole place looks like it's fresh from a 70s catalog.

"When was the last time anyone lived here?" I ask.

"I think the 80s," Grayson says, scuffing along behind me as I poke around all the downstairs rooms. My whole backside sizzles.

I wonder if he's staring at me. I glance over my shoulder; his gaze is waiting for me. An expectant shiver runs down my spine as I recall the intensity of his touch on my couch the other day.

I shouldn't want more of that, but I do. It's the only thing I want anymore, and it doesn't make sense.

"Can we go upstairs?" I ask.

He leads the way, our footsteps clunking up the wooden staircase. Upstairs, the hallways are a bit dark. Things feel closed in. My skin prickles as I imagine a skylight going in. That would give the place a major refresh. He could do a hundred tiny things to make this place more desirable to the average buyer. And about a million more that I could suggest to suit my own personal tastes. I don't know if he cares enough to make the most basic changes, though.

"It's really a cute house," I finally say, after the brief tour of the bedrooms. We're paused in the master bedroom, looking out at the tree-lined street. Cute is an understatement. It's the house I wish I'd bought, with its wraparound porch and tree-shaded backyard. I love my house—I really do. This house would be so fun to fix up. "Obviously the location is amazing."

"So what do you think you can get for it?" He rests his palm on the wood trim around the window, rustling something around in his pants pocket as he stares out to the street below.

"Well, that really depends on what sort of updates have been done. I'm talking water heater, roof..." I use my pen to point out the hot water radiator sticking out from the wall. "That right there is not a great selling point. They get hot; people get burned. You get a family with three kids under five looking to buy, and there's a serious issue with safety suddenly."

Grayson looks annoyed. He swings to face me. "Okay. So what can I get for it?"

I sigh, running my fingertips over my hairline. "Ballpark? Probably three-fifty. But that's strictly based on location and the current market. You'd probably be driven down by a savvy buyer who recognizes that the purchase of this house means redoing the heating and roof. I'd say a realistic closing price might be around three hundred."

Grayson works his jaw back and forth, his eyes made of pure storms. "That's not what I want to hear."

"You wanted me as your real estate agent; I'm not going to lie to you."

"The lake is a block away," he says, gesturing north.

"But the house has been abandoned since the 80s."

He sighs, rubbing at the back of his neck. He takes a few paces across the room, then swivels my way again. "I need that number to be higher. Much higher."

"The more buyer-ready you make this house, the better the price you'll get for it," I say, shrugging. "Some small but important renovations could really jack the price up on this one. My recommendation would be to do as many renovations as possible. But you can sell it as-is, of course."

Grayson doesn't look enthused about this information.

"Truth is...this area in tourism season is *hot*," I go on. "You've got thousands of visitors streaming in daily because of the amusement park in the next town over. Why don't you want the property? You could do so much with it."

And it's true. I'm seeing dollar signs everywhere I look. Not only the dollar signs that go into my pocket from the sale of this house, but the *potential* of it. He could turn it into a trendy home share. I can already envision the cute little wooden sign on the wall that says *Lake. Sunset. Wine. Repeat.* The houndstooth bathmats with a fake fern in the corner.

It would be incredibly fun to turn this into a rental property. And it's something I'd take on myself, if I had a fraction of free time, or, I don't know, a partner who could keep up with me.

"Are you serious?" Grayson asks, the acid practically dripping from his mouth. "Owning property in Bayshore is the *last* thing I want to do with my life. I fought for eighteen years to get away from here—and now that I'm out, I'm never anchoring myself here again."

I roll my lips inward, all the sexiness that had accumulated over the weekend dissolving in a weak puff.

"Bayshore has changed a lot since we were kids," I say, feeling like I should defend Bayshore, even though it's pointless. Grayson's position is clear.

"Maybe so. But it's still Bayshore. Way too small for what I want to do with my life."

I clench my teeth, fighting back the slew of retorts that come to mind. Getting into it with him right now is not the wise choice. I need to capitalize on his desire to sell his house, make my money, and move on.

But still, I feel like Grayson is fundamentally wrong about our hometown. I don't understand why he hates it so much. Maybe he doesn't either. I shouldn't spend a second longer wanting to change this man.

Besides, what am I thinking? That the sparks I felt over the weekend might catch fire and grow into something bigger, something more satisfying?

I realize right then that I've been deluding myself, if on a very abstract, unaware level. That's where all the best delusion occurs, after all. Part of me was hopeful that Grayson might actually prove to be a breath of fresh air. That unexpected romance I've been craving. That equal-witted partner I've only dreamed about during my adulthood.

But no. He's none of that.

He's just the same competitive, unhappy asshole he's always been.

Except now? Unhappier. Even more of an asshole.

And that is the last thing I need in my life.

CHAPTER EIGHT

GRAYSON

Funerals suck. It's a universal fact. Maybe you don't care about the relative or long-lost friend that much, or maybe you do—either way, funerals turn into a pressure cooker of emotions and nostalgia, and everyone loses their goddamn minds.

I'm no exception. The second I step into the big, Catholic church in the center of town, my dark mood turns black. Like black hole-level black. Nothing escaping its clutches. Thankfully, people are supposed to be quiet in churches, which means avoiding eye contact and conversation. Sign me up.

I knew something was wrong that morning when I snapped at Hazel the way I did. It wasn't even part of our ongoing competition. It was strictly the Bad Mood Bears coming out to play. My footsteps scuff softly against the tiled floors as I make my way to the front row of the church, where the entire Daly clan is sitting. Mom's in the center of the pew, flanked by Dominic to her left—of course—and then to her right, Dad, Weston, Maverick, and Connor.

I stop at the end of the aisle, and all my relatives turn to look at me. Six sets of electric blue eyes. Mom is dabbing her nose with a tissue. Dad, a hulking man with salt and pepper hair, is stuffed into a black suit.

"Move over," I hiss at Dom.

He furrows his brows, giving me a look that says, *What the fuck?*

"I'm sitting next to Mom," I clarify, starting to step past Connor. Dad clears his throat loudly.

"We can scoot down, you know," Connor gripes.

"Gray, that's my *foot*," Maverick says. I try to step more carefully. Disapproving frowns form in the rows behind me.

"You could get here on time," Dominic says as he leans forward, sending me a stern look that almost pushes me over the fucking ledge. Like he's my dad. Like he's anybody's dad.

"You could shut your mouth," I return, as the organ music crescendos. Muffled coughs echo through the vast church.

Our actual dad sends me a glare. "Sit down."

"I'm trying," I hiss.

"Has your ass always been this big?" Weston asks.

"Let me sit down," I demand. "I'm the second oldest. I should be next to Mom."

"Oh, honey," Mom says, her voice thick with emotion. Like she doesn't have the energy for any of this. I wedge myself in between her and Dom. Dom gives me a death stare as he slides further down the pew to make way for the shift in people. All of us boys have spent our lives fighting over Mom. This is nothing new.

"How are you doing, Mom?" I ask, wrapping my arm around her shoulders. She nods and pats my chest. Up on the chancel, the closed casket sits. My throat tightens and I jerk my gaze away, to anywhere else. To the stained glass windows towering above us, to the ornate columns spiraling up into the domed ceiling. The last time I was in this church, I was probably about thirteen—and with Grammy Ethel. Everything about this place reminds me of her.

I knew this was going to be an unpleasant day. Emotions and all that. Honestly, it's part of the reason why I wanted to start it off with Hazel. To keep my mind off things. To distract. It didn't work terribly well—really, it might have made things worse.

The service is short and sentimental. I'm a pall bearer, along with all of my brothers and our dad. We form a train of cars leading to the cemetery. I'm thankful for the space, because it gives me time to address the pressure building inside my chest. All I can feel is magma and discontent. It's swirling and pushing at my ribs, like a shaken champagne bottle. But it has nothing to do with my grandma. That much, I can tell.

I'm sad, and regret not spending more time with her before she passed. But this pressure inside my chest feels like muck that's bubbled to the surface. Like a tar that's been coating my insides and finally burbled free. My phone buzzes, and I snatch it up to look at it. This wild, unhinged part of me wants it to be Hazel. Even though there's no reason for her to be texting. Even though she doesn't have my number.

Instead, it's work. My assistant, Chad. His text message is concise: "Kratz wants a meeting with you Monday, what should I tell him?"

That's a week from now. I put in for a four-week vacation, fully intending on staying out of the city that long, if not longer. Rage is simmering in my gut now, a caustic, thick stew that's been sitting there for too long.

My chest gets so tight I almost can't see for a second. I grip the steering wheel and when the processional slows, I slam on my brakes. The truth bubbles up to the surface.

You're fucking unhappy and need to quit.

It's not the first time this revelation has occurred to me. But each time it arrives, like an unwanted religious visitor at the front door, I'd rather wait it out in the shadows instead of confronting it.

Backing down from the life I've created—the life I've fought to have—isn't on the table. I have everything I need. Everything I thought I wanted. There's no place for unhappiness in Brooklyn, in my sweet apartment, with a high-powered job and investment opportunities nearly drowning me with how plentiful they are. I mean, sure, everyone's sort of unhappy in Brooklyn, but it's a collective misery. The sort of *we're all in this crazy shit together* impersonal camaraderie that you can see gleaming on the faces of my fellow scowling New Yorkers.

It's everything anybody should want.

Besides, what are my options? Go to the already-popped tech bubble of San Francisco, relocate to Seattle and pay the same rent for an even smaller apartment, or...what? Move home to Bayshore like a resigned loser, tail between my legs?

This feeling will pass.

Except I'm not sure it's ever truly passed, not really. When it comes up, it stains the air around me. Urging me to fix it. Do something. Even just acknowledge it.

But I can't. I don't know where else to go. So it's easier to ignore. Ignore and distract.

It's occurred to me, like the most inappropriate joke whispered in the middle of a quiet room, that getting my four-week vacation and planning to spend it in Bayshore was something of a test run. It's not like I've ever seriously considered moving home. It's a non-option. But the thought sometimes hangs there, bulky and uncomfortable, like a doctor sticking his finger up my asshole during a routine visit.

And when that feeling persists, you do anything you can to ignore it. Numb it. Move on.

The service at the burial site is emotional. Final. The priest drones on while I fight tears. My brothers and I linger near the plot, tossing roses on top of the lowered casket. Dad mentions that he's already purchased his and Mom's plots nearby.

"And you didn't get ours too?" Weston asks, trying to lighten the mood. We'd all just glower and stomp around, but Weston tries to pick up our spirits. He's really the nicest one of us all. I'm not entirely sure how he came out so free-spirited and happy when the rest of us are generally assholes. Except Mom, of course. "Isn't there a Groupon for stuff like that?"

Dad grunts. "I don't know what this Roopon stuff is."

"Groupon, Dad," Maverick sighs.

We head back to the house in a daze. I have my arm around Mom's shoulders, but she's stony-faced and silent.

Grammy Ethel wasn't only her mom; she'd been her best friend too. One of her rocks had departed this earth. Honestly, I'm glad I'm going to be around for another three and a half weeks. I need to make sure Mom is good before I go. Dad is a rock for her, but not in the way that her mom was. He's more of a pension-holding sort of rock and less of an emotionally supportive rock.

Back at Mom's house, we fill the driveway and part of the street with our cars. I shut my door right as Connor and Kinsley step out of his rental.

Connor looks legitimately distraught. Kinsley's cheeks are pink and puffy, like she's been crying. I'll admit, I underestimated my brother's relationship with the daughter of our rival family. I thought he'd done it just to piss Mom and Dad off.

But Connor slides his arm around Kinsley's waist as if he's been doing it for years, and I realize that my brother has an entire life in California that I know nothing about.

He's the only Daly son with a girlfriend. Maybe I need to take lessons from my little brother.

"You two okay?" I ask, mustering a smile. Kinsley nods and sniffs. Connor squeezes my shoulder, the sun catching his sandy blond hair. Slowly, we all weave our way into the house. Our childhood home.

No matter how long I've been away, no matter what I think about Bayshore, the smell of home can bring me to my knees. It's not that she uses any special perfume or anything inside the house—no randomly spurting air fresheners. No, it's the smell of our family, baked into the wood floors and the sunny corners and the familiar paths through the rooms. It's the thirty-plus years of living in the house, mixed with children's tears and adolescent rages and the inescapable grief and joy that accompanies any ounce of life.

I wish it was a perfume, so I could bottle it and take it with me to New York. Take a sniff anytime I felt down. Even though I'd probably sniff the bottle away within a week's time.

We're all loosening ties and kicking off shoes at the front door. Soon, my childhood home is full of chatter. Mom drifts toward the back windows and sighs while looking at the backyard, where my dad is puttering around the grill.

"You should go get a massage this week," I suggest as I stand beside her, trying to suss out what she's staring at. Maybe it's the cardinals at the feeder. Or maybe it's the uneven edging along the back walkway, completed by yours truly because, hey, I've been living in a big city for a decade. I don't utilize lawn equipment anymore. "I'll pay. I can make the appointment for you."

She heaves a sigh, shaking her head. "You know what would be nice?"

"What?"

She turns to look at me, her eyes so clear and vibrant they're practically icy. "If all my sons were home."

I tilt my head. "Mom. We are home. Right now."

"That's not what I mean." She sighs, wrapping her black shawl tighter around her arms. She breezes past me then, joining Kinsley in the kitchen.

"Do you ever think about moving back to Bayshore?" she asks Kinsley.

Kinsley blinks a few times, studying the countertop. "Well...actually, yes. Rent is ridiculous in California."

"I couldn't move back," I say, joining them in the kitchen. So do Dominic and Connor. "My job doesn't exist in Bayshore."

"You act like you're the royal shoe shiner or something," Dominic chides.

I narrow my eyes at him. "That's not even—That doesn't make sense."

"Tell you one thing I missed about home," Connor says with a sigh, easing onto a stool facing the women in the kitchen. "The lake."

"See?" Mom's smile glimmers hopefully. "I'll just need to find my own way to lure each of you home."

"I live an hour away," Dominic reminds her.

"But she won't be happy until you have the deed to a house in your hand with a Bayshore address," Maverick says, joining the conversation. He's got the darkest head of hair of all of us, and combined with his gaunt features, he looks a little angry almost all of the time. It's like Resting Bitch Face, but for dudes. Let's call it Resting Dick Face.

"I wouldn't say no to that," Mom admits.

Weston joins a moment later. He's already changed into long linen pants and a soft tee that says PEACE. "Is everyone moving home? You mean I have to go find my own place?"

"You should have your own place by now," Dominic reminds him, and I suppress a smile. I'd been about to say the same thing.

"It's not worth it for me to rent." Weston opens the fridge and stares inside. He's twenty-four but looks every inch a teenager as he stares dully at the contents. "Besides, no landlord would rent to me for just a few months. You sign leases for a year at a time."

His response sounds practiced. Like he's repeated it to Dad a million times. Weston is on the move a lot. I'm not really sure what he does or how he affords it.

"Where did you go most recently?" I ask, as Dad comes lumbering through the sliding glass door to the deck.

"Massachusetts," he says, then shuts the fridge without taking anything out. "There was a con."

"Ah." I shove my hands in my pockets, trying to locate anything relevant to this tidbit. I've got nothing. I really should know my family better. "What's that again?"

Dad snorts. They've probably had this exact conversation before.

"A convention," Weston says. "You know, like Comic-Con, Star Wars Con..."

"So you go dressed up as Jabba the Hut?" Connor asks, grinning. At least I'm not the only one who doesn't know what's going on.

"No. I mean, it's not required." Weston runs a hand through his light brown hair. Of the five of us, Connor got blessed with the blond tresses. I used to be so envious when I was little. But when I grew up, I realized the whole *tall, dark, and handsome* combo was as potent—if not more so—than the *dinner, movie, and wine* combo.

"What do you *do* there?" I ask, unable to keep the question inside. It shows how little I know, but I suspect Dom and Connor are wondering the same.

"I work." Weston shrugs, looking at each one of us in turn. When silence settles over the kitchen, he asks, "What?"

I can already sense Dominic's fatherly disappointment, which grates the fuck out of me. Probably because Dad is standing right next to him, and they've both got their arms folded across their chests in *the exact same way.* And then I realize—I do too. It's like we're related. I love but also hate how similar we all are.

I hurry to drop my arms and add, "Well, that's cool. Drifting around to different cons." I work my jaw back and forth, debating whether or not I want to say the next words. "Sometimes I'd give anything to drift away from my job."

"Office got ya down?" Dom asks.

Fuck. Shouldn't have said that in front of him. There's the ammunition he's been looking for. "Handling millions of dollars a day is stressful. Sometimes it would be nice to float, is all I'm saying. Like what you do—" I wave my hand in the air dismissively. Dom is a doctor at a hospital in Cleveland. "Sounds relaxing. Just need to see patients and be done with it."

Dom works his jaw back and forth, and I try to squash my grin. It's fun to irritate my big brother.

"People and paperwork, right? A breeze." I tap my knuckles on the countertop.

"I save people's lives," Dom clarifies, exactly the level of miffed I'd been aiming for. "When's the last time you've performed an emergency surgery for someone hanging onto life by a thread?"

"Boys," Mom begins in that tone reserved exclusively for extinguishing fights before they've technically started. Dad heads to the fridge, and a second later a beer cracks open.

"It's important work," I go on, satisfaction flickering inside me. Dad starts handing out beers. I'm not sure if it's to quell the pending explosion or goad it into something larger. "I'm just talking more about the type of people we serve. You're doing important work on the ground. I'm...a little higher up. The upper echelon."

Connor snorts while Dom glowers.

"Yeah, wiping the ass cracks of petty billionaires sounds like a pretty great way to make a living," Dom mutters.

"I'm not wiping ass cracks," I say, sipping at my beer, "but I'm sure cleaning up."

"Gray's going to be the one footing the bill when we're in the nursing home," Dad cracks as he heads back to the patio. And somehow, that remark means a *lot* to me. Probably because Dad has always made it more than clear that he favored Dom's profession simply because it was in the same industry: healthcare.

Dad has worked as the CEO of the local hospital for the past thirty years, and Dom became his pride and joy once he announced his decision to attend medical school. Cue the ensuing years of disappointment as the rest of his sons took varied paths: investment banking, software engineering, drifting travels, and then the indecision of the youngest whose only real profession seemed to be getting drunk and fucking.

"Could you toss a million my way?" Maverick asks.

"Come work for me for a year, and then maybe I could."

He looks like he's considering it.

"You're not going to Brooklyn too," Mom warns. "I already lost one son to the Big Apple; you're not making it two."

"Ehh, I don't think I'm cut out for what Gray does," Mav says with a sigh. "Whatever it is."

"Does nobody in this family know what the other does?" Connor asks. Kinsley snickers as she cuts up pieces of fancy cheese.

It was meant as a joke, but it thuds through the room, leaving a sick taste in my mouth. He's right, and for the first time in my adult life, it doesn't feel good.

It's easy to forget about people when they aren't in your circle every day. When they're hundreds or thousands of miles away. It's easy to forget why they matter. It's easy to forget the past, the words and the people that formed you.

But being back in Bayshore, with all four of my brothers around me for the first time in a decade? My mom smiling sweetly at all of us, while my dad lights up the grill outside? There's something relieving here, even amidst the awkwardness and the emotion. If I close my eyes, it's almost like I'm sixteen again, and little Mav is zipping around the kitchen with his toy truck, Dom is poring over college application paperwork, while West hangs from the treehouse in the backyard and Connor secretly whispers on the phone to his middle school girlfriend. It's weird how much I still feel like that kid—that sixteen-year-old in the middle of all the noise and family.

It's weird how far away from that New York takes me.

Even weirder is how good it feels to be back in it.

CHAPTER NINE

GRAYSON

I take a day to let my emotions harden back into the immobile glacier they used to be. But on Tuesday night, something's hammering inside my chest I can't fucking ignore anymore.

This pressure pushes me down the street to the little quick mart by the beach around sunset. The lake and sky reflect goldenrod and crimson back and forth between them. I pause outside the store for a moment, lifting my sunglasses to behold the spectacle. Fuck, this place is gorgeous in the summer. I've been here less than a week, and my stress levels have plummeted. Lake life, and all that shit. Hitting the Jet Ski daily probably has something to do with it too.

Inside, the smell of cumin and floor cleaner greets me. Ms. Singh is a self-proclaimed incorrigible vegetarian, and the smell of her veggie creations have permeated this storefront for decades now.

"Grayson," she drawls as I come inside, my boat shoes scuffing over the dirty linoleum. "It's good to see you back."

I extend my arms for a hug. She's a squat and squishy woman, made of pure love and wry humor. And, of course, cuminy vegetables.

"I'll be around for another few weeks," I tell her. "Then it's back to NYC for me."

"Pity," she says, grabbing a dishtowel. "Bayshore needs more men like you. So many new arrivals around here recently. Nobody cares about Ms. Singh's store like you and your brothers."

It's true—we probably supported her throughout the 90s based on our gum and magazine purchases alone. Now, though, I'm here for more sophisticated things.

Like wine and whiskey.

"You know that this is my only stop when I'm in town," I promise her. "Don't Weston and Maverick come around?"

"Oh, Maverick's in here basically every day," she laughs. "Weston stops by occasionally. When he's not jumping trains or whatever it is he does out west."

I lift a brow. Apparently, nobody knows what Weston does, or he really is a secret jack of all trades. "Out west?"

"Yeah. He did some mining thing in Nevada…?" She waves her hand. "I'm not sure. It's hard to keep up with him."

That's the truth. I make a note to bring this up later. If Weston went west, maybe he met up with Connor. I feel like this might make my mom feel better. And I'm trying to gather all the feel-good tidbits possible.

I peruse her famed wall of liquor and wine. I get the most expensive bottle of whiskey she has, as well as her best bottle of dry red. Something from California. She rings me up and throws in a pack of gum for free. For old times' sake.

With the sunset blazing at my back, I walk away from the lake and back into the neighborhood, swerving toward the next street over from my mom's house. The farther I walk, the more my heart rate picks up. I shouldn't be this nervous—I'm a twenty-eight-year-old *professional bachelor* for God's sake. I could use Tinder while in a coma. But the closer I get to Hazel's house, the louder my heart hammers.

It's because this is scandalous—and I know it. These bottles of alcohol are an olive branch. The last time I offered one of those—the metaphorical olive branch, not rum—we ended up dating.

It's just that Hazel is the only person I want to be around, even with all the barbs and the spitfire and the heavy history. There's something reassuring in our rivalry. And I need it more now than ever.

I start whistling once her house is in view, as if trying to convince myself that everything is fine on my insides. I can already see her brow arching up into the clouds. Questioning my presence. Stepping aside to let me in. Regarding me with that sexy suspicion that will melt away into certainty and passion.

The bottles clink together in my arms a bit as I step up the brick path to her front door. Everything is as neat and appealing as the last time I saw it. I knock three times on the front door and swallow the last bit of my nervousness. Hazel can't catch a whiff of it, or she'll seize it to her advantage.

We might have spent the last ten years apart, but I still know this woman like the back of my hand.

The door doesn't open. It didn't occur to me that she might not be home. I check my phone—almost nine p.m. The late sunsets of early summer are particularly magical, and I feel like I'm on stolen time. Just as I raise my fist to knock again, the door opens.

Hazel is in front of me suddenly, her cinnamon hair pulled back from her face, a few wisps loose and wild. She looks at me with an expression that is so pure, so honestly confused, that for a moment I am taken aback. I have no words. I have no response. I can only take her in.

"Hazel," I finally muster. My gaze has trekked across her face thirty thousand times in the ten seconds we've been staring at each other. And God, I want more.

"Gray?" she asks, her brows knitting together.

And that's when I notice the interior of her house. The slight movement behind her. I don't know what pulled at my attention, only that when I look up, I see she's not alone.

Hazel has company. And he goes by *Bryce*.

"What are you doing here? Is everything okay?" she asks. I catch a whiff of her scent, the orange blossom and floral musk that has begun to haunt my dreams.

I force my gaze off Bryce and back to her. I tighten my grip around the necks of the bottles in the paper bag. "Yeah. I, uh...I was walking by and thought I'd say hello."

Each heartbeat reinforces my disappointment. The implicit rejection of finding her here with *him*. I have no reason to be jealous. No reason to be angry. Yet I am. I'm so fucking jealous I could haul him off by the collar and make sure he leaves her alone for good. Heat flashes through my limbs. The paper bag crinkles beneath my grip.

"I don't want to bother you though," I hurry to add, hoping my face doesn't betray an ounce of the devastation trembling inside me. "Just thought...you know." I flash a smile, but it feels more like a grimace. My legs are carrying me away. This is retreat mode.

"Well—" she begins.

But I'm already halfway down the path, and halfway decided to chuck the bottles against the sidewalk. I had everything planned in my head. *Hey Hazel, let's spend the evening together. Netflix and dry red, amirite? Or Netflix and whiskey. You pick. But it must involve Netflix. And heavy groping.*

My mind buzzes as I head for the next street over, as fast as I can go without breaking into a run. I might duck away from her house in an embarrassed dash, but hell if I'll look as desperate as I feel. Once

I hit the next block, some of the tension in my shoulders lessens and I can *think* again.

And what hits me is the disappointment. Not in her—in myself.

Finding her there with Bryce shouldn't have hurt. But it did. Because I still carry this stupid torch for Hazel. No amount of denying it or ignoring it made it disappear over ten years. That's clearer than ever now.

And once again, old habits die hard. Hazel picked someone else. Someone lesser. Someone not as good looking, not as successful, not as smart.

I know that she has no reason to pick me. But fuck, I want her to. I've always wanted her to. Back then, I would have done anything to get her to pick me, and still she chose someone else. Even changed schools to get away from me.

This feels like an unnecessary rehash of something I should have learned eons ago.

And you know what? It's time to learn the lesson.

I'm done carrying this torch.

Time to burn it and bury it.

CHAPTER TEN

HAZEL

The front door shuts with a final *click.* Signaling the end of the opportunity I'd been secretly craving since age nineteen.

"Was that the asshole from the boat the other day?" Bryce asks.

My mouth flops open like a dead fish. I am as stunned as if Jason Momoa had stopped by my house on a whim. In fact, I previously thought there was a greater likelihood of Jason Momoa showing up over Grayson on a goodwill mission.

"Yeah." I nibble on my lip and return to the couch. That brief flash of Grayson is all I need to help me make up my mind.

My evening had been bombarded by two unexpected male visitors. First, Bryce, who'd walked me home from a group dinner with friends and was making his moves to try to spend the night.

And now, Gray, the fireball from left field.

"What's his deal?" Bryce asks, stretching out on the couch. He'd not-so-subtly invited me into his arms no fewer than five times.

"I honestly don't know." I curl up on the farthest edge of the couch from him, studying my cuticles as I talk. "He's probably just lonely and looking for someone to bother."

"Glad they didn't invite him to the dinner tonight," Bryce scoffs.

I try to muster my agreement, but the comment makes me sad. Grayson should have been there. He would have had a good time. Hell, I even missed him a little. Part of me wonders what it might be like to have him back in the group. My forearms light up with goosepimples imagining it.

For as much as it burns, I want the fireball.

"So, what, you two were friends back in the day?"

"Hardly," I say, voice sounding hollow. We were so much more than friends, and so much less. We've covered every notch on the spectrum between love and hate.

"Yeah, I can tell. Dude doesn't even know you. You know what he said about you on the boat?"

My neck flushes hot, and I hazard a glance toward Bryce. This isn't going to be good—the tense prickles in my shoulders warn me of it. "What?"

"He said you were a lesbian."

I almost laugh, even though it's so annoying. That's Grayson, all right—up to his old tricks. Even ten years later. I shake my head.

"Like he was trying to throw me off your tail, you know?" Bryce says. "Didn't work on me, though."

"What'd you say to him?"

"If you were a lesbian, well, better for me." He laughs like he really got one over on Grayson. "I mean, if you're into that, I know a couple girls we could invite over..."

I blink dully at him, something about his response settling bulkily inside me. Like boulders plummeting to the bottom of the ocean, tugging the last of my respect for him along with them.

It's not the ménage aspect that irritates me—to each their own, seriously. But whatever it is glinting behind Bryce's gaze reminds me that he's not what I'm after. Not even in a bid to have someone on my arm at the Bicentennial Ball.

Grayson might not be the best choice, but Bryce *definitely* isn't. I don't want him here. And maybe that's what Gray did for me tonight—reminded me that this half-assed excuse for male company isn't worth the effort.

"I think it's time for bed now," I say, my voice flat. So there's no question.

"So early?" he asks.

"Yeah. You should go." I stand up and head toward the door. I pull it open and offer the plastic smile reserved for my least favorite clients. "Gotta get up early for work."

Bryce doesn't say anything else and brushes past me. So much for that friend. The door thuds shut behind him, and I'm left in a churning mess of doubts.

Grayson showing up blew the lid off all these suppressed thoughts I've been having about him. Maybe he's got an ounce of these doubts too. I know how much of a gesture his showing up at my house must have been for him. I'm not stubborn enough to overlook that. And really, it makes me want to march over to his mom's house and demand he return.

But no. I've got more finesse than that.

I spend the night going over my game plan. This deserves immediate action. And I know exactly where to begin.

Early the next morning, I'm curling my hair against the backdrop of a blue-gray dawn right before it explodes into daffodil sunrise, counting the minutes before I can text Grayson.

I've rummaged up his number from my work database. The text has been typed out and ready to go since last night. My shoulders are tense from waiting, and I honestly think I'm going to explode.

I pore over my outfit choices, settling on a high-waisted black skirt coupled with a ruffled blouse. I add a fake flower to my hair for good measure—a pinch of tropical in my otherwise business-casual attire. I smile at my reflection, asking the woman in the mirror the question that's burned through me for the past week: *What do you want with Grayson?*

I still can't answer it, not even after I breeze into my office and hit SEND on the text that's been waiting for twelve hours. I know that I want *something* from him. More than that, I *need* it.

HAZEL: Can you be at the house today @ 4:30?

Grayson's response comes about fifteen minutes later.

GRAY: Why?

HAZEL: Interested buyer, I think you being there will help the walk-through.

GRAY: Not a big house, can't get lost.

HAZEL: History helps sell a home.

GRAY: You know the history of the house as well as I do.

I nibble on my lip as I reread his responses. I expected this. I'd seen the dejection flash across his face when he walked away last night. Grayson doesn't take well to failing at anything.

God, is it wrong to feel bad for him? I want to scoop him against my chest and reassure him that I actually would have massively preferred to spend the evening with him, exploring the contents of that paper bag under the stars, peering up at the moon, checking the clock every half hour and allowing myself a little bit more time at his side...

I press a hand to my forehead. I must have drunk some sort of mind-altering juice somewhere over the past week. *Willingly spend a work night with Grayson?*

I don't know who I've become, but this new Hazel is freaky. Practically unrecognizable.

HAZEL: Do you want to sell this house or not?

GRAY: See you there.

Fine. So I manipulated him into showing up. Now I just have to whittle away the rest of my day, anticipating the moment I see him.

The day passes blessedly fast. My phone rings off the hook, reminding me that I actually needed a secretary six months ago. I haven't had the time or energy to draft the help wanted ad. Besides, it's a whole thing, inviting another person into my space, into my process. Teaching them, getting them acclimated to the pace. I'm not mentally ready for all that. I'll do it by myself until I can't anymore.

I lock up the office around 4:20 and pull up to Grayson's house, being sure to park several spots away from the front door. The landscaping is still abysmal, not that he's had time to really make any changes, what with his family still in mourning.

I realize, after a full minute lingering on the sidewalk in front of the house, that I haven't taken a single breath. I'm so focused on looking casual and furtively scanning the horizon for Grayson that I don't realize when the couple looking to buy strolls up to me.

"Are you Hazel?"

I start, whipping around to face them. I'm never caught off guard. That's not what "Ask Hazel" is about. I blink rapidly, feeling the ready-made smile take over. "Yes! Hello! You must be Mr. and Mrs. Whitehall."

We all shake hands, cooing over the quaint street and the abundance of leafy trees nearby. My Spidey senses already tell me Mrs. Whitehall is ready to buy—Mr. Whitehall, however, needs a little push. I clutch my folders to my chest as the three of us start a slow walk toward the front door. I grit my teeth as we step over the cracked cement steps.

Right before I reach for the front door, Grayson shows up. He's sauntering along the sidewalk, his palms pressed to the back of his head. The front of his T-shirt is stained around the neck, like he's been sweating. Black workout shorts swish softly around his narrow hips, and the backward ballcap over his dark mocha tresses steals the air from my lungs.

"Here's the..." I can't finish my thought as he comes nearer. He doesn't look at me, which makes things worse. Gives me free reign to *ogle*. "The owner," I wheeze, right as he reaches the group.

"Hey there." He sounds a little winded, like maybe he just got done with a run. I can barely tear my eyes off the dark leg hair sprinkled down his muscly calves. He rests his hands on his hips.

"Grayson, please meet Mr. and Mrs. Whitehall," I say, gesturing toward them, eyes riveted on the swell of his bicep as he offers a hand to each of them in turn. "This house has been in his family for over four decades."

The cooing from Mrs. Whitehall is enough to prove why I supposedly needed him here. Even though, honestly? He's irrelevant right now. Irrelevant to anything other than a pulsing desire between my legs.

"Maybe it can be in our family for four decades too," Mrs. Whitehall says, lifting her eyebrows as she reaches for her husband's hand.

I lead the way, careful to keep my polite smile pressed in place as we walk through the house as I last saw it. Grayson lags, sticking to doorways and halls as I talk this place up as much as I can. I can feel his gaze sizzling over me. I hazard a glance once we've reached the kitchen, and as soon as I do, I trip over my words.

"The bicep—" My cheeks flame "*Basement* stairs are in excellent structural condition, but the railing does need replaced." I barrel on, unwilling to let Grayson bask in my mistake. Behind the Whitehalls, he begins scratching idly at his bicep. Lifting his sleeve up. *Tempting me.*

"But that's enough about this part," I say, fluttering my hand in the air as I lead them toward the staircase. "Let's see the upstairs!"

It becomes a mental test to give security clearance to every phrase in my head before it passes my lips. Just to be sure that no other subliminal thoughts escape like Houdini. Like saying *penis* for *pine trim*, or *sexy sweat stains* for *single family home.*

Luckily, I make it through my tour without any gross slipups. I am able to ignore the way Grayson props his hands on the top of the door molding, watching me with enough intensity that I'm worried the sun might catch his glare and light my blouse on fire.

By the time the tour is over, the Whitehalls are still divided. The Mrs. wants to restore everything as a pet project, but the Mr. wants move-in ready. Once they say goodbye and leave the house, it's Grayson and me in the foyer.

Staring at each other with so much restrained emotion I'm not sure if the next words out of my mouth will be "fuck you" or "fuck me now."

CHAPTER ELEVEN

HAZEL

"Was I really so needed here?" he asks, his voice so dry it could make a desert seem moist.

"I thought you wanted to sell this house," I say, cocking a hip. "Doesn't that entail doing everything possible to ensure that it moves?"

"I provided nothing," he says. "This was a waste of my time."

"Oh, so forty-five minutes out of your Wednesday during your vacation to be available for questions," I return, crossing my arms. "Seems like a real struggle."

He sets his jaw. "Whatever. Are we done here?"

I purse my lips, frustrated—but not surprised—that the man who'd shown up at my house with a sack of goodies last night is nowhere to be found now. Instead, he's the same grumpy, holier-than-thou asshole I've always known and hated.

My frustration bubbles up inside me like the Old Faithful geyser, because there is nothing more reliable and faithful than this feeling when it comes to Gray. I'd thought—stupidly—that maybe he'd be capable of more. That maybe he'd turned a new leaf or grown a new stalk altogether.

"Why did you lie to Bryce about me?" I blurt, unable to control the words as they hurtle past my lips. I don't have time to regret it though. His brows knit together.

"What are you talking about?"

"That day on the boat," I say, feeling my cheeks heat up. "You told him I was a lesbian."

He squints at me as if I'd suddenly asked him if he remembered the fundamental theorem of calculus from high school. "What does this have to do with anything?"

"You lied about me to him," I say, trying to keep my voice steady. It's never been easy to face this man down. "I want to know why."

He scoffs, as if this whole topic is so beneath him. Grayson rubs at his forehead for a moment, then says, "Because he was acting like a douche."

"So why tell him I'm a lesbian?" I won't let this go. I want to hear him say it.

He holds my gaze, those stormy eyes as beautiful as they are fearsome.

"I thought you liked girls," he says, the start of a shit-eating grin on his face.

"Girls are great friends, but you know I'm one hundred percent about the dick," I say before I can think better of it. His eyes flash. Got him. "Do you have a problem with the thought of me being on Bryce's dick?"

The air between us grows taut; time and space have shrunk in an effort to bring us closer. I swear we've both moved five steps closer without anyone moving an inch. I can't believe I'm saying these words, but that's Grayson. Pushing me to do the most absurd thing possible.

"I don't give a damn what you do, Hazel," he says, his voice low and threatening.

His words hurt, but only for a second, like a papercut. I take a definitive step closer. We're an arm's length away now. Every inch of my skin is crawling from wanting him, needing the heat of him against my skin. Even the brush of his thumb against that sensitive hollow behind my knee could send me over the edge right now.

"Why'd you come to my house last night?" I ask, my voice huskier now.

His stormy gaze doesn't waver from mine, but I can see the conflict flashing there. His jaw flexes, but he says nothing.

"It doesn't matter," he finally says, ripping his gaze away.

My heart pounds as the words escape my lips, almost without my consent. "Are you jealous of Bryce?"

He laughs, but it's humorless.

"Or are you jealous because he was the one inside my house?"

Gray's gaze hits me like a whip, and for a moment I wonder if this has all been one narcissistic fantasy on my part. I've got it all wrong. I'm just a small-town girl stuck in my small-town world, wishing that my high school frenemy would still want me. He only needs me for my realty services, and I've been reading too much into this whole damn thing.

"Jealous is the last thing I feel when I look at you two together," he spits. "Besides, you make a great pair. The douche and the attention-seeking realty princess. Couldn't be more perfectly matched."

This time, his words sting. He always used to hurl "princess" at me as an insult during high school, but now, it has a whole new layer of hurt. He thinks I'm some sort of pampered brat who sits back and has it all. And the fact that he overlooks how fucking hard I worked to get here—that's the part that makes me angriest of all.

I ball my fists. I'm done trying to provoke him, trying to win this battle. I thought we were on the same page, but we're not even reading the same book. I give up.

"Bryce and I aren't together," I clarify, trying to keep the emotion out of my voice. "But thanks for thinking so highly of me."

I spin on my heels, eager to put as much distance between this asshole and myself as I possibly can. I might even leave the state for a night, just to feel more secure in the distance. But before I make it three steps away, Grayson grabs my wrist, spinning me back to face him. I gasp as I land against the steel wall of his chest.

"What do you want to hear from me?" he growls, his big palms sliding up the sides of my arms. Traitorous goosebumps flare in their wake. "You want me to tell you how sad I am because pretty boy Bryce thinks he's such a big man because he's got you?"

If this is Grayson's version of mending fences, he's shown up to the job without any tools. I scoff, walking away. "Please."

He grabs for me, this time backing me up against the nearest wall. "Or maybe you want to hear about how, every time I see him near you, I have to physically restrain myself from pushing him off the nearest boat?" His hands have moved to my waist, tracing the line of my body through the crisp material of the blouse. My breath hitches as his fingers graze the swell of my breast. Jesus Lord in Heaven, I need to keep myself together.

"You want to hear about how much I have to jack off in the shower thinking about you? What is it, Hazel?"

I can't tell if he's speaking in hypotheticals, but the idea of him jacking off in the shower while thinking of me snaps the last of my resistance. Now I can't remember what we were talking about. Why I was angry. What my full name is. Not when his fingers are on me like this, and all I can sense is the sweat-laced scent of Grayson, pure cedar and manliness. I draw a fortifying breath while I fist his shirt in my right hand. Like this helps anything.

"Actually," I clarify, trying to keep my voice steady, "I would really rather you tell me if you're going to fucking kiss me or not."

A smile jerks at his lips. His blue eyes sweep over my face, as if assessing where to attack first. "You'd like it too much."

I huff, trying to push away from the wall, but Grayson keeps me pinned. There's no getting past him, and apparently his game plan has turned into pure teasing.

"Or maybe not at all, anymore," I shoot back, my pussy pulsing with desperation. God, I just need him *in me.* Fingers, cock, anything. Being around him reminds me that I've been craving him without knowing it all these years. His essence is baked into mine, and being around him again reactivated it. But it also brings with it a shit ton of frustration.

It doesn't matter. I need Grayson.

But, of course, he won't make it easy. Neither of us will.

"No, you'd still like it," Gray promises, then his hands drift over the tops of my breasts. He swipes his thumbs over the stiff points of my nipples, visible through my shirt. "I can tell."

Traitor boobs now, too. I huff. "Any other evidence you'd like to acquire? Maybe we can draw some blood? Do an MRI?"

He laughs. Genuinely. His head drops as he looks down at our bodies. He won't press himself against me, giving me the joy of learning what's happening on the lower half of his body. His palms crest the swell of my hips, and I hear what can only be described as a defeated sigh escape him.

"Oh, fuck," he says, then his hands smooth over the mounds of my ass.

"What?" I tease. Whatever battle he's fighting on the inside, I'm winning. I arch myself against him, coming up off the wall. There's no pretense of being held there against my will. We both want this. So badly I'm surprised we aren't frothing at the mouth.

He drags his eyes up mine. There's a warning in his gaze. One I understand as soon as he jerks my blouse out of the waist of my skirt.

"You gonna pop all my buttons off?" I tease. "Rip my shirt in half with your teeth?"

He tuts and shoves his warm hands beneath my blouse, cupping the sides of my rib cage. The heat melts me on contact; I wilt against the wall.

"The shirt stays," he says, his voice raw at the edges. He wets his bottom lips, gaze scanning my face.

And then he surges forward, capturing my lips in an eager kiss. The heat and scent of him consume me, prompting a tidal wave of emotions that I hadn't counted on, couldn't have even imagined. I whimper through the kiss, wrapping my arms around his neck. Every cell in my body is rioting beneath him, needing more of him, desperate to draw this out for as long as possible.

Because, right now, the worst thing that can happen is that Grayson prohibits this from going any further. I wouldn't put it past him.

His lips part, tongue surging forward to find mine. He grunts through the kiss, his big hands tracing the curves of my waist, pushing up over the satiny cups of my bra. The way he's kissing me right now makes me feel like I'm blind. Like every bit of energy inside me has exploded, and I'm caught in the middle. Useless and ecstatic.

Nobody has ever kissed me like this. Jesus Christ, Grayson probably *is* my soul mate. How twisted is that?

"Hazel," he says, his voice cracking. Sounding like a plea.

I coax another kiss out of him, tugging on his bottom lip with my teeth. He growls, grappling for the zipper on my skirt. His chest heaves as he fumbles, fails, and then finally tears it down.

"Might have broken that," he mumbles through a kiss.

"Don't care."

A groan rips out of him as he palms my ass cheeks beneath the fabric of the skirt. His fingertips digging into my flesh is a high unlike any I've felt before. He shoves the skirt down over my hips; it crumples to the ground. He slides a hot palm down the backside of my thigh, urging my knee up to his hip.

"There's no one else on their way, right?" he asks, his voice full of heat and grit.

I shake my head, unable to form words anymore. He grunts and hoists me. I gasp, cinching my arms around his neck as he carries me toward the kitchen, leaving my skirt in a heap on the empty living room floor. I squeeze my thighs around him, humming with approval as he sets me down on the countertop in the kitchen.

"Are you sure you want to defile your grandmother's house?" I ask him, locking my heels behind his back. He pushes the heel of his palm up the side of my leg while his lips leave damp trails along the side of my neck.

"It's my house now," he says, voice sounding faraway. "And I say we defile it."

"Not unless you take this stinky shirt off," I chide. It's the farthest thing from stinky. I want to take it home and curl up to sleep with it. I wouldn't wash it for weeks. I'd leave it until dust bunnies claimed it. I just need to see what's underneath.

Gray smirks and tears the shirt over his head, exposing tanned washboard and all. His ballcap pops off with the shirt, leaving his hair messy. I finger the stray strands.

"You already have sex hair and you haven't even fucked anyone," I murmur.

He sucks at his teeth, squeezing the fleshy part above my hips. "Watch your mouth."

"What was the naughty part about what I said?"

He grunts, jerking me closer to him so that our groins collide. That's when I notice the stiff ridge in his workout shorts. That divine hardness that I've been dreaming about for days. Or years, if I'm being honest.

"Everything you say is naughty," he says, his eyes on my lips. Then he dips down and captures my mouth in another kiss. We make out hot and heavy for a few moments. When we part, his fingers dance along the seam of my groin.

"Hazel," he whispers. His fingertips are like electrical pulses against my skin. All I can see or think about or feel is the sensation. His thumb swipes over the crotch of my panties, nicking the hard nub between my legs. I jerk against him as my breath hitches.

He smiles, slow and wide. "You're wet."

"No shit."

He presses his forehead to mine, dipping two fingers beneath the scrap of fabric covering my pussy. He wastes no time, plunging his thick middle finger inside me. My entire body goes rigid and hot. I cry out, arching against him.

"Fuck, Gray," I hiss.

"You're *really* wet." His voice is gravelly, and it makes me need him even more. I jerk against him, urging his finger to move in and out of me, but he just leaves it there. Enough to tease, and not enough to get me off.

"Come on," I urge, squeezing my thighs around his hips. "I need it."

"*Mmm.*" He swirls his finger in a slow circle, which makes my breath hitch. "I like to hear you beg."

That annoys me as much as it turns me on. I roll my lips inward, determined not to say it again. He draws his finger out of me, and I can feel myself leaking. There's probably a pond beneath me on his grandmother's 70s countertop, decked out in goldenrod and brown and pussy juice. Future buyers will love this. I'll be sure to point out the stains on my next walk-through.

"You're such a fucking—"

He plunges two fingers inside me, and the sensation is so surprising, so fucking *good* that my words bleed into a moan.

I toss my head back, bucking my pelvis toward him. "Come on, Gray. I need it!"

"What do you say?" he drawls in my ear, but I can hear the desperation edging his words. The primal takeover happening under his skin.

I grit my teeth. I hate him. But God, I like this a little too much.

"I say you better fuck me like I need you to." My voice comes out wispy against the assault of sensations. He's swirling his fingers around inside me again, and I'm bracing for whatever comes next. He slowly curls them, and I rock my hips against his hand. His thumb brushes my clit, and I whimper.

I'm so turned on I feel like I might come if he even breathes on my earlobe. His other hand drifts to my bra while his useless fingers are buried deep inside me, teasing me from the inside. The pad of his thumb makes lazy, inconsistent grazes across the stiff peak of my clit. Each time it makes contact, my entire body jerks.

"Fuck you," I wheeze.

"You wish." But this time, something in his voice has shifted. He's losing control. He pinches one of my nipples through the fabric of my bra, and my breath hitches again. "Now what do you say?"

I try to catch my breath as Gray keeps his fingers impossibly still inside me. I squeeze around him as hard as I can, like this might change his mind. He buries his lips in the hollow of my neck, and then he curls his fingers again.

A moan rips out of me, and I can't play his game any longer. "Please, Gray," I whisper into his jawline, the barely-there stubble scraping the sensitive flesh of my lips. His breathing is ragged now, and I can tell the last of his composure is slowly dissolving. I knew his fight wouldn't last long. Not when I'm laid out like this, on the kitchen countertop, fucking begging for it.

Grayson might be an asshole, but he's an asshole with a libido. He can't say no to this. To *me.*

To drive home the point, I gather up the mental clarity to feel my way down his exposed six pack, all the way to the waistline of his shorts. My fingertips meet the fleshy head of his cock. Peeking out from the waistband like a voyeur.

"Oh my," I say, laughter in my voice. My thumb traces the seam of his bulbous head, and he jerks beneath my touch. He begins moving his fingers inside me, as if my caressing his cockhead has allowed him to begin fingering me the way I need it. I don't want to come around his fingers—I want to come around his cock—but I'll take what I can get. At this point, if I don't come, I will *perish.*

"Careful," he warns, like I've never handled a dick before. "You're approaching the point of no return."

"We already passed that, homie," I tell him, bucking against his fingers. His thumb crashes into my clit again and tiny fireworks explode in my vision. Fuck, I'm so close. And he knows it. It's why he's denying me it.

He grunts. "I don't have a condom."

"Don't care." I shove down the waist band of his shorts to drive home my point. "Fuck me, Daly."

This must have been the password he was waiting for, because he pushes his shorts and briefs down over the massive mound. His cock springs free, bobbing heavy and framed by tightly trimmed dark hair. I inhale sharply as he grips me by the ass cheeks, arranging me on the countertop for prime entry.

"Fuck, Hazel," he hisses, and then he eases himself inside of me. Once the cockhead clears my entrance, I wilt. He scoops me up, bringing my chest crashing against his. A low moan escapes him as he flexes against me, finding a few more inches. And then another inch. And then another.

He sinks inside me until his entire cock has been claimed by my pussy, and I collapse forward, already spent from the sensation. I haven't come yet, but I could die happy. The heat of his cock pulsing inside me is more than just sexy—it somehow feels like completion. A fullness I've been seeking without finding. I sink my teeth into the ridge of his shoulder, and he hisses again, rocking his hips against me.

His big hands cup my ass, and he jerks me closer to him, finding another couple millimeters of space inside me. I gasp. He wastes no time in starting to fuck me—*really* fuck me—sending my breasts jiggling and the fleshy slaps of our bodies echoing through the kitchen. My head tilts backward as the pleasure riots inside me. I'm a breath away from orgasm after .35 seconds of fucking with this man. A new world record.

His fingertips dig into my ass as he thrusts into me over and over again, his pace both frenzied yet controlled. There's a method to his madness. Sweat collects at his temples, and I'm hanging on for dear life. Onto his shoulders. Onto my composure. Onto this feeling that everything is right with the world, if only for this fleeting moment.

"Graaaay," I moan, arching against him. I can't beat this back anymore. The friction and the heat and the steel inside me and the cedar and the sweat and the moans—it's too much. It's too fucking much, and suddenly I'm coming, my pussy clamping around him like a vice while the explosions turn my body into bright light and buzzing, and I tilt my head back and scream.

Grayson doesn't quit, though; he fucks me through the blinding peak of my orgasm all the way to the second tier and even third tier of residual pleasure, thanks to his thumb working its magic between my legs. Suddenly he pulls out, just when I've gone legally blind and deaf from the pleasure, and grunts as he spurts onto the kitchen floor in a perfect arc.

His chest heaves as he runs his hands through his hair, looking up at me like we've done something very bad. But bad in the best way.

I clutch the edge of the countertop beneath my ass, still lost in the clouds. My entire body is Jell-O, and I'm not sure I could stand if I wanted to.

"Holy…" I begin. Three more labored breaths. "Shit."

He swallows and nods, fisting the front of the hair as he looks down at the floor. "I came on my grandma's linoleum."

I don't know what it is—the words or the moment or the heady combination of both—but I burst out laughing, and I can't stop.

Grayson laughs along with me, and his laughs stoke my laughter.

We laugh until we've both got tears streaming down our faces.

CHAPTER TWELVE

GRAYSON

It wasn't until I came all over my grandma's kitchen that I noticed how ugly the flooring really was.

Burnt orange and white, mixed together in some heinous floral pattern. They say trends always return, but I really don't see this one coming back anytime soon. It belongs to—and died in—the 70s.

Hazel hadn't failed to mention about a hundred times how my resale value could skyrocket if I did some renovations. And I don't know—call it the clarity of an orgasm—but after I fucked Hazel in the kitchen, I decided to replace the flooring.

I figured I had enough time to get some basic things done, and if a few basic things might help me net an extra ten or twenty G? Worth it. Besides, everything is possible with YouTube.

I spend that whole night and the next day watching informational videos about the type of project I want to pull off. Within twenty-four hours of spunking all over the kitchen that started the Daly family, I have my toolbox and flooring equipment purchased and ready to go.

Home renovation is new to me, admittedly. But something about it has always attracted me. When I was a boy, I wanted to be an architect, which spoke to my love for cool houses. In my regular life in NYC, I don't get many chances to work with my hands or get dirty. Everything revolves around the office and the gym and the transportation in between. Hell, if I could get laid like last night even once a month, I'd be on cloud nine.

But of course I wouldn't have that chemistry with any of the random Tinder hookups of recent history. *Of course* the person who is able to set fire to every single nerve ending in my body is Hazel.

Murphy's Law or something like that.

Even thinking about Hazel's juicy pussy has my cock stiffening beneath my gym shorts. I haven't texted her, and she hasn't texted me. I don't plan to, either. It doesn't feel right...mostly because I still don't know what the fuck happened in this kitchen last night.

It wasn't a truce, but it wasn't part of a cold war, either. Per Hazel Protocol, it was something that exists in an abstract category, which defies expectations and reason. If Hazel were a mathematic equation, she would absolutely involve imaginary numbers because nothing about her makes sense, and she would appear in italics every time she was mentioned.

It takes me two full days, working over twelve hours each day with the help of Weston and Connor, to pull out Grandma Ethel's hideous burnt orange injustice and replace it with the slate gray wood-like laminate flooring I picked out. Once it's in, it's not just a breath of fresh air, it's a windstorm. Mom can't stop cooing about the pattern. And Weston was oddly an enormous help, proving once again what a strange wheelhouse my brother has.

"Your plans for the kitchen are amazing, Gray," Mom says, thumbing through the paint swatches I laid out on the countertop.

"If you did the whole house like this…" She tuts, shaking her head. "It would be the best house in the entire Daly family, for sure."

"Wow, now that's offensive," Connor says in mock injury. "You haven't seen the changes I made to my apartment in San Fran."

"Yeah, and what about my house that I'm never going to buy?" Weston asks. "You're shitting all over my future, Mom."

Mom sighs, a smile on her face. Of course she can count on her sons to hassle her about everything.

"I would like to disqualify my current apartment from the contest," I add, "Because I hired an interior designer to do that, so it shouldn't count. I want to win this distinction fair and square."

"Yeah, because now that there's any hint of a competition, Gray *has* to win," Connor says.

"Just don't tell Dom," Weston adds ominously.

I shake my head but say nothing because I definitely can't deny it. The only rivalry greater than the one between Hazel and me is between my older brother and me. And they're right. If Dom got involved, it would turn into a war.

"Whatever, guys," I finally say, stepping over the discard pile of ugly old tiles in the front sitting room. "You're salty because you know I'll win."

My brothers snicker while Mom drifts toward the front window, looking out at the yard. "Do you want me to help clean up the landscaping out here? I can put in some rose bushes, some lilies, maybe a weeping willow over there."

"That would be awesome, Mom." My phone buzzes.

HAZEL: Last minute potential buyer. 3p okay??

It's 2:45 right now. I text back that it's fine and address my family.

"Hazel's on her way with a potential buyer. We should clear out."

"Okay, okay." Mom sighs, heading for the front door. "You tell that sweetheart I said hi."

"I will."

Connor grabs for the open beer he left on the countertop. He's enjoying vacation as much as I am. He's only got a few more days left, though, whereas I still have weeks. A fact I love to shove in his and Dom's faces.

"We doing the bathroom remodel next?" Weston asks. The kid is genuinely interested in helping.

"Yeah, bro. Let's start it tomorrow."

"I'll go pick up some plumbing stuff," he says. "I know a guy who'll lend us what we need."

Of course Weston has the plumbing contact. I slap my brothers' backs on their way out the door, and then I get to work trying to tidy up the mess in the living room. There's a soft knock on the front door, and then Hazel pokes her head in a moment later.

I turn to look at her, and all the air in my lungs fizzles away. She's got skintight vinyl-looking leggings on with high heels, and a loose, flowing sweater that hangs off one shoulder. She's not retro today, like she normally is, but her lips are still fire-engine red. Gorgeous as always. My abs tense as I drink her in.

"Hey there," she says cautiously, her gaze jumping between the piles of crap in the living room. "What's all this?"

The trepidation in her voice tells me she wasn't expecting it. A couple comes in behind her, wide-eyed and smiling.

"Hi, guys," I say, surging forward to offer my hand. My tool belt jostles as I move forward. "I'm Gray. I was just cleaning up."

Haze's lips are pinched into a very particular sort of grimace-smile. She meets my gaze.

"Why didn't you tell me about this?" she asks, her words measured.

"Ahh..." I rest my hands on my hips, trying to think of anything she might accept. "I wanted it to be a surprise. I'm sure you'll be surprised when you go into the kitchen. But hey, don't let me get in the way. You guys do your tour. I'll be around if you need me."

Hazel moves past me stiffly, her heels clicking on the floor. I twist around to watch her go, wetting my bottom lip as I drink in the curve of her ass and that soft arc of her shoulder. Fuck. So apparently once wasn't enough with her. I adjust my jeans and get back to work cleaning up the debris. Listening to the husky lilt of her voice as she shows the house gets me lost in yet another Hazel fantasy while I sweep the living room floor.

Fifteen minutes later the tour is over, and she's chatted the couple out the door. She waves at them in a final goodbye and then pushes the front door shut.

She turns to me. Arms crossed. Eyebrow lifted.

"Why are you looking at me like that?"

"What is this?" She gestures at me kneeling on the floor. "What are you, Bob the Builder?"

I snort. "Didn't you tell me the resale value would improve if I did some renovations?"

She huffs. "Yes, but..." She gestures angrily at me again. "I didn't say you had to pretend to be some sort of construction model."

I sit back on my heels. "You want me to take my shirt off again."

"No, thank you. I got that out of my system."

"Right." My pulse quickens at the thought of what we did two days ago on the kitchen counter. Hell, the memory of my fingers buried in that juicy pussy might haunt me for the rest of my life. When I close my eyes, I see her face as she unraveled around me. Getting it out of my system is a non-option. I could fuck Hazel until the end of our days and still want more. "So, no thoughts on the kitchen? Just gonna body shame me for wearing these old jeans?"

She huffs again, but I see the start of a smile on her lips. She swings her head toward the kitchen. "It looks awesome, honestly. And if you finish the paint job and update the cabinets, you'll have buyers salivating over it."

"Great." I come to standing, wiping my hands off on my jeans. I can sense her eyeing me again. The tension in the house quadruples, and I swear to God the air is *buzzing* between us.

"I'm up here," I say, pointing to my face.

Hazel's rocking back and forth on her heels, looking at me like she wants to say something. Instead she spins on her heel and heads out the door. "I've got another appointment. Bye."

I watch her storm down the driveway and hop into her car. She basically peels out of the neighborhood. And maybe she's right to run away like that. There's something explosive burbling beneath the surface with us. I feel it too, except I don't want to run from it. I want to strip her down and bury myself right into the heart of it.

It's a little weird to think that we had as much sexual chemistry at age seventeen and eighteen as we do now at age twenty-eight. It makes me think there really has been something between us, simmering since time immemorial. It's as dreamy as it is upsetting. On the one hand, people like that story about soul mates and meant-to-be love. Except nobody knows what they're talking about, and "soul mates" is simply code for two people who are in love.

And if that's the only requirement, Hazel and I will never be soul mates.

On the other hand, something really has sparked between us since day one, starting in the hospital when we were born minutes apart. Like life designed a path for us to follow together. Though we diverged early on and tried to veer away from each other, here we are.

Butting heads in Bayshore again.

I fight the urge to go after her, even though I'd love to march her back inside this house and pin her against the wall one more time. Maybe this time, I'd start in the living room and work my way upstairs. Fuck her on every flat surface in the house. I could bring in additional flat surfaces and fuck her on those, too.

Something about the additional flat surfaces makes a lightbulb go off.

I should get some furniture.

Sure, fucking Hazel on new furniture *is a consideration* for this idea, but really, I want to see what this finished kitchen will look like. My mind races as I figure out my game plan. I could rent things temporarily while I'm here, but why not just buy? That way, I can pass them off to Maverick or Weston when I'm done. Like giving them a bachelor's leg up. I'm their big brother. I should do shit like this.

And the more I think about it, the more excited I get.

I should use my time in Bayshore to be as productive as possible. But that doesn't only mean physical labor.

It might also mean being a better brother and son.

CHAPTER THIRTEEN

HAZEL

It's eight thirty on Sunday night when a harsh knocking sounds on my front door. I jump out of my skin, not expecting anybody. In some places, people wouldn't show up without texting or calling first. Like sane twenty-first-century technology addicts. But no, in Bayshore, we're still small town and proud of it. Hence the unannounced visits that could send a cat bursting through the roof.

I pull open the door. The evening outside is bathed in gold and red, the air holding that unmistakable scent of early summer.

And in front of me, Grayson Daly.

Hotter than fucking ever.

"Are you alone?" he barks.

I narrow my eyes, trying to conjure even an ounce of irritation. It's hard, because all I can feel is relief. God, I've been pining for this man since the second he pulled himself out of me on Wednesday night. And now that he's decided to cultivate his construction-worker chic side, it's harder than ever to keep my libido at bay.

"Not if you count the entire cast of *Grey's Anatomy* waiting for me inside my television right now," I say.

He grins. He's at it again, in those worn jeans and stained white T-shirt. When he gestures for me to follow him, I notice a hole near the armpit, allowing me a glimpse of wiry, dark armpit hair. My pussy clenches.

"Come with me, then."

"But they'll be upset if I leave."

"Hazel." My name on his lips is a warning, and I slip my feet into the flats I keep by the front door.

"Okay," I grumble. I shut the door behind me, not bothering to lock it. I have a loose tank top on over leggings, and I cross my arms over my chest to keep the fabric from billowing up around me as a light breeze wafts through. Gray's boots scuff over the sidewalk, and I keep a couple paces behind him. Out of defiance.

"Where are we going?" I ask.

"My house."

"Your mom's?"

"No, the house I own." He glances back at me. "The one you're selling?"

"Right, but..." I drift off, distracted by the ochre center of a recently opened sunflower. In this golden light, everything looks magical. *Especially* Grayson. "You talk about it like you live there, but you don't."

"Don't I?"

His cryptic comment settles strangely inside me. As soon as we round the corner onto his street and we're within viewing distance of the house, I can tell he's been working on it. The landscape is neatly formed—still sparse, but it's been heavily weeded. There's actually an edge to it now. He's pulled up all the weeds that formerly dominated and cut back an unsightly juniper bush that had become a shapeless eyesore.

"Holy shit," I murmur as we draw nearer. He looks back at me, pride creasing his face.

"Thought you should see the latest developments," he says, hooking his thumbs in the beltloops of his jeans. We walk up the stone path to the front door, and as soon as I step inside, I'm hit by the presence of *furniture.*

Two big love seats fill the sitting room, facing the picture window. The original wood floor is still there, untouched. Into the kitchen, I can see a new fridge and a high-topped table. Some of the countertops are missing, and it's clear that his project has moved to the cabinetry.

Still, I turn to him with my mouth parted. "This looks so much better."

He nods, then jerks his head toward the stairs. "Come up here."

We clomp up the wood stairs, and when he shows me the master bedroom, I gasp. A king bed, fully outfitted with a boxy, black leather headboard and sheets and all, faces the big bay window. There's not much else—a closet door where there previously was none, and a nightstand—but holy shit. What a difference a king bed makes. I run my fingertips over the down comforter, eyeing the comfy-looking bed.

I'm a sucker for nice things, and this bed looks brand new. I hop onto it, sinking in. I groan and flop backward.

The bedroom door clicks shut. I glance over at him, and he's watching me with unmistakable hunger. Grayson smiles like this was his plan all along.

"I didn't think it would be this easy to get you into my bed," he says, a new huskiness in his voice.

"Oh, was my magic pussy the motivation behind you getting furniture?"

He scoffs but doesn't correct me.

"I'll have to remember to put that in my dating profile. Sex so good you'll furnish a house you don't live in."

"Not the craziest thing I've done to get laid."

"Oh? What's got the top spot?" I'm almost offended that dropping thousands of dollars in renovations and furniture isn't purely a reflection of how top-notch our sex was.

"One time, a looong time ago, I let a girl win at tennis so I could get into her pants."

My cheeks grow hot as he scuffs his way over to the bed, a shit-eating grin on his face. He fills the space between my feet hanging over the edge of the bed. Waiting for me to bite. I've already fallen into his trap; now begins the torture.

"I won that match fair and square," I counter, but my voice wavers as this little nod to our shared past inevitably sends me spiraling into nostalgia.

"So you think." He takes care to enunciate each word succinctly.

"And losing one tennis match is worse than dropping thousands of dollars of your hard-earned money?" I ask, my eyes on his palms indenting the comforter on either side of my legs.

"Totally." He wets his bottom lip, dragging his fingertips up the side of my calf. I inhale sharply when his fingers reach that sensitive hollow behind my knee. He knows exactly what he's doing, and he *loves it*. "Because money comes and goes. But nothing is better than winning."

I huff, fidgeting as he swirls his fingers back and forth over the hollow. "And what makes you think you're gonna win this time around? You don't know how good I am at beating you."

His smile spreads wide, full of mischief. "You'll have to make me lose."

I don't know what we're after, I just know that I have to win. Hell, he probably doesn't know either. It's so baked into our DNA that it's become a biological imperative. Eat food. Procreate. Beat Grayson.

The sunset blazes into the master bedroom as Grayson's hands drift toward my hips. He jerks me toward him, and I gasp.

"Fine. So what are we even competing for?" I ask, my voice shaky. He's got me wrapped around his finger right now. My pussy is basically leaking already from wanting him. Fuck, this man still knows how to push all my buttons. And then some.

"You know what it is," he murmurs. "It's the same thing we've been after the whole time."

His words don't make sense—what have I been after the whole time except peace of mind?—but the confusion dissipates as he lifts my hips in his big hands. I fight to stay annoyed, but it's hopeless.

"So now you're exploiting our adolescent rivalry for a chance to break in your new bed?" It's hard to joke when he's squeezing both my ass cheeks. "You could have used Tinder, you know. Gotten a random booty call."

He grunts, and climbs onto the bed, kneeling with my legs on either side of him. He jerks me again by the hips, bringing my pelvis crashing against his.

"That's no fun." The look in his eyes is pure fire. He'll eat me alive, and oh my God, *I want it.*

Except I shouldn't. I'm conditioned to resist whatever it is that he wants. And if he wants me? Then he can't have me.

"I already told you," I say a moment later, and the words barely leave my lips. "Not interested anymore. Got it out of my system."

His hands push up to my waist, but I twist away from him. And that's when it clicks. He stills, and I can practically hear the record screech. He stares at me for a moment, then he lets go of me.

"Fine." He climbs off the bed. The thick ridge of his cock is visibly tenting his jeans, and I almost whimper. Almost. "Sorry if I misread this."

His quick retreat leaves me stunned. That's not what I wanted. Not *really*. I can't move. I only want that encroaching heat on me again. The weight of his body denting the mattress around me.

I force myself to sit up, feeling disoriented and lightheaded as I assess him. He crosses his arms over his chest, avoiding my gaze.

"Just go then," he says, but there's something in his tone that tips me off. He's goading me. Pushing me to see if I really mean what I said.

Gray might be a master in innovation when it comes to our competition, but I am the master of endurance. I can hold out so long that his bones will turn to dust. And I can't wait to prove it.

"Thanks for the tour," I say and then hop off of his bed. Each step away from him feels like a mistake, but I can't take it back now.

I'm almost to the door when he barks out, "Hazel."

I pause, my hand on the doorknob. "What?"

"Am I really wrong about this?"

There's something in his gaze right now that splits me in two. Suddenly, this isn't part of our competition. This is Grayson, confused and worried, asking me a real question. I soften for a moment, and against my better judgement, I answer, "No. But you told me to make you lose."

CHAPTER FOURTEEN

GRAYSON

If Hazel leaves this room right now, I'll fucking explode. I didn't buy this king bed *for her,* but I did buy it *because of her.* This whole thing is because of her.

And this hard-on right now?

Also because of her.

I shake my head, heading for her where she's still paused at the door, hand on the knob. Like she's waiting for me to stop her.

"Leave then," I challenge her. "You know where the front door is."

She looks up at me, regret written all over her face. I'm eating it up. Time to see how dedicated to the game she is. She slowly turns the knob and pulls open the door, eyes never leaving mine. Like a puppy waiting for the signal to jump.

But I'm not going to give it to her. She wants to act like she doesn't want it, then I'm here to test her resolve. Nothing ever came easily between us; why would sexual satisfaction be any different?

"Fine," she says, a slight waver to her voice. "Nice bed. Bye."

She walks out of the bedroom and heads down the hall. I grip the doorframe above my head, watching her go until I can't see her anymore. Her footsteps scuff down the steps.

And then the front door closes.

Fuck.

Doubt ripples through me. Maybe I read that whole damn thing wrong. If she could walk away from these fireworks, then maybe I was the only one holding the lighter.

I fist the front of my hair, equal parts frustrated and disgruntled. I could almost laugh, if my cock wasn't throbbing. *Nice bed. Bye.* I can't tell if those words are the pinnacle or the rock bottom of my career as a virile man.

The front door slams shut a moment later. Footsteps thundering up the stairs.

Hazel pushes into the bedroom a moment later, looking like she's run all the way home and then back again.

I can only stare.

"I forgot my shoes," she breathes, and then she heads straight for me.

Those black flats securely on her feet.

She makes a running leap for me, and the air whooshes out of me once our bodies connect. Her hands fist in my hair and her mouth is on mine, wild and wanting. Our kisses begin furious but bleed into something so passionate that it makes me crash backward against the window.

"Should have gotten curtains," she mumbles through the kiss.

"And ruin this glorious sunset?" I squeeze the balls of her ass, a groan ripping out of me. "Fuck, Hazel."

"What?" she demands, nuzzling into the hollow of my neck. My vision goes spotty for a second when she starts nipping at my earlobe. It's my weak spot. She hasn't forgotten.

I grunt, hauling her over to the bed. I toss her easily, and she bounces a little on my new memory foam mattress. This shit was expensive, almost seven grand, and fucking Hazel in the red rays of sunset is the best way to break it in I can think of.

"Time to see how nice my bed is." I unbutton my jeans, my hands shaking like it's the first time all over again. Hazel was my first, after all, and I'd been more nervous than this. But as a successful man in my late twenties, I didn't expect my gut to be the size of a peach pit.

The other day had been different. An out-of-the-blue thaw that turned me into a Neanderthal. Like Brendan Fraser emerging from his cave. But this? This was premeditated. This is a step toward something I know I shouldn't be heading for. Something I know can only end poorly in the long-run, even if it provides a spectacular light show in the interim.

"Part of the real estate checklist," Hazel says, wriggling out of her shorts, then toeing off the flats she'd never forgotten. "Personally testing the staging furniture."

"Mm-hmm." I run my palms up the sides of her legs. Her belly caves in and then rises as she watches me, eyes on my hands. "One could call it a blessing for the next owners."

She snorts with laughter at that, and then I flip her onto her stomach and tug her panties down, exposing both her ass cheeks. She moans into the down comforter.

"Graysooon." She fists the comforter, already writhing against the bed. I've barely touched her, but I can see the juicy slit of her pussy. Leaking already. My heart rate skyrockets, and I step out of my jeans and briefs, tugging my shirt over my head.

"Jesus, Hazel." I run the heels of my hands up the bumps of her spine. She inhales sharply, wiggling her ass in the air. "I can tell you *really* didn't want to come back."

"Nope," she grunts. "Forced against my will."

I smirk, tilting my head to drink in the sun-drenched lines of her body, her dark hair pulled back into a messy ponytail, glinting honey. My cock is straining into the air, desperate for any amount of contact with this princess.

Except she's not like the princesses that fairy tales talk about. This is the type of epic warrior bombshell who runs empires *and* counsels others on moisturizing routines. She's as motivated and high achieving as the best of them. As motivated and high achieving as I am.

Fuck, at one time, I wanted her to be *my* princess.

Maybe I still do, but in her own way. Not in the helpless, pretty princess way I'd always use as an insult against her.

In this moment, I want her as my warrior princess. Building empires and taking names.

"If this is going to be a staging-furniture real-estate blessing," I say, my voice gravely as I jerk her up to all fours. "Then I think we should do it with a view." I guide her around on the bed so we're facing the brilliant sunset. The lake sparkles choppy teal in the distance, framed by oak trees leading to the beach. My chest tightens as I drink it in, the heat of Hazel's ass pressed against my groin.

Outside, it looks like paradise. But sinking into her luscious pussy *is* the actual paradise awaiting me. I even bought condoms as part of my master plan. I reach for my jeans and tug the condom out of my back pocket. She sighs, looking back at me.

"Do we have to?" she asks.

I stare at her. This woman is perfect. "I mean…"

"I'm on birth control," she says. And that seals it for me. I toss the condom aside and spread her ass cheeks, lining up my cockhead with her swollen lips. She jolts as my dick brushes her pussy. I can tell I've hit the mark when she shivers as if a winter chill ran through her.

"Please, Grayson," she whimpers, wilting a little. Her eyes pinch shut as if she's been waiting for years instead of minutes.

She doesn't need to ask me twice. I surge forward, all the air in my lungs escaping me as I enter her. A river of heat and electricity swarms me. Sex has never felt like this with anyone else. Sure, I've had plenty of *good* sex. But with Hazel, it's *fucking awesome* sex. It's *life-changing* sex. It's *make me consider residing permanently in Bayshore* sex.

An animal moan rips out of her. Her ruby fingernails pierce the comforter as I bury myself to the hilt. She is velvet and juice around my cock. I don't even need to thrust twice before the warning prickles in my gut tell me I could come already.

She wasn't lying about her magic pussy.

My breath escapes in soft grunts as I rock against her. She drops to her elbows, allowing me a deeper angle. With this view of her ass, with this vice grip around my cock, I've got another minute if I'm lucky. I draw myself out of her and pause, bending down to press kisses up her spine.

"Don't stop," she rasps.

"I'm timing it," I say, steeling myself against the urge to bury myself in her once more. I'll probably be fighting this urge for the rest of my life. "So we can come with the sunset."

She laughs, dropping her forehead to the bed. "That's cute."

"Part of the blessing," I say, and then I crack my palm against her ass cheeks. She hisses.

"That was for lying about your shoes," I tease.

"I really forgot them," she insists weakly. "By the front door."

"Mm-hmm. Even though you never took them off."

She dissolves into laughter. "Shut up and fuck me, Daly."

I surge forward again, claiming every last inch of her pussy, a shiver racing up my spine. The bedroom is full of red and gold and the scent of freshly cut grass. I've never been so turned on and simultaneously at ease. My heart hums with contentment, a feeling that breaks through the sex fog.

Right now. Right here. Life is perfect.

I fuck her hard. And I mean *hard*. My fingertips leave indents in her hips as I hold her in place against me. We're both grunting and groaning and sweating. I can't pretend to hold on much longer.

"Hazel," I grunt. She arches her back, her pussy clenching around me.

"I knooow," she wails, and then it turns into something else. Primal and guttural and from the depths of her being. She's coming, and her orgasm prompts my own. My cock spasms, and I pull myself out of her in time for my spunk to arc through the air. It lands on the small of her back, my hips jerking with additional rounds of residual pleasure.

She sinks to the bed like she's a deflated balloon. Chest still heaving, I wipe my forehead with my forearm. "I came on your back, Hazel."

"Nnnngh," she says.

That's a good sign. I sigh, trying to get my legs to work. I have nothing to clean her up with. But I'm not going to leave her like that. I reach for my T-shirt and wipe up the tiny pond of semen. I toss it aside and then collapse on the bed.

I'm pulling her into my arms before I can think twice. Before I can think better of it. She nestles back against me, and we're both facing the last rays of brilliant red that stain the sky. The bloated sun has just sunk beneath the horizon.

I tighten my arms around her, and she sighs.

Yeah. This is Bayshore-level perfection.

But this is a new type of perfect.

One I didn't realize I'd been searching for.

CHAPTER FIFTEEN

HAZEL

We've reached an armistice. At least, this is how I rationalize it.

Not a truce and not a peace treaty. Simply a lowering of our weapons while not declaring peace quite yet.

Besides, we need some way to continue this mind-blowing sex without becoming total hypocrites.

This is about sex. Nothing else.

Which is why I've seen Grayson every single day since we broke in his king bed. Because of the sex. It's also why we've started ordering takeout and eating it in his newly remodeled kitchen and why I've spent the night twice and gotten up extra early so I could walk-of-shame it back to my own house.

Only because of the sex, which the armistice allows.

It's mid-next week when Gray finishes the renovations on the upstairs bathroom, turning it into a pebbly paradise with one of those rainwater showerheads. Now I officially want to live *here* instead of at my own home, which is not great.

His brothers have spotted me here on more than one occasion. Luckily, I work late most nights, so it's not like they see me waking up here or anything. It seems wrong to let anyone know what's going on, though I'm sure the neighbors are *more than aware* that I roll up to his house every night and never leave. This neighborhood is full of porch lovers. Neighbors who sit outside from about seven-thirty onward, soaking up the evening and the people walking by.

They're also very effective spies and gossips, so I'm sure rumors have started circulating.

Gray texts me before I'm done with work that Wednesday. We've started texting throughout the day, which is also related to the strictly-sex arrangement. There's nothing else going on here.

GRAY: I made dinner plans for us.

Excitement swells inside me. Looking forward to seeing him each evening makes me lightheaded sometimes. The sex is that good.

HAZEL: Oooh. Downtown, beachfront, or something else?

GRAY: I'll tell you when you get here.

I wrap up work as quickly as I can, fumbling with the lock on the front door in an attempt to get the hell out of the office. As I'm hurrying up the brick walkway to Gray's house, he steps outside in a gray T-shirt and dark shorts.

I pause. The sight of him actually takes my breath away, which is not something I expect. I grew up with this guy. I've seen him more than probably any other human being on the planet except my dad, especially given our recent escapades.

Yet still, my heart flutters each time I see him. The same way it always has. Even when I've hated him or been annoyed by him or been ignoring him.

"I'll take your stuff and put it inside," he says in lieu of a greeting. His tone makes it hard to argue.

"Okay," I say, handing over everything except my phone. I try to tamp down the excitement. I love surprises. I love it when a man is on my level. I love *Grayson.*

The thought sears through me, hot and awkward. Thank God it was only in my head. I can delete that thought history and pretend it never happened.

"How was work?" he asks, guiding me back down the path. We start a slow stroll down the sidewalk. I lean into him, resting my head on his shoulder. I'm tired from the day, but seeing Gray has given me a jolt of energy.

This is nice. Actually, this is way more than nice.

This is perfection.

"Busy as usual," I say. Our hands brush, and he takes mine in his a moment later, giving it a squeeze. "Where are we going?"

"My parents'," he says, a smirk on his face.

I search out his gaze. "Oh? Are we...outing this?"

His jaw flexes, and his blue eyes burn on the horizon. "No. We'll just...I dunno. We don't need to tell them anything. You're a family friend."

His response—typical male not thinking ahead—reminds me I have no idea what's going on between us. Neither of us knows. We haven't talked about it, because why would we? Except now, his mother will *want to know.* Everyone has long suspected our inevitable love affair. Showing up together will only add fuel to the fire.

"But, uh, hello? Your mom? She's been our number one fan since day one. We're holding hands. She's going to order wedding invitations during dessert."

He snorts. "Fine. I won't hold your hand."

But he doesn't let go.

His parents' house is in sight now, and my heart rate picks up. The anxiety is real. Besides, it's not like we can tell her we're fucking. *Your son has a magic dick, and I'm riding him like a pogo stick.* Not what you tell the sweet woman who bore your current fuck buddy.

Even though thinking of Grayson as a fuck buddy isn't quite right. He's so much *more* than that. But no—it's just sex.

That's it.

"Grayson and Hazel!" Annette Daly hangs out her front door, waving at both of us as we approach. Gray finally lets go of my hand, but he's too late. Annette clamps her hand over her heart and tilts her head.

"Did you come from work, honey?" she asks me as I step onto the small porch.

"Yeah," I say with a little laugh, and she pulls me into a hug.

"You work so hard," she murmurs in my ear. "So, so hard. You're the star of Bayshore, you know that?"

"Mom," Gray says.

"What?" Annette pulls back, sending a glare at her son. At least we know who her favorite is. "Our Hazel needs to be recognized."

"I do get recognition," I say, following her into the house. She's leading me by the hand. She's practically waving a banner that says *Grayson, you better make this woman my daughter-in-law.* "I was voted Best Realtor in last year's People's Choice Awards."

"I voted for you *every day* in that contest," Annette confides as we walk down the short but bright hall leading toward the kitchen at the back of the house. The voices of Grayson's brothers and their dad reach us. The dining room is full of the Dalys, and when we arrive, the conversation kicks up to a commotion.

"We're all here!" Annette declares, and busies herself with bringing out the dishes.

"I can help," an unknown woman says, but she looks familiar. Something about her cheek bones. She offers a smile as she walks past, and then, as I look at Connor, it clicks together. "Hi, Hazel. Remember me?"

"Kinsley Cabana." Connor offers a toothy white grin. Kinsley was in Connor's grade, and the middle child of the Cabana clan, AKA the Daly family's arch nemesis. I don't know how I forgot that Connor was dating a Cabana daughter. Grayson leads me toward the two empty seats reserved for us.

"More on that later," he whispers hotly into my ear.

Their dad, Damon, booms his greeting to me and immediately launches into a terse but polite rundown of my business success. The man has always been extra success oriented, which both helped and hurt his offspring. I think most of his sons resent him in some way, while also owing most of their success to him. But isn't that how most parent-child relationships end up?

Maverick and Weston nod their greeting, and Dominic smiles broadly as he comes over to me to offer a hug. I was always closer to Dom, Gray and Connor. By the time I graduated from high school, Weston was just about to enter, and Maverick was still a year behind him.

"I can't believe we're all here at the table," Annette enthuses, setting out plates of roast beef and scalloped potatoes and a corn casserole. Even though Kinsley helped her bring out the dishes, I'm not sure Annette glanced her way. Damon sends occasional icy looks toward Kinsley, as if he's keeping tabs on her. Making sure she doesn't launch into a pro-Cabana diatribe or try to stab a Daly with a bread knife or something. I don't know the bulk of the Cabana-Daly beef, but it's so bad it's lasted for decades and turns the normally gregarious Dalys into quiet, icy hosts around Kinsley.

Grayson's elbow brushes mine as we lay napkins on our laps and settle in for dinner. Oddly, joining their dinner doesn't feel as awkward or ill-fitting as I'd have imagined.

There's always been something a little too comfortable about having Grayson at my side. On my arm. Lurking around the edges of my life.

"Thank God for vacation time," Connor says, scooping a big serving of scalloped potatoes onto his plate.

"Some of us have more of it than others," Gray adds, grinning like an asshole. It makes me grin too.

"You were overdue," Annette says. "You hadn't been home in years."

"I didn't even recognize you when you showed up," Maverick says, scoffing.

"See? You scared your brother." Annette purses her lips as she forks some roast beef onto her plate. "Hopefully you two will be coming around more often."

The "two" must be referring to Grayson and Connor, her east coast and west coast transplants, respectively.

"I'll visit more," Grayson says, sounding a lot like he's placating a child. "At least in the summer."

I make sure my smile doesn't waver as his words sink into me. They're a reminder. This thing between us is about sex. Just as I knew. As I feared. As I claimed to be fine with.

Was it so wrong of me to wish that my first love and current sex partner might want to stick around Bayshore a little more?

"You should come back for the Bicentennial Ball," Annette says before she stuffs a bite of potatoes into her mouth.

"No," Grayson says, and it's definitive. My smile droops a little.

"When is it?" Connor asks.

"September, I think," Annette responds.

"September ninth," I clarify. Not like it's in my phone calendar, two work calendars, and scribbled on my paper planner at home or anything.

Annette clucks her tongue and sends a mysterious smile toward Grayson and me.

Yeah. September ninth—the day we were both born. Funny happenstance that the ball falls on our Saturday birthday this year.

"Ohhh, we'll be back in California by then." Connor frowns at Kinsley, who scrunches up her lips. They're an unlikely pair, if only because of their families' history. But still, all bad blood aside, the two of them side by side *are* cute.

"Are you going to the ball, Hazel?" Annette asks me. My heart drops for unknown reasons, and I smile brightly at her.

"Of course. I've had my ticket since the day they went on sale."

"I should have figured." Annette lowers her chin, staring directly at Grayson. "A pretty woman like Hazel deserves a man on her arm at that party."

I agree with her, but maybe not for the same reasons. I deserve a man on my arm because I'm ready for the next step in life. I deserve a partner who wants to keep pace with me. I deserve a boyfriend who wants to take me to the most important city-wide ball because he loves Bayshore and our life here as much as I do.

But maybe that man doesn't exist.

And out of all the men in the world, there's still that part of me that still only wants the man to my left.

Grayson shoves a forkful of scalloped potatoes into his mouth, saying nothing.

I should be thankful for it, really. It's the reminder I need in the middle of our amazing sex-a-thon.

Grayson isn't that man. He won't be that boyfriend. He can never be mine, no matter how much the seventeen-year-old inside me is still hoping.

Dinner churns on happily, and there's something infectious about being with all the Dalys at once. I always loved their big family. It was the opposite of what I had growing up—a mother who existed only in photographs and a hard-working single dad who did as much as he could. No siblings to play with. Not many cousins to count among my family ranks.

In a way, during our childhood, Grayson was the brother I never had. Until he became the crush I never counted on. And the first heartbreak to shatter me.

Once dinner wraps up and Annette has hugged and complimented me out the door, Grayson and I are walking lazily toward the sidewalk. Down the street, the flames of a tiny front yard bonfire lick through the steel cover. Laughter reaches us from farther up the street. The crickets are out in full chorus.

I already know how tonight should go. I need to go home alone. Break the spell of what we've been doing over the last week. Get back to my single-girl routine.

Gray's fingers lace through mine. When we reach the street, he faces me, running his thumb along my jawline.

"We should go work those scalloped potatoes off, huh?"

I snort with a laugh. "You want to head to the gym? At this hour?"

"Thought maybe we could substitute my bed for the elliptical."

I smile, but there's sadness in it. "I think I need to go home tonight."

His face falls. "Really?"

"I haven't slept in my own house for days. Besides, the extra stop each morning to pick up the things I forgot...I've been getting to work late."

"You own your own business."

"Even so, my boss is a bitch."

His smile nearly topples me. "I've heard."

"Yeah, I bet you have." I pretend punch him in the side, but he seems reluctant to let me go. His rough hands cup my face. In the dim glow of the streetlights, I can see the storm in his eyes.

"You don't need anyone to keep the other side of your bed warm?"

His question slices me in half. Any resilience or willpower I might have accumulated over dinner—totally gone. Evaporated. Goodbye single-girl night.

"Yeah, I think I do." I smile up at him. It's hard to say no to him. Especially when he's being sweet like this. When he's showing the side of him that I've always fallen for, head over heels, without any hope for rescue.

"I could help keep your side warm," he murmurs. We've started swaying gently, out here in full view of the porch sitters and the passersby. Nobody has passed by yet, but somehow Bayshore still knows. I can feel it.

But I don't care.

Not when we're caught in this fantasy bubble. Something seductive and warm, a tapestry only he knows how to weave.

"Let's go to my place," I say, and I lead the way.

CHAPTER SIXTEEN

GRAYSON

I've been home for two weeks, and it's felt like two years.

But I'm not sick of Bayshore yet. Not even a little bit.

Some things feel so new here. The town has grown, matured, become more bustling in its own beachy way. What used to be a tiny drug store on the outskirts of town has now been developed into a huge shopping plaza. Neighborhoods are popping up on the edges of town. People *want* to move here, which is maybe the biggest change from my childhood.

But one thing that hasn't changed?

I'm falling for Hazel. Like the last time I lived here.

Maybe it's the fact that we've spent the past seven nights holed up together. Laughing like teenagers, fucking like rabbits, and connecting like the mature adults we actually are. We're not playing the game anymore—or maybe it's on hold. Whatever's going on, we're both on board. Without having said a word.

Just like when we were seventeen at the end of junior year, when things thawed for the first time. Our downhill race happened blistering fast. We went from enemies to lovers, and by the end of senior year, lovers to enemies.

I can't handle her returning to enemy status again. Not after this whirlwind week we've shared, allowing ourselves to be tender and scorching, vulnerable and bristly.

But that's the part that messes me up. How can she hold any status once I'm back in New York? I'm not naive enough to think that we can make a distance thing work. I need to see this woman more than once a month. Really, I need to see her daily, and sometimes hourly, but I can settle for slightly less.

I've been thinking about this shit all day while she's at work, sending me sexy selfies in her pinstripe blouse between clients, the natural light spilling into the office behind her. She always makes sure to give me kissy lips with that big red pout of hers and to show some cleavage.

She's the most gorgeous woman I've ever seen. The smartest. The most motivated. When people talk about her, they gush. Hazel is the Bayshore sweetheart. And in so many ways, she's the only woman I've ever wanted.

But the pieces aren't aligning quite yet. Good thing I'm a master at puzzles.

Hazel's working extra late tonight, so I head for the beach around eight to sit by the water and catch the sunset. As soon as I roll up to the lakefront at the bottom of my neighborhood, I see familiar faces gathered by the shore.

There's Luke and Anthony, standing with beers in their hands around a cooler, while Callie squats in the sand fiddling with sticks to start a fire. I saunter up and clap Luke on the back.

"Gray!" he shouts, and then punches me in the shoulder. "You're still in town?"

"Got two more weeks." I shove my hands in the front pocket of my hoodie. It's an unseasonably chilly evening, so this beachside fire seems like an extra good idea. "What are you guys up to?"

"Oh, you know, making the weakest link light the fire," Callie mutters from the ground.

"I would help if you'd just *ask*," Anthony says.

"No, no," Callie says, voice dripping with sarcasm. "I've got it."

Luke and I snicker. He reaches for a beer in the cooler and passes it to me.

"Stay awhile. Some others are coming later. Hey, Cal, did you tell Hazel?" Luke glances at me, as though suddenly realizing what he's said. "You're cool with that, right?"

"Totally." The beer can goes *crraaack* as I open it. "We're sorta, ya know…" The appropriate phrasing escapes me. Fucking? Dating? Deluding ourselves? "Reconciling our differences."

"About damn time," Callie mutters.

"You need help there, Cal?" I ask, kneeling down to look at her attempts.

"Can you do it?" she pleads.

"Give it to me." I take the lighter and the sticks she's using and make the appropriate pile with the skinniest log pieces collected nearby, Boy Scout style. Within a minute, I've got a little fire going. Callie grins, and I sit back on my heels and take a long pull at my beer.

The sun sits low on the horizon, but there's already a cold snap in the air. It's not too cold for shorts, which we're all wearing, but it's that perfect combination of chilliness and summer. Hoodie and beer weather. Like fall, except warmer and with a later sunset.

Best damn time of the year.

"I'll text Hazel that we're here," Callie says, but I've already started typing a message to her.

"I got it," I say, then hit *send* and pocket my phone. "And let's *not* tell Bryce, okay?"

She lifts a brow. "Wow. Texting Hazel, huh? You must have done more than reconcile your differences."

Anthony cackles. "I have so many good comebacks for that one right now."

"Let's hear them," Callie says.

"Gray might beat me up if I say them," Anthony says, winking at me while he takes a pull at his beer.

"Nah, Gray's a pacifist," Luke jokes as he drags over a smoothed log perfect for sitting on. We've got a mishmash of lawn chairs, coolers, and logs around this fire pit. "He would never challenge anyone like that."

I snort, kicking at Luke's leg as he sits down.

"You're damn right. And if you disagree, I'll pacify the shit out of you," I tease.

We all break into laughter. Callie unrolls a thick beach towel and settles onto it, facing the lake. It doesn't take long for Anthony to abandon his lawn chair and join her on the towel. I watch the backs of their heads for a moment as Callie props hers on his shoulder. Anthony's arm goes around her waist.

"When's the wedding?" I call out. Anthony flips me the bird without turning to look at me.

"Right after yours and Hazel's," Callie responds.

I snort, but the idea doesn't sound as ludicrous as it might have once upon a time. Even two weeks ago. It's not like I'm planning on it or anything, but the taste of it isn't so bitter anymore.

"You'll have to come to New York for that." I take another sip of beer. Honestly, I can't get the vision of Hazel in New York out of my head. I can already see her waking up with me in my apartment, the gray rays of an early winter morning cutting through the wood slats. Going for coffee at my favorite spot around the block where they sell repurposed journals with old book spines. Checking out erotic bookstores and tiny fashion boutiques. Lazy Sundays in the park with the swirl of the city around us.

Hazel embodies that *thing* I've been searching for in New York. The thing I've been missing. The thing that will make life perfect.

It's the type of idea that sparks right into a firework with its rightness. I just need to bring it up to her. She might be hesitant at first, but I'm sure she'll see the benefits of a move to Brooklyn. Her real estate business would soar. She'd quadruple her income. Hazel belongs in a place like Brooklyn. No more playing small in Bayshore.

She needs to spread her wings and *soar*.

The idea leaves me equal parts excited and anxious. I know it'll take some convincing, but if she's feeling half of what I'm floating in right now, then this is the only way to make it work.

The four of us hoot and holler as the sun goes down. A couple more friends arrive, an old buddy from high school and a new Bayshore transplant with a guitar. Smooth chords fill the beach now that twilight has settled. Since this is a private residential access beach, there aren't a ton of people out here besides us. A few teens further down and a small family sitting in Adirondack chairs.

Between the humid, earthy scent of the lake, the murmur of waves lapping at the beach, and the easy laughter flowing among the group, I'm not sure I could feel more relaxed than this.

In fact, the past two weeks in Bayshore have jostled me out of the vice grip New York had me in.

I forgot what the rest of the world was like. What home was like. What real relaxed happiness felt like.

Squeals from Callie tells me Hazel has arrived. When I twist around, I see Hazel sauntering toward us. She's still got her work face on, but her hair is in a messy bun and her form-fitting skirt has been replaced with mesh shorts. Instead of a busty blouse, she's got an oversized, red OSU hoodie on.

But it's her bare feet that draw my attention. My gaze locks onto those slender ankles, her little toenails painted black. When she gets within reach and is saying hi to everyone, I run my fingertips up the side of her leg.

She grins down at me, and I yank her onto my lap. She settles with a giggle.

"Differences have been *reconciled*," Anthony jokes.

"Did you tell them?" Hazel asks me in a low voice.

"They already knew," I answer her, and then press my lips to hers. Because I physically can't *not*. Because when she's within arm's reach, she needs to be in *my arms*. Because finding each other again has shown me that we had our differences, but there's more in store for us if we choose to follow what's blossomed here.

"Are we that obvious?" Hazel asks to our group of friends.

Callie snorts. "I knew it the second we saw Gray on the Jet Ski that day."

My grin turns to shit-eating grade. "Did you?"

"Oh yeah," Callie says, poking the fire with a stick. "The way she looked at you when you showed up at the dock. Had wedding bells written all over it."

"Yeah, that glare was really romantic," I tease, nudging her shoulder with my chin.

Hazel dissolves into laughter. I thread my hands into the front pocket of her sweatshirt, fingertips tingling with the promise of finding more. I've been with plenty of women and dated my fair share. I've never felt like *this* with anyone before. Like my insides are melting into lava and turning into dry ice with excitement at the same time. Like I need to start counting the hours and minutes I have left with her before I go back to New York. Before a day needs to go by when we're apart.

"So you two want me to call Bryce, right?" Luke asks.

I point at him menacingly, and Hazel loses it into my chest.

"I told you, Luke," I warn. "I will pacify the shit out of you."

Anthony looks over my shoulder toward the road, a big smile coming over his face. "Look who else showed up!"

Luke hoots, and Callie waves. I turn around to see Connor approaching with Kinsley in tow. They're all grins.

"Hey, brother," Connor says, slapping me on the back as he comes up to the group. Everyone exchanges greetings, and normally timid Kinsley seems more outgoing now that she's outside of the Daly house. My mom hasn't been exactly warm with her; although, I give the woman credit; she's handled the appearance of a Cabana relative inside her home remarkably well.

"Where are the rest of the brethren?" Luke asks.

"Dom went back to Cleveland," Connor reports. The news makes me frown. Typical. Doesn't even say goodbye. Just leaves, because he's too important for siblings or giving a damn about anybody other than himself. "West said he had to go help someone decorate their new yoga studio."

"At ten at night?" I ask.

Connor shrugs. "And Mav's out being a ho."

We all laugh. Maverick is twenty-three and living it up. I would almost be jealous of him, except I'm sort of over the endless-sex days. Scratch that. I'm totally into the endless-sex days, as long as it's with the right person. With Hazel.

"And your mom and dad?" Hazel asks.

"Curled up in front of the TV shouting at the Real Housewives for being idiots," Connor reports, settling onto an open cooler top before inviting Kinsley onto his lap. The way she looks at him includes a mixture of adoration and amusement. Like she's hanging on each word. Really lapping him up.

When they first showed up, I had my doubts. But those two are in love. And good for them. There's something poetic about Connor falling for Kinsley.

Almost as poetic as Grayson and Hazel, the enemies that fell for each other not once, but twice.

I squeeze my arms tighter around Hazel, wishing I could mold her against me so that she could never move. So that I could visit the delicious weight of her on top of me whenever I needed. So that her sweet clementine and freesia scent would always be a breath away from me.

I press my forehead to her arm as the guitar music swells and turns to a slow, earthy rendition of The Beatles' "Something." All I can think about is Hazel as the dreamy lyrics flow through me.

Nobody's love story will ever be as epic as ours. Nobody else was born on the same day as their rival. Nobody else spent decades trying to outstrip their one true equal. Nobody else has been avoiding the one person that everyone else knew was meant for them.

Hazel and I, we've got a love story that beats the competition.

And doesn't that just fucking figure?

CHAPTER SEVENTEEN

HAZEL

It's not like I've started a paper chain or anything, counting the streak of days that Grayson and I have had sex. It's ten, of course, but I'm not *tracking it*.

I just know it in the back of my head constantly.

It's part of the armistice.

The armistice that looks and feels suspiciously like an extremely happy long-term relationship.

I don't know what I'm doing. I don't even know what I think I'm doing. I'm simply going with what feels right. If I'm any indication, ignoring the big future questions is what late-twenty-somethings should do when hooking up with a man who lives hundreds of miles away.

Gray suggests tennis that Saturday. I work a few hours in the morning, as always, but I leave the office early so I can change before he picks me up. My blood has been humming from the moment I woke up about the chance to take him on in tennis. I'm going to whoop his ass so bad he'll be limping for a week. The limp comes from how badly his ego will get beaten by my tennis superiority, of course.

The best tennis courts in town are behind the high school. *Our* old high school. Even though I live in Bayshore, I barely come around this part of town. As we pull into the empty parking lot facing the fenced-in tennis courts off to the side of the football stadium, memories come flooding back to me.

And all of them involve Grayson in some way. Whether I was trying to join the men's tennis team or picking his locker so I could rearrange his books and ensure my advantage in the after-school sprint to the cars, damn near everything about my time in these halls revolved around this man.

"You okay, Hazel?" he asks as we enter the courts. The sun glints off his tanned skin, a simple white T-shirt stretching over his broad chest. He looks good enough to eat. Good enough to marry.

The thought sears through me.

"I'm fine," I say, but my voice doesn't sound fine.

"You forget your homework?" he cracks.

"Nah, I turned it in yesterday." I offer a smile, trying to regain my breezy mood from that morning. "A full twenty-four hours before you did, as usual." But as time churns on, it's harder to avoid thinking about what we're doing. Every passing day demands an answer from us. Louder each time. *What is this?*

I don't know the answer. Not even a little bit.

"Better get your head in the game," Grayson warns, "because I'm not going easy on you."

"You've never gone easy on me."

"I might have once or twice," he says, bouncing the tennis ball against the red court. The smile he sends over his shoulder steals my breath. Gray admitting he's gone easy on me is about the same as him telling me he loves me. Because there may be no greater act of love from him than willingly coming in second.

"I don't believe it," I tease. "You're just saying that because you want to get into my pants."

Grayson smiles and takes his place on the far side of the court but doesn't deny it. He bounces the ball high, tossing the racket in one hand.

"You ready to get your ass kicked?" he asks.

"I'm ready to remind you why you had to move away from Bayshore," I say, trying to keep the laughter out of my voice.

He lifts a brow. "You think you were *that good* at tennis?"

"I know I was." God, I love stoking this fire between us. "You're not the first man I've driven to relocate."

Something flashes in his eyes. Maybe it was because I questioned his skills, or maybe it was the mention of another man. Either way: Game on. Gray serves the ball *hard*, and we launch into a grunting, dashing, extremely serious tennis match. For each point that Gray grabs, I snag another. We edge up evenly in the score, until we're sweating bullets and breathing heavy, and dammit, I never get a better workout than when I'm playing against Gray.

"Okay. Okay. This is match point." I bounce the ball against the court, trying to corral my breathing. I'm exhausted by the end of the second set. Before today, I'd only been playing against Bryce on occasion, and he always made sure to let me win, if he tried at all. I *hated* that.

"You played a good game, Matheson," Grayson says, using the collar of his shirt to wipe at his upper lip, allowing a gut-clenching glimpse of that washboard. "Not bad for a rookie."

I block out his words and serve. We volley back and forth intensely. I push myself to the limits, diving to return the ball. My racket hits at an unintended angle, pushing the ball into the farthest corner of Gray's court. I watch in suspense to see if it stays in bounds. It does.

And Gray misses it.

I win.

Dark clouds swarm his face as I hop to my feet, pumping my fists in the air. I laugh incredulously.

"Hoooly shit!" I bounce over to him. He's got his hands propped on his hips, studying me like he's trying to figure out if he'll devour me verbally or maybe sexually. Once we're home. My entire body is on edge waiting for his reaction. To see which spikes he'll start with.

"That was out of bounds."

My jaw drops and I laugh again at the absurdity of his claim. "You are *nuts*! That was totally valid!"

"We need a rematch," he says, raking his hand through his hair. He is impossibly sexy and sweaty right now. He uses the bottom of his T-shirt to wipe at his face again, and this time I get a full view of his tanned chest.

"Yeah. In *bed*," I tease, sauntering up to him. "Don't be salty that you lost. Just accept it."

A smile plays at his lips. "There's only one consolation prize I want."

"And what's that?" I drop my racket and throw my arms around his neck. The man is radiating heat like a nuclear reactor. If he were any other person, it would be uncomfortable. Too hot. Too sweaty.

But with Gray, I want all of him. Even in the blazing sun, on a tennis court, dripping with sweat. I'd sooner spend the rest of the day sweating with him at my side, than enjoy air-conditioned comfort without him.

"You," he says, tugging at my ponytail, "on top of me."

"Jeez, is that it?" I push up onto my toes and press my lips to his.

"Outside."

"Here?"

"Tonight. By the water."

I lob a sigh, like the request is so unsavory. But I love it. Now I can't *wait* for tonight even more. "Fine. We'll find our own little secluded place on the rocks for you to fuck me until I scream."

An evil smile curls his lips. "Perfect."

We pick up the rackets and our ball, heading back to the parking lot. We played for a solid hour, and my legs are wobbly from the Grayson-level workout. Giggles and conversation reach us as we weave out of the tennis courts. A small group of women head toward us, and I offer a small smile in their direction as we pass.

"Grayson Daly?"

One of the women stops in her tracks, turning toward Grayson with a shocked smile that says it all. It takes me a moment to place her, but those big, puppy-dog eyes and chipmunk cheeks click into place a moment before Gray says her name.

"Aubree." Grayson's got that tinny tone to his voice, the kind everyone has when they've run into an old acquaintance or schoolmate they haven't seen in a decade. "Long time no see."

Aubree slaps her knee, glancing back at her friends. "We went to high school together!" she explains to them. Smiling at Grayson, she says, "Who would have thought the prom king and queen would be back together again at BHS?"

Her words kick up a secret storm inside me. Not only has she not acknowledged me, but she's referencing probably the worst period of my life. Right before prom, when Grayson and I didn't just break up, we *shattered*.

"It's been a hot minute," Grayson says, wiping at his forehead. "Hazel and I just kicked each other's ass on the courts. Like old times."

Aubree nods and glances my way.

"Good to see you, Aubree," I say succinctly. Fuck her for ignoring me, but I won't sink to her level.

She sends me a plastic smile before barreling on. "So, what are you doing here? I thought you lived in New York."

"I'm back for a little bit," he says, crossing his arms, biceps bulging in the white shirt. It's clear what she's after: Grayson. And for some reason, my presence at his side means nothing for her quest.

"How long?" She steps closer. Her friends behind her have receded into their own conversation, and I don't bother hiding the sigh that rockets out of me. "Will you be around in September? You know, there's the Bicentennial Ball going on. We should totally go!"

I twirl my racket in one hand, contemplating what cracking it against her head might feel like. Whether or not I'd have the guts to actually try. My muscles are pretty tired right now—I better not.

Grayson glances back at me, and I can see the indecision written in his face. "I'll see you there—I'm going with Hazel."

"Oh!" Aubree's smile turns to stone and she blinks rapidly. "Well, that's great! There's nothing better than supporting Bayshore's birthday in style!" Her pinched voice gives me a vapid type of satisfaction.

"You ladies have fun," I interject suddenly, waving at all of them. I'd use my middle finger if I could. "See you at the ball, Aubree."

We make a quick exit, and neither of us speaks until we're back at the car. Only after Gray unlocks the doors and I slide into the passenger's seat do my shoulders drop.

"Holy shit," he murmurs, looking into his rearview mirror. Like checking to make sure Aubree hasn't followed us.

"Wasn't it so nice to run into the prom queen?" I ask sarcastically, then scoff. "Jesus, she didn't even *look* at me."

Grayson turns the car on, and the Muse we'd been playing during our ride to the tennis courts comes blasting through the speakers. He turns it down quickly.

"Mega bitch," Grayson agrees, sounding distracted as he buckles up.

"Are you serious about the ball?" I ask suddenly.

He hesitates, not looking over at me as he navigates out of the parking lot. "Well, no. I'll be in New York. I just said that to get her off our backs."

That's right. He'll be back in New York. Where he'll be again in a matter of weeks. The news sobers me, dousing my anger at the encounter with Aubree, dousing the high of my win. Almost extinguishing all the bliss I'd been simmering in for the past ten days.

"Oh. I thought maybe you'd come back for it," I mumble.

"Why is everyone so obsessed with this stupid ball?" His question is lighthearted and joking, but the words spear me. Wounding and reminding in equal measure. "I don't get it. It's the adult equivalent of a school dance. If you need me there that bad, I mean I can try to get the time off. But wouldn't you rather I used my vacation for something a little bigger? Like, I dunno, taking a weekend in Paris? Skiing in Colorado?"

Sunlight filters through the oak trees lining this road, and to the west begin the rolling corn fields. It's a picturesque day, but my insides are grumpy as hell. Everything that has come out of his mouth is wrong. The Bicentennial Ball, my life here, Bayshore in general—none of it really matters to him. And I don't want a pity date to the ball. I don't want a pity anything. I want someone invested in my life, and my life is in Bayshore.

"No, don't worry about it." My tone comes out clipped, but I can't help it. "It's just a stupid thing in Bayshore, you know, so who cares?"

Silence thuds between us. There's a storm raging inside me, and I'm doing my best to control it, but let's be real, it's not going well.

"I don't understand why it's so important," Grayson admits.

"Yeah, I guess you wouldn't." I stare out the window, watching but not really seeing the trees as we zip down the street. "You haven't worked in the community for the past ten years. You haven't helped cultivate it from a forgotten beach town into a thriving tourist destination. A place that people are proud to do business in. You leave for a decade and come back and still know people's names, and that's nice, but you don't know what anybody here is *doing* for the community. The ball is to celebrate that. To honor our history. Our hard work. But you could give a fuck-all about this place."

His grip on the steering wheel tightens.

"You don't have to say anything," I rush to add. "Because honestly, you don't belong there. You *shouldn't* go. The party is for people who care about this city and want to see it prosper. Not outsiders who come in and scoff because it's their tiny hometown and that means it's stagnant and backwards."

I can't control the words tumbling out of my mouth. I'm over-reacting and I know it. Doesn't change things, though.

"I never said it was stagnant and backwards," Gray says through gritted teeth.

"No, no, you're right. You called it *sluggish and uninteresting.*"

He expels a sigh. "I was annoyed that day."

"You were speaking your truth," I remind him. "And it's fine. Believe what you want, but don't come back for the ball because you think it's going to make me happy. It won't. It'll piss me off. Save your vacation time for Paris."

Tense silence stretches through the car, and my entire body is rigid as we weave back into town and toward his house. My mind is running a mile a minute. Doubts crash through me like lake waves on a stormy day. White caps and all. I'm fucking drowning in it, and for the first time in a long time, I can't see the surface.

When he parks, I've got the door open before the car is off.

"I think I need some time," I say to him quietly, avoiding his gaze.

"Hazel—"

"We've been really up each other's asses, you know?" I try to keep the tremble out of my voice. I need to appear strong. Unaffected, maybe. I don't want him to know how hard I've fallen for him again in such a short time. This was supposed to be about sex, and maybe it can return to that. But only after I take a day or two to fucking *breathe.*

"Okay." He's still white-knuckling the steering wheel, staring ahead at the one-car garage of his house. "Give me a call when you're ready."

I tear out of the car, beating back the tears until it's safe for them to spill.

This feels a lot like a breakup.

It never should have felt like this.

I never should have started this at all.

CHAPTER EIGHTEEN

GRAYSON

Two days.

That's how much I give her. That's the most I can stand to give her.

Because once forty-eight hours go by without Hazel, I'm a tightly wound mess, itching from the inside to see her. We've been texting, but it's not enough. She hasn't even sent me a selfie. I'm ending this needless stalemate because I've got a week left here, and though the future is uncertain, my present is more than certain.

I need Hazel.

GRAY: Okay, you've had your time. Get yr sweet ass to my house. Making you dinner tonight.

HAZEL: Ugh fine. What time?

GRAY: 7. And pack clothes for tomorrow.

Once she's on board, I head to the grocery store to pick up ingredients for the meal I plan to make. Except no visit to the grocery store is ever just about buying what you need. No, I run into about three hundred different people I know—almost the entirety of Bayshore—while I'm circling the perimeter of Bayshore's most popular grocery store, The Daily Shop.

I always used to think it was named for our family until I realized the spelling difference a little too late, around age nine. But oh well. A part of me still likes to think it's my namesake and possible future inheritance.

I manage to pick up shrimp and salmon, just in case I can't decide on what I want to make, plus a whole array of vegetables to roast. I've also crossed paths with Mrs. Whitmore from the next street over, Mr. Hank who is a regular at the bar on the beach, Corey from high school, Tabitha who used to babysit Maverick, Ms. Koch who heard about my success in New York and wants me to talk to her son, and even *my own mother.*

"Grayson!" she exclaims, like she didn't see me two hours ago.

"Mom, I gotta go," I tell her while I press her into a quick hug. "If I don't leave now, I never will."

"Let's head to the bar and get a drink real quick!" She points to the bar that The Daily Shop recently constructed. Smart move, letting your shoppers get drunk and loose with their snack cash.

"Mom," I tell her. "I've spent the past forty-five minutes socializing in the bread aisle. I need to get out of here."

"Fine, fine. I'll see you at home." She pats my arm and wanders off past the display of lilies. I bolt for the checkout line and heave a sigh of relief once I'm safe inside my car. One hour and fifteen minutes. That's how long it took me to complete what would have otherwise been a fifteen-minute run. Except, I admit, in New York it would have taken longer. Once you figured in traffic and the insane lines at Whole Foods *and* whether the ride share could circle around onto my one-way street on the first try or not.

At least here I could catch up with some people I haven't seen in ages. I'm interested in helping guide Ms. Koch's son. Maybe I could give him a few pointers, the same way people helped me when I was finding my path in life.

Back at the house, I throw myself into dinner prep. It's only three thirty, but still, I need time. This is going to be the best meal I've ever made, and Hazel deserves it. *We* deserve it.

Besides, it's high time I tell her about my idea for preserving the "we." I know she loves Bayshore. But she's got to see the monetary opportunities just *waiting* for her outside this city's limits. How much she could be raking in if she'd take the leap and move to a bigger city.

Mom loaned me all her unused cooking stuff to use while I'm in town, so I've got a decently equipped kitchen. West got me an apron, like a weird housewarming gift. The picture on the front is a bodybuilder, naked from the waist up.

While I prep food, music pulses out of my laptop, switching from jazz to hip-hop to rock. Cutting vegetables and making foil packets of produce gives me ample time to think over the spreadsheet I've been working on for the past two days. Sort of my formal proposal package to Hazel. Hey, what else am I going to do with all this time off and no way to occupy the math-oriented side of my brain? I'm used to crunching numbers in a big way. It makes sense to crunch the numbers on Hazel's behalf so she can see what an opportunity a move to New York would be for her career.

I spared no imaginary expense, either. I drilled down to moving costs (provided we hired a moving company for her), realty investments (I could help her with thirty percent of it), half of my apartment's rent (I wouldn't really expect her to pay though), and the time costs of re-licensing in the state of New York. This will be the supplemental documentation to follow my pitch.

I don't mess around when I have a goal. I'm in it to win it.

Hazel's coming to New York.

Around five o'clock, the kitchen starts getting *extra* hot, so I tear off my shirt and leave the apron on over my mesh shorts. Shortly thereafter, my simmering white sauce pops with the heat and splatters the back of my shorts. I take some time to remove the stain and stay in my underwear, since the kitchen is still so damn hot. I've got someone coming tomorrow to install a central air system for the house. It'll sure beat this 80s unit I've got in the side window that puffs out air that smells like it's a hundred years old.

"Gray?"

I whip around at the unexpected voice. Hazel is peering inside the kitchen, looking both fascinated and quizzical.

"Hey! Hazel! What are you, uh—" The tea kettle starts screaming. Hot water for the French press coffee I suddenly decided I needed. "What time is it?"

She sends me a tight smile, and that's when I notice she's clutching a folder to her chest. Something isn't right. It's too early, but then again, I haven't looked at my phone in at least an hour. I snap the heat off for the tea kettle.

"Did you see my message?" Urgency thickens her voice.

I feel around the front of the apron. No phone. "No, I—"

"Oh, this is *lovely*," coos a new voice, and that's when two wide-eyed prospective buyers step into the living room behind Hazel.

My jaw drops. "Oh. Hey!"

I am wearing very tight briefs right now, so this is fun. I back up against the counter, trying to keep my front angled toward them, but the apron doesn't help matters. It only makes things worse.

"Mr. and Mrs. Parker, I'd like you to meet Grayson Daly, the current owner of the house."

"I'd shake your hands, but I'm covered in shrimp juice," I offer. *And basically nude behind the apron.* I see Hazel stifle a smile.

"It's a pleasure to meet you." Mrs. Parker looks particularly amused. "We're excited to see the changes."

"Grayson has been hard at work," Hazel says.

"And very hard at work at dinner right now," I add. "I'm wining and dining our realtor tonight."

Mrs. Parker lifts a brow, looking between the two of us.

"This shrimp juice is all for you, Hazel." I send her an exaggerated wink. Hazel lowers her chin, sending me a private smile before spinning on her heel and beginning the tour. While they creak and step around the house, I track down my phone—I left it on the bathroom sink—and send Hazel an SOS text.

GRAY: Bring pants from my bedroom?? PLEASE

HAZEL: But those briefs really show off your quads.

GRAY: Should I take off the apron too?

HAZEL: No. That's for my eyes only.

GRAY: And lips.

HAZEL: Stop. I'm trying to work.

GRAY: My cock is for your lips, mouth, tongue, hands and eyes only.

She doesn't reply to that last one. I grin as I set the white sauce aside to thicken. A few moments later, footsteps thud down the staircase. Hazel rushes in with a pair of workout shorts. As she hands them off, I jerk her toward me for a kiss.

"Mmm." The scent of her washes over me, and whatever doubts or questions might have cropped up over the past two days are entirely gone. This woman is for me.

"Watch your shrimp juice," she teases and then hurries back up the staircase.

The tour is quick, and now that I at least have pants on, I take some time talking to the couple about the renovations and the upcoming changes. In the past two weeks, I've completely redone the kitchen, downstairs bathroom, and painted all the walls in the entire house. The upstairs hallway isn't quite ready yet, and the back porch

I might not get to before I leave. But the house is a total one-eighty from when I inherited it.

And there's still so much more I want to do.

Really, the past two weeks have brought me closer to Weston and Maverick, who have been my unofficial right-hand men. It's occurred to me more than once that it would be awesome to start my own renovation company. I could even hire those two. We'd be the Daly Brothers, Inc. It's got that small-town charm that *works*.

Before the couple leaves, they take a moment by the front door, discussing something heatedly. Then Mr. Parker marches up to me.

"Would you take three eighty?"

The offer thuds through me. I immediately look to Hazel, who's got a big grin on her face, squeezing that folder to her chest. That's a full thirty thousand more than Hazel thought I could initially get; eighty thousand dollars higher than her worst-case estimate.

I haven't sunk more than five grand into the renovations, either, from doing it with my brothers. This is almost easy money.

"I need to think about it," I finally say. "Let me get back to you tomorrow."

The Parkers look a little crestfallen, but Hazel counsels them as she leads them out of the house. I know better than to accept on the spot as a general business rule. But more than that, I have some serious reservations. My gut tightens thinking about selling the place as it is right now.

When Hazel reappears, I can tell she's out of work mode. She breezes up to me, and I catch her in a hug before she can dodge me. I capture her lips in a kiss, and then another.

"You took too much time to yourself," I murmur before stealing another kiss. "Now you're going to make up for it."

She's all smiles, wrapping her arms around my naked body apron and actual half-naked body. "Consider me a willing hostage." Her gaze slides to the stove. "What's going on in here, Chef Daly?"

"The best flavors are about to assault your senses," I say, moving toward the stove with my arm around her shoulders. "From head to toe."

"Does that mean you're going to pour the sauce all over me?"

"Yep. In the new bathtub. It'll be sexy."

She snickers, then she swats at my chest. "So why'd you shoot down the Parkers?"

"It's not smart to accept the offer on the spot," I say, bringing the wooden spoon up to my lips to taste the sauce. "And I didn't want to break their hearts."

"You're not going to take it?"

"I don't think so." My gaze lands on the French press loaded with ground coffee, but suddenly it seems like it's time for wine. I'll save that coffee for tomorrow.

"But it's thirty more than I quoted you," Hazel says with an incredulous laugh. "You'd be crazy not to take it. They're motivated to buy. This is essentially the retirement home of their dreams."

"I'm not ready to sell," I say simply, moving the two of us toward the far counter where I have the wine selections set out. "I think I can get more money once I finish the renovations."

Hazel is quiet, her arms still wrapped right around my middle section. I get out the corkscrew and open the sixty-dollar merlot I picked up for tonight's dinner.

"Fancy a glass?" I ask.

"Absolutely."

I pour out two generous glasses, and then she finally dislodges from me so that we can clink glasses. We grin and sip, and I take her in. Her loose chestnut braid curling over her left shoulder. The sheer black tank top she's paired with slate gray slacks and peep-toe heels.

"This is *nice*," she admits.

"I got it from The Daily Shop on my three-hour trip down memory lane in aisle five."

She laughs. "It's hard to go anywhere without running into every-one from high school."

"Yeah." I smile, tasting the wine again. "But it was nice."

We clink glasses again. For no reason this time.

Still, it feels definitive.

Like we decided something.

Like now that the Parkers are gone and I've rejected the offer and dinner's about to be ready, we can get back to what really matters.

Hazel and Gray.

CHAPTER NINETEEN

HAZEL

Thirteen tiny shrimp and two bottles of expensive wine later, Gray and I are racing down to the private residential beach.

He wants to make good on our idea to fuck on the beach from earlier that week, and at this point? I can't deny him.

The two days apart to "take some space" have nearly crippled me. I spent each second apart from him thinking about him, which means that when he finally goes back to New York, I'm going to *physically perish.*

I should be smart and start taking my space now. And I tried. But while he's living within two blocks of me, I can't stay away. Not when I show up at his house and he's in a naked bodybuilder apron. Not when he's made shrimp scampi *just because.*

Once our feet hit the sand, we start racing like children. I lunge for him and tumble, hitting the sand. A laugh pops out of me and he circles back to help me up, and then we keep running. Sand flies underfoot, and the scents of lake water and fish reach us in equal measure.

Grayson leads me toward a shadowy alcove of trees above an outcrop of rocks. It's a secluded area—honestly the first place I'd pick for fucking in public at night—and we climb carefully over the bulky stones stacked up along the shore. When Grayson finds the right spot, he sits down and pulls me on top of him.

"Here," he growls, and then he captures my lips in a punishing kiss. It feels like a reprimand for the time I've separated us. My hips open and I straddle him, our groins colliding. His heat washes through me despite the damp night air dancing over my skin. The waves lap against the shore as his hands scorch up my legs, then tug down the lounge shorts I changed into after dinner.

I gasp when the night air breezes my ass. Nobody can see us from here, but still, it feels scandalous. And totally awesome.

"Now this is a pretty tasty dessert," I mumble through a kiss, fisting the hair at the back of his head.

He grunts, and a moment later, he tugs his own shorts down. The warm cockhead grazes my folds, and the sudden pressure against my swollen clit causes my breath to hitch. His biceps are straining on either side of me as he lifts me, guiding me into position.

"This is the only dessert I want anymore." His voice is rough at the edges, betraying his straining composure.

"Mmmm." My lips find the sweet spot by his ear. Gray shudders beneath me. His words mean so much more than our little public sex outing. But this is all about the naughty stuff right now. "Then go on and give me your honey."

He laughs a little, but then he eases himself inside me, and all my thoughts zap into nothingness. All I can feel is the heat and stretching and the steel of him filling me, against the harmony of the lapping waves and the crickets all around us in the darkness. This moment is perfection, and I know I'll never find someone else to make me feel like this—to fuck me on the rocks after shrimp scampi.

Hell, Gray's the type of guy to do this when we're seventy. Because that's how we'd be.

And I don't want to *be* with anyone else.

Tears prick my eyes as we start a rocking, passionate rhythm. I wrap myself around him, hanging on for dear life, like this might be the last time. Because any time could be the last time. His departure is looming, and nothing is guaranteed. We haven't talked, and I'm scared to bring it up. I just want to exist in this, *right here*, forever. In the warm, languid knowing that we're somehow made for each other, even if time and space doesn't allow us to align.

I can take solace in that. Once he leaves.

I move against him, every inch of my body alert in the night air as we buck and rock and try to tamp down the moans. Grayson's stormy gaze glints in the moonlight. Washing over me, pinpricks and silk. I want to be wrapped around him and only him.

I lift myself off him and then slam down, burying him to the hilt, so deep that it makes me wince. His fingertips dig into my butt cheeks. I rock again, a victim to my own merciless rhythm, spurred by the lapping waves and the wall of man beneath me. My breath whooshes out of me as my knees grind against the stone. He grunts, and it sounds strained. He's as close to the edge as I am.

"Hazel," he breathes into my ear, and there's something in his voice that tugs on the final thread holding me together. My name on his lips is a plea. It cracks me open, and the emotion clenches my throat.

"Gray," I begin, the *I love you* burbling up to the surface like the pressure in a shaken bottle. I rock my hips in a slow circle, but before I can say the words, my orgasm comes barreling through me. Pummeling. Igniting me from head to toe, rushing through the scrapes on my knees to the tips of my toes and all the spaces inside me. I cry out, arching back, but Grayson scoops me closer, like he'd fit me inside of him if he could. Our chests collide, and I can feel him pulsing inside me, his abs jerking as he fills me with liquid heat.

He's the only man I've ever let come inside me, and each time it happens, I fall deeper. Harder. It's intimate in a way I can't express, and by the time my orgasm washes away, I'm clinging to him, and there are tears in my eyes. I gasp for air.

Gray holds me, his breath at my ear a reassuring anchor in the wild and dreamy aftermath.

It feels like hours go by in languid pleasure. The pressure of the rock beneath us finally forces me off of him. I groan as I hike my pants up and nestle in at his side.

"Good thing we didn't fuck in the sand," he says, pulling me onto his lap.

"Your cock would have felt like sandpaper."

"Well..." he says, cocking his head. "I don't know about that. You were pretty juicy. Could have tossed at least a half cup of sand in there without it making a difference."

"A half cup of sand?" Laughter slips out of me as I rest my head against his shoulder. "Sounds like a recipe I don't want to try."

"Yeah, you don't mess with perfection." His lips press against the top of my head.

A lake breeze moves the sweaty strands of my hair at the nape of my neck. I watch the inky waves against the shore through the canopy of leaves and tree branches. "Exactly. And thank you for admitting I'm perfect."

His bass laugh resonates through me. "I didn't say *you* were perfect."

"Oh, just my pussy, huh?"

He hums with appreciation. "No, I take it back. All of you is perfect."

His words surprise me. Grayson Daly laying down the gauntlet? I look up at him, a brow arched. "You aren't going to use this opportunity to one-up me?"

Moonlight illuminates the satisfied smile on his face. "Nope."

"I think this is your formal admittance of defeat, then."

"No, no," he's quick to add. "Just recognizing the strengths of my foe."

I dissolve into laughter. He's as far from my foe as anyone could get. Even though a month ago, he was the definition of my enemy.

"More like your ho," I crack.

"So that makes you the Daly ho."

We both crack up. "There were a few Daly hos—back in high school, at least," I add.

"Mostly Connor," Gray says. "I was a good little enamored boy when we were together."

My smile fades a little. "Until you took your lover."

He tenses beneath me. "I never took a lover."

"Yes, you did. We ran into her earlier this week at the tennis courts. She, by the way, is still in love with you."

Grayson scoffs. "She was never my lover. She was the prom queen."

"Right, but you totally ditched me before prom to be with her," I remind him, as though he hadn't fully participated in that string of events.

"I didn't ditch you," he said, an edge in his voice. "You ditched *me*. I found out that you were going with Mark What's-His-Face, and I got pissed."

"I only went with Mark What's-His-Face because you ditched me first!" I exclaim, sitting up.

He sighs, rolling his eyes. "Come on. I was head over heels for you, Hazel. It really fucking hurt when you changed your mind."

I'm breathing heavily again, but not because of sexual ecstasy this time. I search his face in the dim moonlight. Something doesn't make sense, even all these years later. "I swear to God. I took him as a last resort. Besides, Aubree made sure to tell me in *explicit* detail the exact rules and regulations defining the prom king and queen attendance as a couple. She could have recited the student handbook by heart."

There's a long stretch of silence. Finally, Gray says, "She *what*?"

"It was a couple weeks before prom. She cornered me at my locker to pressure me into not going with you to the dance because of *the rules*. I said she could fuck her rules with a baseball bat."

"Typical Hazel ho," Grayson murmurs.

"But then you went with her anyway. So, good job following the rules." I try to laugh a little, but it sounds weak. Probably because we're almost thirty and still discussing high school events as if they matter.

But they did matter once. And Grayson was such a huge part of my life at that time. We'd been planning to go to NYU together. Hell, if things had panned out like we planned, I'd probably be living in New York with him now. We'd be blissful and rich in Brooklyn, together. But it didn't pan out. And now here we are. Ten years into our cold war, and things are just beginning to thaw.

"Hazel," he says, his voice softer now. "I only went with her because she tipped me off that you were going with Mark, and he even confirmed it." He pauses. "But now, I'm thinking that probably Aubree was behind it."

The idea thuds through me. She's a very obvious common denominator in this saga of miscommunication.

"So why didn't you talk to me after that? We could have cleared it up," I say.

"I don't know. Because I was eighteen and a hothead? I was *mad*. It didn't occur to me that Mark would lie about that. I don't remember what he said exactly. But he told me you guys were going together and I…believed it."

"Mark asked me to prom, but it was four days beforehand, and I was desperate."

Grayson scoffs. "Fucking ridiculous. It was Aubree. It had to be."

"She's always been in love with you." I pick at the hem of his shirt while something like an orb of satisfaction encases me. It's a relief to know that your high school sweetheart didn't actually spurn you. Even if you spent the following ten years believing it. "She's the perfect candidate for the crime."

"I should have called her out on the tennis courts," Gray says.

"Or challenged her to a match."

"Her against both of us," Gray adds.

"We would have slaughtered her." I cackle, and Gray offers his hand for a high five. Somehow, this feels like redemption. Like we can finally team up to gain the victory we deserve.

A few more moments of silence drift by, and finally Gray says what's been on my mind.

"What would have happened if we hadn't graduated hating each other?"

His question makes my chest hurt. I don't like thinking about how the past ten years have been a mistake. Like Aubree has stolen something from us by getting in the way. The past decade has been fruitful and productive and successful.

But it's also been lonely. Even though I have plenty of friends, and customers for miles around…I've been lonely. I've been missing Grayson. Even as a foe.

"I don't know if I can think about that," I say into his chest, hoping he can't hear how tight my throat is.

Gray rubs my back. "I've thought about it a lot."

I tilt my head to look up at him. "You have? Even though we hated each other?"

His smile stretches wide. "Hate is just love that got all twisted up."

The words trickle through me. Fuck, he's right. I've loved Grayson since the beginning. Since we were six years old and running through the kindergarten playground to see who could scare more classmates.

And now at twenty-eight, I love him more than I can properly say.

"I hate you," I whisper to him. He grins and captures my lips in a kiss.

Because he knows what I mean.

"I love you too, Hazel," he whispers back.

He's always known.

CHAPTER TWENTY

GRAYSON

The soft sounds of Hazel moving around the bedroom at six a.m. rouse me to consciousness the next morning. The bedcovers go *hushhh* as she sits down and pulls on leggings. I roll over, blinking lazily as I watch her get ready for the day.

This is my favorite part of the morning. Admittedly, it's partly because I'm the one staying behind and not going into work. But also because I get to watch Hazel in the lazy, early rays of daybreak. When she's bathed in cobalt and then sunflower yellow, and she's brimming with energy for the day.

"Not gonna wear my favorite skirt today?" I say, my voice groggy.

She looks back at me and smiles. "Not today. My knees are all scraped from our escapade on the rocks."

I tut. "We'll bring knee pads next time."

"No, I wear these scrapes with pride. Except, secretly."

I laugh a little, and she stands, pulling the leggings up to her waist. Then she breezes into the connected bathroom and a triangle of light spills onto the bedroom floor. I listen to the sounds of her rummaging through drawers and opening makeup cases.

My eyes drift shut, and I try to imagine being in my apartment again. It's been so long, I can barely remember what life is like in New York. It's amazing how quickly I've forgotten, even after a decade of calling it home. Three weeks back in Bayshore, and I feel like I'll never leave again.

Except I am soon. In less than a week, actually. Panic streaks through me, jolting my eyes open. I've been content to put it off until "the right time." But the clarity of dawn helps me realize that time is now.

"Hazel," I call out.

"Yeah?" She's got that distracted voice she gets when she's putting on eyeliner.

"I'm leaving in five days."

Silence ripples out from the bathroom. Finally, she clears her throat. "Is it wrong that I wish you were staying?"

I manage a weak laugh. "Not wrong. Trust me, I don't want to leave yet either."

"Then stay."

I sit up in bed, rubbing at my face. It's not that easy. We both know it. When I look up, she's in front of me, earnestness written all over her face.

"Morning, beautiful," I say, grinning as I take her in. I'll never get tired of waking up with her. Of admiring her cute nose and the line of her collarbone or the sexy smirks she reserves just for me.

She looks at me expectantly, and I sigh. "I can't stay. You know this."

Hazel looks crushed, and she starts picking at the comforter.

"But I have an idea." I say the words slowly, trying to find the words I've been practicing over the past few days. "I don't want this to end. It's a little crazy, but...hear me out."

"Okay," she says, and moves the fiddling to her cuticles.

"I think you should come to New York."

"Like to visit?"

"Like to live."

Silence forms a gulf between us. Hazel is staring at me, but I can't read what's swimming in her eyes. It's something I've never seen before. She's still, like stone, and the only sign that she's alive is the intermittent blinking.

"You can live with me," I say, anxiety pulsing under my skin. "You always wanted to come to New York. And now, well, this is the perfect opportunity. You would make a *killing* out there. I can promise you that. Relaunching your business might take some time, but I've started crunching the numbers for you." Words are flowing now, more of an effort to fill the icy silence than anything. "I'm one hundred percent confident that you could quadruple your earnings out there. And you've got your in. You've got *me*."

She blinks but still says nothing.

"Hazel..."

She jerks her head away, and it's then that I notice her chin wobble. My stomach shrinks to a fist, and she heads for the bathroom.

I'm pretty sure this isn't going well.

But there's still hope.

"You don't have to decide now," I call out. "But Hazel, this thing between us is *good*. I don't want it to end."

There's more rustling in the bathroom. She still hasn't said a word.

"*Hazel*," I say again, frustration making my voice harsh. "Aren't you going to say anything?"

She emerges from the bathroom a moment later, her makeup bags packed. She comes over to the bed, sets everything down, and then starts stuffing her clothes from yesterday into her small duffel. I sigh, running a hand through my hair.

When she speaks, her voice is as cold as a glacier. "Moving to New York City is the last thing I want."

I pinch my eyes shut. "And moving to Bayshore is the last thing I want."

Her nostrils flare as she sweeps her heated gaze up to meet mine. "Then I guess we made our decision."

"No," I blurt as she slings her duffel bag over her shoulder and stomps toward the bedroom door. "Hazel, *think about it*. That's all I'm asking."

She pauses in the doorway, twisting around to look at me. "Do you even know me? Have you listened to a single thing I've said since you've gotten home? Or do you only see me as some sort of filler for sex and intimacy, since you apparently can't get laid in New York?"

I scoff, rolling my eyes. "Yeah, that's it, Hazel, I'm using you for sex and plan to import you as my pleasure doll."

"Whatever. We knew this day was coming, so we might as well start accepting it now. I tried earlier this week, but this time I'm not going to fail. Goodbye, Grayson."

She storms out of the bedroom, leaving me rigid and mulling over her words. The bedside clock switches to 6:23 as the front door slams shut. Her car starts a moment later, and I listen until I can't hear the hum of her engine in the distance anymore.

Then I collapse backward and stare at the ceiling.

That went worse than I'd imagined. But I'm not going to be swayed by her display of aggression. She thinks this is over—well, it's not. Not until we've talked this out like adults, instead of the hot-headed teenagers we both are inside.

Besides, I'm convinced my idea has merit. I haven't shown her the spreadsheet yet, which is *extremely* convincing once we get into the financial projections tab. She reacted angrily. Fine. Once she cools down, we'll talk more about it.

She *wanted* to live in New York once upon a time. And now I can make that a reality. Hazel knew from a young age who she wanted to be and what she wanted out of life. Which is why I know that there must be some part of her still curious about taking a stab at life in the Big Apple.

But waiting doesn't come easy for me. I toss and turn in bed for another ten minutes, mulling over things, before I realize that more sleep is totally off the table. I'd get dressed and go straight to her office except that I don't want to mess up her schedule. I'll wait, even if it kills me, for the right moment to continue this conversation.

In the meantime?

It's back to renovating. Which is the other thing about Bayshore that's got me hooked. These quiet mornings, scuffing around the house between sawdust and paint chips. Imagining new styles and then making them a reality. If I had more time, I'd stay here and see this through to completion. But for now, I've got to get as much done as I can before I start the drive home.

Returning for a few weekend trips is an option, one that I'll offer to Hazel as a sort of compromise. But it won't be anything long term, and it certainly won't scratch the itch we're sure to have.

Besides, once she sees what it's like without these sweet touches as part of the daily grind?

She'll be Team New York in no time.

I can guarantee it.

CHAPTER TWENTY-ONE

HAZEL

I'm in mourning. I'm inches away from ordering a black netted fascinator on Amazon, but I stop myself before I one-click the funeral accessory.

But this fantasy of Grayson and me?

Officially dead.

My insides are steaming for the rest of the day after he suggests his "solution." Which sounds a lot like "give up your life to come live mine."

I know better than that. But what makes me angrier than his suggestion was the fact that my first reaction was to consider it.

Sitting there in his bathroom, staring at the reflection in the mirror, I could almost hear the honks and shouts of the street beyond the window of his Brooklyn apartment. I really went there—fantasizing cab rides, Broadway, the occasional three a.m. hot dog *just because*—but the whole thing doesn't feel right.

And not because I don't eat hot dogs.

I'm pissed that this was his only solution. He hasn't been listening to a damn thing I've said the entire time.

I'm cycling between hurt and astonishment so hard I feel like I'm out on a Sea Ray on choppy water. Being jolted back and forth between bow and stern, the spray from the white caps coming up to dampen me. There's nothing straightforward about this. Because, on the one hand, he wants to be with me. And yes, that's very alluring. Very redeeming. But on the other hand, he wants me to abandon my life.

He wants me to abandon *this*. My gothic desk situated at the perfect angle in the perfect sunny office, with the perfect view of Briggs Bay due north. My father, who lives three miles away. My amazing group of friends, whom I see weekly, and sometimes daily. He thinks I'll have the energy to start up a brand-new realty business in the most competitive city in the world, *and* go make a whole new friend group after that?

He wants me to give up this sparkling lake, where I can count three sailboats out on the water in my direct line of sight.

He wants me to give up my *house*, which I hand styled from the inside out. All the way down to my little crabapple tree in the front left corner of the yard. Sure, you can find a house in New York, but not with my fifty-year-old lilac bush in the backyard, and certainly not without paying five times as much.

And honestly, I don't know what's more depressing, the fact that we've spent the past ten years hating each other because Aubree manipulated us into breaking up, or the fact that we've reconnected, fallen in love again, and will ultimately fail because the distance manipulates us into breaking up.

But maybe this is something I need to learn as a twenty-something successful woman.

There are very few men I'd consider forever with, and those who I would are destined to not work out.

Great.

Grayson calls me on and off that day, but I silence all his calls. I don't respond to texts, either. I'm actually busy with clients all day, and that evening is a meeting with the city about an abandoned downtown building I invested in, with the goal to renovate it and attract more businesses. It's really a collaboration between the city and me. I'm not a developer; I just happened to snag the deal when I saw it and like the idea of participating in downtown's renaissance.

I'm in meetings until eight, because we can't find a good renovation company who isn't price gouging. Afterward, I head to the hipster taco joint so I can finally grab dinner and try to unwind with a margarita. No Grayson. Not if I know what's good for me.

His text comes through after my first bite of taco.

GRAY: When are you getting here?

HAZEL: I'm not coming over tonight.

GRAY: And why not?

HAZEL: It's called weaning. We need to start.

I finish my taco and start on the second when his next message comes in.

GRAY: You haven't even seen my spreadsheet.

I still my fingers before I call him a nerd. That could be construed as friendly or flirting. I must stop all those activities immediately. I need to put emotional distance between us now so that the physical distance doesn't kill me.

GRAY: I'll send it to your email. I broke it down by expenses in the NY market based on an interview I had with a realtor friend.

I soften a little. The man has done research on my behalf. He's speaking my love language. Except his end goal is something I absolutely do not want to consider.

But maybe I should.

GRAY: I miss you, babe.

After that last text, I swipe my phone closed and turn it onto its face. Tears are stinging my eyes. If I can miss him after ten hours at the office, how am I going to survive weeks away from him? Months? Years?

Because I need to face the damned truth. Once Grayson leaves, my love for him will not magically extinguish. No, my feelings for him are resilient. They'll survive fire and ice and earthquakes. My love for Grayson is the biological equivalent of a cockroach. It really doesn't matter what you do to it—it's going to survive.

It's so non-romantic I should get it cross-stitched and gift it to him for our birthday.

But, again. Weaning.

My superbug-style love for Gray is why once our Bayshore time is over, I'll still be just as hung up on him. Probably no matter how much time goes by. I've loved him for the past ten years—more, if I'm being honest. Wanted him without even realizing it. Pined for him when it didn't make sense.

So him going home to New York? It'll be no different. I'll still be here, rocking the realty game, investing in my community's future, while my heart throbs for the one man I can't seem to snag.

Once I'm full of tacos and sadder than ever, I drive to my dad's house. He's on the front porch with a beer, talking to a friend. As I pull into the driveway, his friend says goodbye, and my dad pats the rocking chair next to him.

He's a big old biker. White haired, big bushy mustache, and love handles to rival the best. I grew up around hot cars and fast motor-cycles. He's a gearhead and a homebody and had to be both mother and father to me as I grew up. Though he looks like a beast on the outside, inside he's softer than melted butter.

And the hardest part about leaving Bayshore might be the thought of not being able to drop in on him weekly like I do.

"Hazeyyy," he croons in his ex-smoker's voice. We hug, and then I sit next to him in the familiar old rocking chair. I sigh, looking out at the last crimson rays of sunlight blanketing the world. In his driveway, his Harley is parked right behind an old '64 Ford truck. That's not even half of his collection.

"Hi, dad," I say, unable to not sound morose. I already want to curl up in his arms. "Just thought I'd come and say hi."

"I saw your new billboard the next town over," he says before taking a pull at his beer. "Looks great, as usual. Hey, you want one?" He holds up his beer.

I smile, but it fades fast. *Ask Hazel.* All the billboards say the same thing. Except this is one situation Hazel can't solve. So please don't ask her. She has no freakin' idea.

"No thanks." I start to pick at a nail, the question bubbling up inside me faster than I can control it. "What would you say if I sold the business and moved to New York?"

My dad's salt and pepper brows furrow together. "Move where now?"

"New York." I clear my throat, cheeks flaming. This is so stupid. "I started seeing someone, and he asked me to move with him to New York."

"You seein' somebody?"

"Yeah." I pause, wondering if I want to admit that it's Grayson. My dad hated him alongside me for a long time, out of duty to his only daughter. I have to tell him. Otherwise, the story won't make sense. Why I'd consider abandoning everything and leaving. Why I feel the way I do. "Grayson Daly is back. Temporarily. We were stupid and started something again. Except now he's going back home and wants me to come with him."

A long sigh rattles out of my father. Then he clears his throat. I can tell this isn't gonna be good.

"Are you flippin' crazy, girl?" my dad barks at me.

I sigh, feeling logic and reason click back into place inside my skull. "*Yes.* But that stops now." My dad's response is all I needed to hear. Besides, you'd think that the journals would have been enough. My mother left behind a *lot* after she passed away, days after I was born. One of the things was her journals.

They sat untouched in boxes in the attic for a long, long time. Until I discovered them as a teen, surreptitiously devoured them all in one sitting one day while my dad was at work, and then hoarded them for my own and never told anyone.

He still doesn't know what I read in those journals. But I do know more about what brought them together back in the early 80s. How hard they fought to have a baby. And how much my mom gave up in order to follow my dad to his job here on the North Coast as a union worker.

She'd given up her own wild dreams to follow his path of stability. I don't blame her for it. It's what a lot of smart, forward-thinking moms would do.

But I could read the sadness tucked beneath her words. She'd always wanted to be an interior designer and run her own business. It's one of the reasons I fought to have my own business and took such an interest in interior design, if only as a pet project. She'd dropped out of school halfway through her second year to follow dad here. And sure, they were happy, but she hadn't wanted to come here.

And now my entire life is built here. I often wonder if the mother I knew for three days would have ended up loving it. If she'd have thought of it as home after raising a girl here and having her family.

"You tell that guy he can bring his big apple over my way, and I'll take a smack at it." A laugh cracks out of him. I snicker, swatting my dad's arm. "If he breaks your heart again, I'll smash his apple to pieces."

"Well…" I start, trying to offer him comfort that he can't, at least, do that to me again. But the words don't arrive. I'm not certain I'll escape unscathed. It's never been possible with Grayson. All I can do is manage the consequences.

"But seriously, peach," my dad starts, using the nickname he's used with me since the day I was born. "You're thinking about moving there? When you got all this good stuff going here?"

"I was considering it," I admit, starting back with my cuticles. He's the only person I'd admit this to. Him, and maybe London. I'd be too embarrassed to tell Callie and the boys. "I mean, just weighing my options, you know? But, forget I said anything. I'm not going to move."

We chat for a little bit about other things—how his first run on the boat went, the new paint on the door trim and how he messed it up—and I finally head home around ten, feeling more confused than ever.

I was so sure about what I'd told my dad at his house. But as I'm driving home, I have to physically steel myself against turning onto Grayson's street.

Go home. I need to go home.

I'd said it myself earlier that evening.

This is the weaning process, and it's time to get used to it.

CHAPTER TWENTY-TWO

GRAYSON

It's Friday evening and I'm at my mom's house, trying to take stock of my life now that I'm about to head back to New York. Drops of white paint dot my forearms and fingertips. Weston and I finished up all the trim in the house today, and I sanded the back deck.

The amount of satisfaction and—dare I say it—joy I've taken in this project is overwhelming. Honestly, the sensation feels foreign after a decade in the city. I've forgotten what personal projects are like. What slowing down can do for a person. But the happiness is dampened by one little detail.

The fact that Hazel isn't here to share it.

It's been over twenty-four hours since I brought up the idea. I have full faith she'll be looking over my spreadsheet and getting back to me with a whole list of logistical questions. I need to give her time to stew.

"You look like you need a shower," Mom comments as she breezes into the kitchen where I'm staring out the back window.

"Yeah," I say. "Just got done working for the day."

"How are things coming along?"

"Pretty great. Reno-great, I should say."

Mom snickers and rummages in the fridge and then pulls out a bowl of fruit. She pops grapes into her mouth as she assesses the backyard.

"Any offers on the house?"

"I got one earlier this week." My heart rate picks up at the mention of the Parkers, because it reminds me of the epic sex that followed their visit to my house. "But I turned it down."

Mom's eyes almost pop out of her head. "You did? Did they lowball you?"

"No." I pause, wondering if I should admit this. It feels...revelatory. In a bad way. "They actually offered me thirty thousand over what I was expecting."

Her eyes widen more. They're close to popping out of her skull. "And you didn't accept it *why*?"

"I'm not done with the house," I say simply, grabbing for a handful of grapes. I don't like her inquisition. Or that tone she's using. Or the way she's studying me like she's *cracked a code* or something. "Once I finish all the renovations, I'll be able to get a higher price. You watch."

Mom doesn't respond right away, which unnerves me. Instead, she's narrowing her eyes at the fruit bowl now, clucking her tongue. "Uh-huh," she finally says.

"What?"

"No, no. I get it." She waves me away, like suddenly my presence is unnecessary. "You don't need to say anything else."

I chew another grape, watching as a little smile quirks her lips. "Mom, what are you talking about?"

"You're making memories there." Her voice suddenly dons a wistful tone, and she's moving around the kitchen like she's floating on clouds. "And those memories have everything to do with our Hazel."

Every time she references Hazel, it's *our*. Except Hazel is now *mine*.

I won't share her. Not even with my mom.

"I don't know about that." I drum my knuckles against the countertop. "It's a wise business move. It means more money for me to invest in this start-up I have my eye on."

Mom doesn't look convinced.

"Besides, I'm trying to get her to come out to New York. It's not about the house."

Mom stops her dreamy saunter through the kitchen and turns to me with an icy look. "What?"

"I asked her yesterday morning. She's still thinking about it. But I think she could make a killing out in New York."

Mom blinks about a billion times, as though she's having trouble processing the idea. "You asked our Hazel to move away from Bayshore?"

"Are you capable of calling her just *Hazel*? And yes, I did."

"Grayson Thomas Daly. What the hell is wrong with you?"

She sounds angry. Like, actually angry. Not the fact that she used my full name, but the tone in her voice. She's disappointed in me.

"We want to be together," I say slowly, succinctly, "but it won't work unless she comes to New York. I have my job there. She can bring hers with her. It's the only thing that makes sense."

Mom scoffs, throwing up her hands. "You seriously think Hazel is going to leave behind her empire?"

The question throws me for a moment. I hadn't thought of it like that before. "She can create a new one over there. She's the best at what she does. I have full confidence in her."

"Like it's so easy to pick up a thriving business and restart it elsewhere?" Mom scoffs again. "I tell you what. Sometimes, the denseness of men is astounding."

Now she's pissing me off. "Oh, come on. What's so wrong with my idea?"

"You need to stop lying to yourself about how you're going to make it work with our Hazel." She's pointing her finger at me and using the tone she uses during arguments with my dad, which makes me feel worse. This all went downhill very quickly. "She's not going to stick around for you forever. You got lucky when you came back this time. But if you mess this up again, she might not be around for a third chance."

I work my jaw back and forth. I feel like she's got me and this situation all wrong. Nobody has looked at my spreadsheets, either. Nobody would be pointing fingers if they'd look at my projections. "This is my attempt to make it work."

"Asking her to drop everything and leave when she's at the peak of her career? Some offer you're extending."

"But she's—"

"Don't you 'but' me, young man." Mom wags her finger at me. "I see what goes on here. I talk to Hazel. I recognize the look in her eyes. That woman wants to start a family. She wants a husband. She wants *babies*."

I sigh, raking a hand through my hair. "I want that stuff too. It doesn't mean—"

"You don't get it. And that's fine. But you're going to lose Hazel if you ask her to follow you." Mom slaps the countertop with her palm. I haven't seen her this upset in a long time. And I certainly wasn't expecting to provoke the beast today.

"I already asked her," I say, the wind going out of me. I'm tired of defending this idea. I want to talk to Hazel and continue the conversation. "We still need to figure things out."

Mom deflates a little, shaking her head. "Have you ever considered bringing your talents back home?"

She pins me with a look and heads for the living room. I watch her go, hearing all the usual protests in my head. There isn't a job for me here, not like I have in New York.

So it's impossible. Case closed.

But what if there's a different job for me?

I can't think about it. The thought is too big; too scary. I'd rather continue along the trajectory I set for myself in college. The path that involves assured paychecks, living well, and making millions. Everything else will figure itself out.

But still, I'm antsy the rest of the evening. I'm waiting for Hazel. For a text. For any hint that she's planning on seeing me before I leave. Dinner comes and goes, alone, at my house. I can't even convince Weston or Maverick to join me. It's Friday night, after all—they're already out partying.

Once I've milled around the house for hours and downed a few beers, I get a text. My heart hops into my throat.

LUKE: Yo buddy, where you at?

GRAY: Home. What's going on tonight?

LUKE: Just got to the bar. Your girl needs you.

My heart starts racing, and I'm lacing up my sneakers before I can consciously decide to. Luke texts with their location—a lakefront bar about a mile away—and I hop into my car for the short ride. I could have walked, but I need to be there *now*.

It's after ten when I pull into the packed parking lot. The marquee sign shows something about a Blues band. I push inside the doors, heart in my throat. I blow past the security guy, who calls out after me for my license.

"I'm fucking twenty-eight," I shout over my shoulder, and then hang a right into the main area of the bar. The scent of beer accosts me, and the dull roar of conversation between musical acts fills my head. I scan the bar, my gaze hopping over women in sundresses, heads tossed back in laughter, lots of ruddy-cheeked men holding Bud Lights. And in the sea of normalcy, I spot Hazel immediately.

My Hazel.

She's dressed for a night out. Like a *girls'* night out. A silky red tank top that showcases the tantalizing tops of her breasts. Red lipstick to match. Hair pulled away from her face in a low ponytail. Callie is at her side, whooping while she holds up a beer. She's facing the band, but nobody is playing. I can already tell she's shit-faced.

Hazel isn't looking my way. I weave through the crowd, keeping an eye on her. Luke clamps onto my shoulder as I approach.

"Hey. You got here fast," he says into my ear, worry in his gaze.

"What's going on?"

"She's tanked." He guides me toward the bar, and I can see Hazel over his shoulder. She's leaning against the bar, and if she's noticed me yet, she hasn't let on. "About one shot away from taking her top off is my guess."

That's when I notice some slick-o sidle up to her. She turns to him like she's been waiting for him. I can hear her throaty laugh, and she leans against him. Heat thrums through me, turning my skin prickly. My hands turn into fists.

"And yeah," Luke says, casting me a worried glance. "There's that guy. Callie told us that you guys are going through a thing. But I figured…" He trails off. He doesn't need to say anymore. Tiff or not, Hazel is mine, and this bullshit is about to end.

I already know what she's trying to pull. That's the benefit of being telepathically connected to your archrival and greatest love. Even when we're miles apart, throughout the years, I still get glimpses of Hazel in my mind's eye. Days when I can't get her out of my mind. Like her spirit can ping me.

We fucking *are* meant for each other.

And maybe she has been my soul mate all along.

CHAPTER TWENTY-THREE

HAZEL

I need to start an advice column.

I already have the first submission for my newspaper debut.

ASK HAZEL: How should I handle my quasi-boyfriend, long-time rival, and hotter-than-sin soul mate dumping me discretely via outrageous ultimatum? Signed, Hazel.

Dear Hazel, or should I say SELF: The answer here is clear. You should absolutely go to the bar, take three shots of Jamison back to back, dance unattractively in the middle of the dance floor until single creepers arrive, and then flirt with anyone. Literally anyone. Just so you can feel like you might have options once the love of your life leaves you in three days. Also, you should trip over yourself while you're at it. And maybe have one boob pop out of your too-loose tank top, which is loose because of the recent weight you lost being puppy-dog enamored with the man who's about to move away. Don't forget to end it with a late-night pity quesadilla and crying in your bathroom.

This is my game plan. It looks suspiciously like my game plan when I first got to OSU and had my "wild streak," which was also born of Grayson-induced trauma. Being nineteen and crazy goes over slightly better than being twenty-eight and sloppy. I can tell Luke, Callie, and Anthony are a little worried. Well, Callie, not so much anymore because I have her taking shots alongside me. See, I'm smarter than I look. Rope in your sidekick.

But they know something is up. All I said at the start of our evening was that Grayson and I were done because he never listened to me once in my life. That's all. Barely anything. Yet the puzzled looks abounded.

It's okay. They don't know how hard I fell. They don't know that I went headfirst into the abyss and cracked myself wide open. Top to bottom. And out came spilling guts and pride and all.

This guy I started talking to about a half hour ago is back. His name is Dan or Darrell or Juan. I have no idea. It doesn't matter. Every time I look at him, I notice that he's not Grayson, and it makes me sadder. I crave distraction, but even the distraction leads me back to Gray.

But weaning is necessary. It's inevitable. And it's going to happen whether I like it or not.

"So you wanna get outta here?" Juan or Darrell asks me. He's looking down at my cleavage, so I push my chest out. Eat it up, buddy. I wouldn't take him home with me, not in a million years. But pretending I would is fun. Pretending I'm not hopelessly in love with Grayson is fun.

"Ohhh, I don't know," I drawl, peeking at him from under my eyelashes. Already this is getting boring. I sigh, shoulders dropping. "I might get another drink."

"Let me get it for you," he says, turning to the bar. As he does, I glance over his shoulder. Just a few bodies away there's Luke, and at his side...Grayson.

His stormy blues are like a fire whip against me. In the gauzy glow of the bar, I can see him in a new light. The off-duty Grayson light. No longer the polished New Yorker wearing suits for days. No, this is the small-town hottie as I always knew him. His hickory hair has grown since he got here, and the longish strands are starting to curl. He can almost sweep it across his forehead. His square jaw is flexing, flexing, flexing as he stares at me. Like he's contemplating whether to walk away or to kidnap me on the spot.

My entire chest cavity seizes, and I suddenly go weightless and rigid. A chorus of angels erupts from somewhere, drowning out the music, and all I want is to run to him and collapse into his arms. The day and a half away from him has, once again, basically crippled me. Which doesn't bode well for the rest of our lives.

He's heading toward me now, and hoo boy, he doesn't look happy. I remember Darrell or Dan. I glance at him, mouth opening to maybe warn him, but what can I say? *Sorry, you've been a pawn?* Gray stalks up to a me a moment later and grabs me by the arm. Brisk. Fierce. He brings me toward him, face level with mine.

"What do you think you're doing?"

He's dressed in all black, which is my weakness. Our outfits actually complement each other *perfectly*, so, you know, one more spear to the heart. His simple black tee shows off his biceps, which bulge even bigger since he started working on the house. Black mesh shorts hug narrow hips. The scent of him, cedar and working man, forces a whimper from my lips.

My arm sizzles where he touches me. The jealousy crashes off him and nearly drowns me. I hate how much I love it that he's jealous. No, scratch that. *I just love it.*

"I'm enjoying a night at the bar with my friends?" I try to act put out, but I can't look away from him. He's all I want to look at. He's the one thing missing in my already-awesome life.

"Yo, man, step off," Juan suddenly interjects, like he's my knight in drunken armor.

"She's with me," Grayson barks, fiercer than I've ever heard him.

"I bought you this drink," Juan-Darrell says, sounding a little miffed. Whatever.

"You can drink it!" I suggest cheerily as Grayson leads me away. God, what a relief. Not only to be rid of the company I didn't want to begin with, but also to have Grayson back at my side. To be able to give in despite fighting it for so long.

"You two leavin'?" Callie slurs, apparently not noticing that Grayson was never here to begin with.

"I'm taking her home," Grayson says as he steers me out of the bar, his hands clamped onto my shoulders. I can't fight the grin, but only as long as he can't see it.

"Bye, drunky," Anthony taunts, while Luke waves us off. It takes work to weave out of the bar, but once we hit the warm night air, the sounds of the bar become a dull murmur behind closed doors. I tear myself away from him.

"I'll walk." It's my last chance to exert any sort of dominance over my waning willpower. I stumble, and Grayson catches me.

"How about no? I drove. Get in the car."

"Grayson, I don't want to leave with you."

"You left the bar with me."

His logic leaves me searching for a comeback. If I were sober, this would be much easier. I wouldn't have to struggle to be snappy. *"You* left the bar with me."

Grayson snorts. That wasn't a good response. My street cred is waning.

"Come on." He grabs for my wrist, but I slink away from his reach. I stand my ground on the sidewalk in front of a huge mound of lilies.

"I don't want to go with you," I say, resting my hands on my hips. As if my posture might help my cause. "We're supposed to be weaning. You're leaving in like *a day and a half* and I—" My voice cracks suddenly, which is just the space needed for all my repressed emotions to come rushing forth. *Fuck.* I stop talking and turn away, swallowing the knot.

"And you what, Hazel?" His voice is softer this time, and right at my ear. His heat surrounds me like the most amazing sweater. I would bathe in his scent if I could. I pinch my eyes shut.

"I can't handle us breaking up for a second time," I say in a quiet voice, looking everywhere but at him.

"Then come with me."

A sigh rockets out of me. I'm not sad anymore; I'm pissed. "Why is that the only solution?"

"Did you look at my spreadsheets?" he demands.

"Yes, *I looked at your perfect spreadsheets*," I hiss. They were a modern work of art. Perfectly bolded text and outlined columns with a level of detail that I haven't seen in...years. It's my level of work. The type of attention I pay to things that really matter. And goddammit, that spreadsheet was *moving*. Like a practiced symphony.

"And?"

"And we need to wean," I say, slicing my hands through the air. "Your numbers are solid. The profit is...*enticing*." I wobble a little. "But I want to have babies, Gray."

He steps closer, smoothing his hands over the sides of my arms. He's all manly tenderness now. He forces me to meet his gaze. "We can have babies. I *want* to have babies with you."

I pinch my eyes shut again. Lord, those words don't help matters.

"When? After I turn forty?" I scoff. "I mean, sure, it can be done. But I was thinking, like, oh, I don't know, in a couple years? But I can't. If I move to New York, I can't. I'll be saddled with debt and working ninety-hour weeks and—"

"Hazel."

"And your mom would *love* to help out with the kids," I barrel on, all of my worries gushing out of me at once. "We need to have a support network, you know? We need to have help, and in New York, we might get some random weirdo posing as a babysitter or, or, or a nanny who puts spoiled goat milk in the bottles and—"

"*Hazel.*" His arms squeeze around me and I melt into his embrace, my worries suddenly quieting. I bury my face in the solid wall of his chest, taking deep gulps of the scent of him. Like this is the last time I'll ever get the chance. "You don't need to decide now. We've still got a couple more days."

A couple more days. The words prompt another whimper. A breeze from the lake reaches me, and I take a restorative breath, propping my chin on his chest to look up at him.

"Can we walk back?"

Gray wets his bottom lip, dragging the pad of his thumb over my cheekbone. "Yes, baby. Whatever you want."

Between sweet nothings like that and his fire spreadsheets, I'm toast. I *need* to be with this man. Each time I try to put distance between us, I fail anyway, so why not give into it? Sadness washes over me, fueled by alcohol and the very real heat of this man. Because in a few more days, he'll be hundreds of miles away. Back to his own life, in his own routine.

And I'll be...what?

Missing him so hard I'll be ready to call the moving company.

We walk down the curved sidewalk leading to the lakefront. There's a boardwalk that traverses the majority of the shore, cutting through downtown, and eventually dumping off near a side entrance to our neighborhood. It's pretty convenient. And quite romantic. Which is another thing that doesn't *help*.

Walking like this—even though I do occasionally stumble—is what I've always wanted. To have the man of my dreams at my side while the lake air whips around us on the perfect summer night. I watch the lake, the dark waves moving against the shore, and before I know it, I'm crying.

Grayson doesn't notice at first, and I try to hide it. But soon my chest hitches, and I have to wipe my eyes, and then Grayson is in front of me, gripping the sides of my arms.

"What's wrong?"

"I don't want you to leave," I wail.

"Aww, you're drunk and sad," he teases, a dimple flashing.

"Yeah. Drunk on Jamison and sad about *you*." I poke his chest, wiping at my eye. I've probably fucked up my winged eyeliner already, but who cares? Grayson sees me pee in the morning, so there's nothing left for us to hide.

We walk down the boardwalk a little more, pausing every so often to admire the water or erupt in an accusatory back-and-forth about who is sadder about his time here coming to an end. By the time we make it back to the neighborhood, I'm tired and way more sober. The humid night air and the walk did me good.

Once we go into Gray's house and I chug a glass of water, I know what's next. If he's leaving in three days, I need to take advantage of this possible last time. Don't get me wrong—we still need to wean. But I'll start tomorrow. The first day of weaning never goes well. Everyone knows that.

I push Grayson's back. He barely moves, only twists around to smile at me. He knows what I want. The curtains are open at the bay window in his bedroom, and the light of the full moon spills in. The room is bathed in ethereal darkness, barely lit enough for me to catch the tanned skin of his belly as he tugs his shirt off. The arc of his biceps as he sits on the bed and beckons me closer. The squareness of his jaw as he tilts his head to take me in as I straddle him buck naked.

Each time with him has been memorably hot. But there's something else happening tonight. There's sadness and raw, aching love spilling out of both of us. We move against each other as if we're about to be sent into outer space on different rockets. End of the world–style lovemaking. His hot palms slide up my back, over the bumps of my spine. My hard nipples graze his smooth chest.

Everything is moving like a dream sequence. The sensuality of the moment forces my eyes closed, but I need to watch what's happening between us. To memorize it. To inscribe it into my soul so that I never forget what true love looks and moves like.

Grayson's gaze is a vortex as I look down at him, my pussy hovering over his straining cock. His breath comes out harsh as he traces the lines of my body, urging me closer. Our mouths connect, desperate, hot, and seeking, as I lower myself down. He sinks into me with spellbinding slowness, guiding my hips with his hands. I'm on top, but he's controlling this as much as I am.

And isn't that how it's always been? Two equals vying for best. But neither of us could be here if it wasn't for the other.

The thought slams through me, making my throat thick, as I arch and rock on top of him. Our game of who's-better and who's-winning was never about being number one, at least not after a certain point. It was a dance to celebrate the fact that we were both together. And I love being together with this man.

Tears prick my eyes as we rock and moan and grind in the moonlight. Every flex and groan from him sends me spiraling, until finally I crash down on him one last time and my entire body starts tingling. It never takes long with Grayson, and I cling to him as the orgasm wrings me out. I'm moaning and crying out and saying his name, over and over again, as the pleasure makes my vision go spotty.

Grayson is jerking beneath me, his thumbs digging into that hollow above my hips, and I can tell he's coming.

When he's spent, he releases a long exhale and then collapses backward on the bed, inviting me on top of him. I laugh and cover his chest, hugging him. He's still inside me. And I want him to stay there.

I want to stay *here*.

Eons of silence drift by. I'm caught in some dreamworld between sobriety, sexual satisfaction, and the hazy aftermath of being drunk. I feel like I could fall asleep but also fuck until daybreak.

There's nothing better in the world than this: the solid heat of him beneath me. The rise and fall of his chest. And the steady thrum of his heartbeat.

"You should just stay," I finally say, my croaky voice something even I don't recognize.

Grayson runs his fingertips through my hair and says nothing.

CHAPTER TWENTY-FOUR

GRAYSON

Hazel knows how to compartmentalize better than most men.

Maybe that's her dad's influence showing. I don't know. But when I wake up the next morning after rescuing her from the bar, she's not in my bed. She's not in my bathroom. She's nowhere inside my house.

She's gone. Because she fucking vanished. Per her compartmentalized plan.

And I'm back to square one. Texting with no response. Calling and getting her voicemail. And lurking on the sidewalk around her house like some sort of asshole.

Except I can't text or call her nonstop. There are only so many hours in the day to stake out a lover's house. I've got *shit to do* during my last two days in town. At least ten hours of reno work per day, if I'm being honest. Not to mention packing, buttoning up the house, and saying goodbye to my parents and brothers.

Mom and Dad insist on taking me and Weston and Maverick out for dinner on my last night in town. I can't argue. Hazel has made no effort to respond to my thirty-five unanswered texts and fifteen calls, so I should take the hint, right? My mom is as sad as I am about Hazel not being there with us, but I've got nothing. I can't convince the woman of anything, much less to follow me to a place she doesn't want to go.

Even though I know she'd fucking love it.

The last two nights in my house are lonely. The house feels empty without her in it, and if I'm being honest, I hardly want to go back to my apartment. Sure, I've got an awesome spot in Brooklyn, but I didn't rehab that place from the ground up. I bought it ready to go. Cookie-cutter perfection. This house, here in Bayshore? This is *all mine.*

It's occurred to me more than once that maybe I should hang on to the house. Stop trying to sell it and keep this place for sort of a...summer house. Or a retirement home. I don't know. It might be worth trying to keep it around, at least for a little while.

By the time my last morning in Bayshore arrives, my chest is thick with anxiety. I haven't seen Hazel since our last night together. Every bone in my body aches with wanting to see her. I said goodbye to Luke and Anthony and Callie the night before when we met up for drinks. Hazel was conspicuously absent, and the four of us didn't even talk about her. We'd all gotten the memo. My guess is she swore them to silence. To act like I was already gone. Or dead.

But I'm not leaving town without saying goodbye to her. She can ignore my texts, but she can't ignore me when I come to her office. I show up just before noon, because I know she'll be there. Her office hours are, without fail, eleven to twelve-thirty. I've got dark slacks and a light gray button-up on as I stroll into her office. As soon as I step inside, I push my sunglasses onto my head. She's behind her desk, staring daggers at me. She's wearing a black tube top with a black cropped bolero jacket over it. Her hair is darker. She died it dark brown, a touch beyond mahogany.

My beautiful, thorny Hazel.

"What are you doing here?" she asks, her voice suspiciously placid.

"Asking you one last time." I walk her way, hands shoved in my pockets. "Come with me, babe."

Her nostrils flare. The only sign that I'm getting to her. Her fingers are poised over her keyboard. I interrupted her mid-thought.

Her silence sends my anxiety skyrocketing again. There has to be some way to resolve this. We're two grown, intelligent adults. Why can't we make this work?

"I'll wait for you. Come on, Hazel. Just let me know you're thinking about it."

Her gaze drops to her desk. She blinks a few times, then says, "A new offer came in on your house. It meets your threshold. Do you want to sell?"

I sigh, my shoulders drooping. "You didn't answer me."

"Well, I can't right now. I'm busy."

"Hazel." I can hear the desperation in my own voice. I'm pleading, and I know it.

She meets my gaze again. Reluctantly. Indecision flashes in her hazel eyes, and then she straightens. Reaffirming her position. I have to act fast. She's gearing up to shoot me down again, and I don't know how much fight I have left in me.

"Let's do weekends," I say quickly. "We'll stick with that for a while. You can fly out next weekend, even. I'll pay. We won't be apart for long."

She's nibbling on her lip now. I can tell she's considering it. And holy hell, if this is the only in I've got, I'll run with it.

"We can do it long-distance until you decide," I go on. "Just...*please*, babe. Give me something. I can't leave knowing that I'm not gonna see you again."

That must get her, because she slumps a little. Her gaze flickers my way, and there are all sorts of emotions there. She's pouting too.

"I don't want to not see you again," she admits in a small voice. And it breaks my heart.

"Then let's do weekends," I urge, coming up to her desk. My skin itches with wanting to touch her. Next Friday can't get here soon enough, and she's still within arm's reach. "Please, Hazel."

A sigh erupts from her, and her eyes drift shut.

And then she nods.

The most reluctant agreement ever, but I'll take it.

I go behind her desk and wrap her in my arms, pulling her from the chair. Her arms shoot around my neck and I find my favorite sweet spot buried between her collarbone and her neck. I hug her like we're saying goodbye for five years instead of five days.

"I'll need to cancel an appointment on Saturday," she murmurs.

"Do it. And hire an assistant while you're at it, okay?"

She laughs a little. "Fine. It's time, I guess."

"Overdue." I pull back and look at her, drinking in her sharp features. I've never felt so simultaneously thrilled and sad at the same time. Overjoyed that she's agreed to give this a chance. Crushed that I need to physically exist without her at my side for the next five days.

"I love you, Hazel," I whisper, and then I dive in for a kiss. The intensity sends her back onto her desk. A few papers flutter to the ground. I cup her face in my hands and I kiss her over and over again, until my lips go numb and half her lipstick is on my mouth.

She laughs when we break apart, swiping her thumb over my lips. "Love this shade on you."

"Looks better on you." I grip the edges of her desk, fighting the urge to christen her office. But it's the middle of the day, and we're in full view through her wall of windows. A few people outside have already stopped to stare.

"You better leave, Grayson Daly," she says, smoothing her hands over the front of my shirt. "Or we're gonna get arrested for fucking in public."

"We'll save it for Brooklyn. Rooftop. View of the Statue of Liberty."

She smiles, patting my chest. "Deal."

I rip myself off her, start to walk away, then snag one more kiss. I'm about to push out of her office when she calls out my name.

"I love you too," she says, the look on her face so vulnerable that I pause to watch her. I don't want to forget this moment. The morning she gave us a real chance.

It means something. It doesn't just give me hope, because I've had that tucked away all along. It confirms my suspicion.

I've been really in love with her for longer than I can even remember. So that makes her my soul mate.

And I'm not letting this fail.

CHAPTER TWENTY-FIVE

GRAYSON

My return to work is the equivalent of a horror movie. I ensured my redundancy while I was on vacation, but on Tuesday morning I show up to a shit show. I work fourteen-hour days Tuesday through Thursday to feel even slightly caught up. Hazel's selfies and my favorite lox bagels from around the corner at work sustain me. I don't care what anyone says. Nobody does bagels better than New York, and I will fight a man who tries to convince me otherwise.

HAZEL: I will see you in HOURS.

I smile down at my phone, but it doesn't last long. I've been holed up in my office at work so long over the past three days that it's erased every ounce of relaxation and goodwill I'd managed to cobble together on my vacation. I didn't need four weeks off—I needed a fucking sabbatical.

I'm leaving the office early today—by eight-thirty—because Hazel's landing at nine-thirty, and they can fucking fire me if they have to. I'm not postponing our reunion even a second longer than I have to.

The only good thing about being insanely busy? Days melt away from under me, like a carnival ride I was pretty sure I wanted to get on but now I'm having second thoughts about. Though it's a blessing for getting through the work slog, it's also pretty depressing. If I spend ninety percent of my life in this office, doing the same activity over and over again? Before I know it, I'll be thirty. And then I'll be forty. And what the actual fuck will I have done over the past twenty years of my career besides sit in an office, move wealth for richer people, and collect paychecks?

So yeah, coming back to work has been difficult.

But time grinds on regardless, and I manage to leave the office by 8:45, which means I show up at the arrivals door at the exact second Hazel glides out onto the sidewalk, her shiny purple luggage rolling behind her.

Butterflies take over my stomach in a coup. The organ is theirs now. I park and get out of the car on wobbly legs. She's beaming at me like she's never been so happy to see me. Like I'm the only one she wants.

Like we're really something and this is it for the both of us.

She's in my arms before I even realize I've walked her way, and I'm so relieved I could crumble. And this is after five days apart, people. I put her luggage in my trunk, and we both climb into the car. I take a deep breath, trying to calm my racing heart, as I ease into the traffic heading away from JFK Airport.

"How was your flight?"

"Perfect." She smiles, looking out the window. "And now I'm in NYC."

She sounds way more excited to be here than I planned for, which already feels like a major win. My plan is unfolding exactly as I imagined—lure her here, make her fall in love, and then help put together the puzzle for her life in New York.

"I can't believe you never made it out here before now." I cluck my tongue as we pull onto the log-jammed freeway. Normally, I'd be sighing and tense. But today? Hazel's here, so all the annoyances in the world could occur at once, and I wouldn't give a damn.

"Guess I was waiting for the right thing to bring me here." She sends a bright smile my way. "And now I'm on *vacation*."

"For two whole days." I laugh a little, then sigh. "I've been back at work for four days, and I'm already jealous of your time off."

"Don't you have this weekend off?"

"Well yeah, but..." I trail off, shaking my head. We're going five miles per hour. This is why they need self-driving cars already. We could be fucking in the backseat by now if I only had a robot to navigate us back to Dumbo. "I'm never fully off. I guarantee I'll get at least one emergency call tomorrow and another on Sunday night."

"As long as you don't have to leave me for a single second," she says, reaching over to squeeze my knee. "That's all I ask."

"I wouldn't dream of it." I smile over at her, and her hand trails up my knee and along my thigh. Soon she's stroking the zipper of my work slacks, and my cock pricks to attention. "You don't waste any time."

"These last four days have been *hell*," she moans, drawing lazy patterns over the crotch of my pants. Her grazing touch stiffens my cock until the bulge is noticeable. I wet my bottom lip, glancing down at her hand between my legs as we creep forward. The sight of her slender fingers and perfectly done red nails stroking my growing bulge makes me even harder.

"Can I?" she whines a moment later, turning toward me. She's fiddling with my belt and has it halfway undone before I can even answer.

"In traffic?" I ask, but it's only a facade of propriety. She could suck my dick in the middle of Central Park if she wanted.

"Yes! We're in the big city, we'll never see these people again. Besides, it's almost dark out." Her eyes glint with mischief, which sweeps me away. This, among so many other reasons, is why I love this woman. Because on her first outing to New York she wants to suck me off in traffic. Because she's willing to take a chance on this. Because she's the most successful person I've ever met and still wants to climb higher. I could list the reasons for a full week and still have more.

"I'm not gonna say no to that," I say, laughing as she unzips my pants carefully around the straining bulge. Her cool hand finds my cock through the fold in my boxer briefs, and suddenly my dick's out in the growing dusk of Friday night traffic. Just another passenger in the car.

"*Mmmm.*" She fists my cock a few times, and I jerk beneath her, white-knuckling the steering wheel. It's hard to keep my focus on the road. I suck at my teeth as she drags her fingernail around the head of my cock. "They didn't serve me any snacks on the plane, so I'm gonna need to eat your cock now, okay?"

All I can do is laugh as her head dips, and then there's the slippery heat of her mouth, consuming the length of my cock. I grunt, smoothing my palm over the silk of her hair as she draws up and down a few times. My thighs go tense under the slurping attention. Hazel's the fucking best.

"*Mrrgghhh,*" she mumbles from around my cock, and I can't even find the words to ask what she was trying to say. I slam on the brakes a little too hard after I creep forward again. Her tongue found the sensitive slit, and I'm about done for.

"Jesus, Hazel," I breathe. My dick is iron in her mouth, and she snakes a hand into my pants to squeeze my balls. I groan, pressing my head to the seat. The traffic is a blur in front of me. This probably wasn't the safest idea, but too late. I'm panting like a dog as she takes another pull at my cock. She comes off with a *pop.*

"So tasty," she murmurs, then dives back down again.

As a rule, I make no eye contact with drivers around me on a normal day, but today I *definitely* don't want to scan the highway and see who might be enjoying the peep show. It's almost dark outside, so there's that, at least. But I won't make it to full nighttime. Not with these plump lips pulling me over the edge.

She swallows my cock again, and then she wraps a hand around the shaft as her lips slip over and around my cockhead. My stomach goes rock-hard, and I fight the urge to buck my hips. Even my toes are curling, awaiting this orgasm. I'm so fucking close.

"Hazel," I grunt, fisting the back of her pretty hairdo. She slurps and groans and then the bliss spills over, heat filling me from head to toe. I make sure I stomp on the brakes as my eyes pinch shut and the orgasm wracks my body.

She's purring like a kitten, swiping her tongue around the corners of her mouth. She took it all and didn't even bat an eye. I struggle to regulate my breathing.

"Traffic moved," she says calmly, and then tucks me back into my pants. I grip the steering wheel and ease forward, taking another deep breath.

"Is that the snack you were looking for?" I tease, swiping my knuckles against the side of her face. I reach over to adjust some of her hair I tugged loose. She lowers the visor mirror and fixes her hair.

"Exactly what I needed," she says with a devilish grin. "Until our main course later, that is."

How could we do anything other than fuck the second we set foot in my apartment? I originally had the silly idea of giving her the grand tour and starting with wine on the rooftop, but no. The second we enter my fifth-floor apartment, I have her pressed against the wall and half undressed. We're kissing like the first time at my house in Bayshore all over again. Like we still have so much to make up for.

Once her skirt is off and her heels have tumbled to the floor, I hoist her against my door. Her breath hitches, the tops of her breasts spilling out from the black satin bra. She is a living fantasy. Soft curves and elegance, whip smart and witty, but still the same sun-freckled Hazel I've been racing bikes with since childhood. Except now our races have led to here—the apartment she'll be calling home soon enough.

"Please, Gray," she murmurs into my ear, digging her nails into the ridge of my shoulder. "I need it."

I need it too. More than I can even fucking understand. While she's pinned to the door, I tug aside the damp scrap of fabric covering her pussy and settle between her thighs. My cockhead slips over her folds, and she moans, head hitting the door.

"Graaay," she groans, desperation edging her voice.

I plunge inside of her, faster than I meant to. But it's so damn difficult to take it slow with her. I want her hard and fast and always. I sink into her glorious, velvety heat, the breath hissing out of me. She wails and arches. It feels too good. It feels too *right.*

Our bodies slap together, the metronome of our passion. I squeeze the mounds of her ass in my palms, burying myself inside her. We haven't even been inside the apartment five minutes, and already I know she is the missing piece to my puzzle. The final aspect to really make this place home.

Not just my apartment, but New York. Hazel is what I've been missing all along.

"Fuck, Hazel." I draw out and then drive back in. Back to the best feeling in the world. Buried to the hilt in the woman of my dreams. "I love you so much, you know that?"

A lazy smile crosses her face, and her chest heaves. "I love you more."

I grunt, prickles of pleasure pooling low in my gut. I'm close. Even after I came an hour ago in the car, I'm ready again. With the silk of her pussy wrapped around me, I can't hold on for much longer. Not when she's saying *I love you more*. Not when she's here in my apartment, in New York City. Giving us a chance.

To the soundtrack of slick flesh and ragged moans, my own orgasm comes barreling forward. I jolt forward, making one last attempt to fuse our bodies together. I come long and hot inside her, buried deep, the most perfect punctuation mark to this day.

Hazel is Jell-O in my arms. She's pure liquid and laughter, and when I lower her to the ground, she can't stand up on the first try.

"That one..." She looks at me with sex-clouded eyes. "That one got me good."

I grin and push a kiss against her lips. "That was the welcome committee," I tease, running my lips over the shell of her ear. "Wait until we start the actual tour of the apartment."

In this moment, I realize that I've never been happier in NYC.

Now I just need to make sure Hazel stays.

CHAPTER TWENTY-SIX

HAZEL

I'm back in Brooklyn, for the second time in a month. It's three weeks after Gray's vacation in Bayshore ended, and two weeks since my last visit.

I'm gazing out the floor-to-ceiling window of Grayson's living room. This would be my everyday view. Cobblestone streets stretch away from me, and the converted warehouses in the distance lend damn near everything a hipster vibe. I love his neighborhood. I love New York. I love taking taxis—legitimate yellow taxis. Even though his apartment is one of those swanky, personality-less places he claimed to be tired of, it has potential.

But none of that really matters. Because no matter how often or vividly I envision my life here, it doesn't quite click into place.

I should give it more time. Except the only way I can keep coming back here is to treat it like a vacation. Like Grayson's place is the sweet home share I found online and all the places we visit are entries for the travel scrapbook.

It's the second visit, but the quiet truth whispers through my bones. *Living here isn't for me.* There's no yard. There are no birds in the morning. The rumble of the bridge nearby is a deal-breaker alone. Not to mention the other hundred things that would annoy me after the first month here.

Probably worst of all is Grayson's schedule. We're both career oriented, but the man barely gets out of work before nine most nights. I'm guilty of the same on occasion, but on this particular Friday, he had a rideshare meet me at the airport instead of him, because he "got caught up at the office."

I believe him. The man is a work machine.

But it's only setting the tone for what life here would be like.

I'd be mostly on my own. Creating my business from scratch. And irritated by street noise.

Great.

A text arrives as I'm contemplating the street below.

CALLIE: Hey girl what's up tonight?

HAZEL: Nothing much. I'm out of town.

CALLIE: Where ru??

HAZEL: NYC.

CALLIE: Hold up. This is the second time! Are you moving there or what?

I toss the phone on the couch behind me. I don't know how to answer that question. Or rather, I have two separate answers. What I'd tell Grayson, and what I'll admit to myself.

And they sound like "I don't know yet," and "Hell no."

Truth is, my intuition knew after the first visit, but here I am again, testing my resolve. Grayson makes it hard to say no. Because if I say no, I'll lose him. And if I lose him, I don't know what comes next.

So it seems wiser to exist in this new, modern version of a stalemate. Where we're living in a stasis until...*something*.

HAZEL: Just visiting Gray.

That's all I can say. Because it feels traitorous to shoot down his idea to anyone else first, even though the deepest, most secret parts of my heart know the truth.

Last time I was here, Gray took me to meet with a real estate mogul in the rare moment we actually broke from sex and left the apartment. We grabbed an expensive lunch under the Brooklyn bridge with Gray's buddy Trace Fairchild—one of those benevolent billionaires the media loved to dig into because he'd started from nothing and maintained a fascinating array of sexual partners. Trace and Gray were old friends from Wall Street, and Trace had the connection to the real estate world that I needed—an on-again, off-again lover named Tarina. Over chardonnay and salmon pate, Tarina dug into the nitty-gritty about what I could expect in real estate here, while Trace laid out some of the financial realities that would await me.

In a nutshell? Even more hard work, lots of time, and a metric shit ton of investment money.

I'd need at least two years to establish myself, with a budget five times as large as back home for multimedia. I'm twenty-eight, so that means I wouldn't even be able to realistically think about getting pregnant until I was in my early thirties. Which is great. Except establishing myself doesn't necessarily translate to financial solvency. I can see myself needing more time to really get in my groove here. To rake in the profit I'm used to.

My guess is that if I let the NYC market dictate motherhood, I wouldn't get pregnant until I was thirty-eight. And that's not how I envisioned things unfolding.

This question weighs on me, clawing at my arms and my legs, every hour of every day. The RAM of my brain is at ninety-nine percent trying to fix this hang up, even when I try to not actively think about it.

Because what happens if I make the wrong choice?

And what happens when both choices seem wrong?

Grayson finally gets home just after nine thirty, and he's rushing around, dropping off his briefcase, tugging off his tie. I get a quick kiss from him before he bolts into the bedroom.

"I wanna change, and we'll leave," he calls out. "Sorry I'm so late. Are you starving?"

I follow him into the bedroom, watching as he unbuttons his work shirt and steps out of his slacks. Two weeks ago, he had me backed up against the door, fucking me senseless. Today, I can practically see the wrought iron his muscles have turned into from stress.

"I'm hungry," I say, easing onto the bed. "But don't worry about it. I had a big snack before my flight."

A smile ghosts his face. "Hopefully not the same kind you had last time you were here."

He zips into the bathroom then, and I hear a heavy sigh. When he comes back out, he's rubbing his face.

"Rough day at the office?" I ask, wincing.

"You could say that."

"It's okay, babe. It's the weekend now." I stand in front of him, searching out his expression. His gaze darts over my face, but it doesn't seem like he really sees me. I smooth my palms up his arms and over his chest. He unwinds slightly.

"I'm so glad you're here," he murmurs, pushing his hands over the tops of my hips. He presses his forehead to mine, and I can feel some of his spark return. "I'd have you laid out on my bed if it weren't almost ten already."

I laugh. "Sex can wait. Sushi cannot."

My stomach is grumbling, and I'm a whiff away from being hangry, but I don't let him know this. He's stressed and teetering on the edge of a bad mood, so Operation Start the Weekend commences. I help him pick out an outfit, keeping it fun and flirty as we hurry to the elevator and make our way to the street. He keeps my hand in his, and even though he's smiling and laughing, I can feel the exhaustion radiating off him.

The streets are bustling and alive at ten 'til ten, and even though it's *so* extremely late for dinner, I don't mind. Because I'm in vacation mode. He leads me to the sushi joint around the corner. It's all dim lighting and low black seats. A waitress with a septum piercing and strange, blocky-cut hair leads us to a corner booth. We slide into the highbacked vinyl seat, and Gray takes me in his arms.

We look at the same menu. He rests his chin on my shoulder and occasionally grunts his approval as I repeat different options.

"You're so tired," I say, twisting to look him in the face.

"I know. Get me whatever you think I'd like."

I tilt my head back and forth as I make the decision for both of us. Grayson yawns.

"Poor thing." I pat his knee. "What time did you go in today?"

"Six."

I knit my brow. "Why so early?"

"I wanted to leave early because you were coming."

It doesn't take a genius to figure out that's a fifteen-hour work-day...on a day he was supposed to leave early.

"Why did you get out so late?"

He shakes his head, eyes drifting shut. "Some of the research my junior came up with got all fucked up. So we had to scramble to fix it for the client. It's one of my biggest accounts, so..."

I've heard this same story from him in passing before. Not about this client, or this exact junior, but the same storyline. Something got messed up, so he spent multiple overtime hours trying to fix it. He lives at his office, but for some reason he won't admit it.

"Let's eat and then go back and go to sleep," I murmur into his ear. He heaves a sigh, tightening his grip around my waist.

"But we need to go out and do something," he insists.

"We're doing it right now. And then once you've had a good night's sleep, we'll do even more tomorrow."

He grunts, swiping his thumb back and forth across the top of my thigh. "Okay, Mother."

The sushi spread comes, and it's truly a work of art. But Grayson is checked out. He eats, but he doesn't even seem fazed. This sushi is *phenomenal*—when it comes arranged in the shape of a serpent, you know you're in for a treat. But he could care less.

And I get it. I really do. He's trying to muster energy when there isn't any left to give. He's bordering on burnout. And the truth is plain to see.

The man doesn't have any space in his life for anything beyond work. Which doesn't leave much time for that happy family I want to create with him.

It's a thought I try to suppress as I inhale wasabi and salmon. I even feed Grayson a few pieces, and he grins while I chopstick the food into his mouth. He's let the front of his hair grow out more, and there is a whole mess of curls forming over his forehead. With the sides shorn almost to shaved, he looks even more like an impossibly trendy New Yorker.

One who's burnt out on work. Who lives his personal life in the half hours before bedtime and after sunrise. Who wants it all but doesn't have time for any of it.

Once we're back in the apartment, Grayson is asleep before his cheek touches the pillow. It's late for me too, so I spoon his snoring frame for a little bit before drifting off.

I won't be mad about not having a late night with him. I at least have him at my side.

Except that sounds like a dangerous mantra.

One that might become the norm if I decide to live here.

CHAPTER TWENTY-SEVEN

HAZEL

The next morning, I'm up at seven, bright eyed and bushy-tailed. Hey, that's sleeping in for me. Grayson is still dead to the world, so I rummage around his kitchen and prep the coffee maker. Sunlight fills his apartment, and I can't help but smile. This place is gorgeous. The view? Stunning.

It's absolutely in my top ten favorite destinations.

The thought throbs through me as I stare at the *drip drip drip* of the coffee maker. There's a difference between *destinations* and *home,* though. My phone vibrates at a quarter 'til eight. My dad is calling.

"Honey, I wanna take you out for some breakfast," he barks.

I smile, nudging the phone between my ear and shoulder as I pull a black mug from the flat white cabinets. The entire kitchen is decked out in white with steel accents. All the appliances are stainless steel. It's sleek and bright and inspiring. Being in the real estate business here *would* be fun.

"I can't, Dad." I would love to take him up on his offer, slip out while Grayson sleeps to meet my dad for pancakes. But I'm hundreds of miles away now. And if I move here, my breakfast trips with dad will be reduced to once or twice a year. "I'm out of town."

"Yeah? Where'd you go this time?"

"New York again." I've kept things kind of quiet about my trip this time.

"Again? Are you really trying to move out there now?"

My stomach pitches. This is what I was afraid of. Facing the beast head on. "I don't know. I'm considering it."

"You told me you weren't gonna."

"I know." I nibble on my lip as I pour myself a brimming mug of coffee. "I know."

A sigh rattles out of him. "You really wanna move to follow this guy?"

"I'm just *seeing*," I say with a sigh. "Besides, I know a woman who followed a man to Bayshore once upon a time. Was she so wrong?"

"Peach," he says, sounding resigned. "Those were different times. Your mama didn't have a ten-million-dollar business."

I smile. He always inflates my success, but I don't mind it.

"Besides," he goes on, "I've seen plenty of friends who started out like me 'n' your mama. And they're all divorced now. People get unhappy about what they sacrificed, and it drives them apart."

I frown. He makes a good point. Grayson wants me to sacrifice a lot. But he doesn't see it that way. And maybe that's the jagged edge of the puzzle that refuses to click into place. He's blinded by something—whether it's his disdain for Bayshore, or his adrenaline addiction in New York, or something else altogether—and it's like he doesn't even realize it.

But still. If this is the only way to keep Grayson...then I should do it.

Even if it's hard.

"I'm just sayin' your mama probably would have been unhappy down the road too. I made her leave her home. You know what I'm saying? She woulda stayed in southern Ohio 'til the end of her days if it wasn't for me. But what do I know? I'm an old fart. I know you two got something going on, but damn. I want you to be happy."

"I'll be happy," I reassure him, snickering to myself. He always calls himself an old fart. "With whatever decision I make. I promise."

"All right, Peachy. Well, Imma go find myself someone else to watch me eat waffles. When you comin' home?"

I tell him I'll be back Sunday night, and we set up a date for the next weekend. When I hang up the phone, I notice Grayson in the doorway to the bedroom, rubbing his eyes.

"Morning, sleepyhead." I grab a second mug and pour him a cup too. He stumbles into the kitchen, wearing shorts and bedhead. I've never seen a sexier sight. He scratches at his chest, and then wraps me in a big hug.

"Morning." He kisses the top of my head about ten times. His voice is groggy and deeper than normal.

"Did you get enough sleep?" I prop my chin on his chest and gaze up at him. This. Right here. This is the moment that will always have me considering abandoning everything in Ohio. The warmth of him wrapped around me. That strong jawline and the indescribable feeling that everything is finally, blissfully complete. As long as Gray is here with me.

"*Mmm.* I feel like a million bucks."

"Just a million?" I tease. "That's chump change out here. Why not a billion?"

"I feel like a trillion bucks, actually." He leans down and presses a minty kiss to my lips. "Who was on the phone?"

"My dad." I pass him his cup of coffee, forearms prickling as I realize he probably overheard my end of that conversation.

"Ah. So that makes more sense." He tugs at the front of his hair before he eases onto a stool facing me on the other side of the kitchen island. He blows at the top of his mug for a moment.

"What does?"

"That you know a woman who followed a man to Bayshore once upon a time."

I cup the mug in my hands, relishing the heat. Grayson keeps his apartment just this side of chilly. "He's a little worried I'm seriously considering moving here."

Gray watches his coffee a moment, then looks up at me, vulnerability written in his gaze. "Well, aren't you?"

"Of course I am." My chest tightens. "I told him originally that I wouldn't. And I haven't really been telling a lot of people about these visits, so both he and Callie tried to make plans with me this weekend. They're curious."

"Callie too?"

I nod, slurping at my coffee. "Nobody wants me to leave."

Gray doesn't say anything.

"But I have an interested buyer already for my house," I say, trying to sound bright about it. Gray's astonished gaze finds mine.

"Are you serious?" The excitement in his voice is a jolt better than the caffeine winding through my veins.

"Yes. I mean, it happened organically. I haven't even listed the house or anything. But the right opportunity sort of...came along." I laugh, but it sounds hollow. I don't want to sell my house. But one of the tours I gave last week was to an old family friend, who said they'd always secretly wanted *my* house and would buy it the second it went for sale. I hadn't even said I was considering a move. They'd seen it while driving past through the years and always admired it.

Coincidence? Or a sign that I should head to Brooklyn?

Just one occurrence of many leaving me questioning what the right path forward might look like.

On the one hand, I could sell my house next week and land softly in Dumbo with a serious boyfriend and a pre-set future ahead of me.

Or I could say no to the love of my life because I want babies sooner rather than later, and because I miss the sound of birds in the morning.

"Babe. That's awesome." Grayson squeezes my hand, something heavy in his gaze. Something meaningful.

"Yeah." My gaze drops back to the coffee. "I don't know if I'll sell though. I'd need it for start-up money out here, but..."

"Sell it or don't. It's totally up to you." Clarity shines in his eyes. He's got that tone that means business. "I can help with your start-up money."

"I saw the amount you offered in your spreadsheet," I say, feeling more doubts rise to the surface. "But I don't think it would be enough. Not after meeting with your friend last time. Really, I think the wisest thing would be to sell my house *and* take you up on your offer. Just to have the cushion for the first two years that I'd need to really see if I can hack it out here."

"Great. Let's do that."

I nibble on my lip, staring at the contents of my mug. "It kinda hurts to consider selling my house."

Grayson deflates a little. The sense I get is that inside his head he's thinking, *Great, so we're back to Square Bayshore.*

"I've spent so much time and money on it. And I *love* it."

"We can totally redesign this apartment, you know."

"Right. But..." I sigh. I don't know what else to say. The doubts are killing me. They're eating away at my sanity and my free time. Even standing here in Grayson's apartment doesn't give me any clarity. I'm just as conflicted as ever.

Grayson's phone buzzes from across the room. He flexes his jaw, twisting around to look at the phone. It buzzes for a while, and then he finally goes after it. He answers it with a thorny voice.

"What is it?"

I don't need to overhear a thing to know that it's work related. He rubs at his face as he comes back toward the kitchen. He clears his throat, easing back onto the stool with a strained look on his face.

"I'm not coming in," he finally says. "You need to figure this out your own damn self. And don't call me for the rest of the day. For fuck's sake. You hear me?"

He swipes off his phone and turns suddenly to hurl his phone at the couch. It lodges itself between the cushions. I stare at it, stunned.

"Jesus Christ, kill me now," he mutters, pinching at the bridge of his nose.

"Um, Grayson?" I ask. I'm not used to seeing him act like that. "If I give up everything in Bayshore and move out here, will you promise to get a new job?"

He drags his gaze up to mine, and there's uncertainty there. Like he's trying to figure out whether to laugh or not.

"I can't quit," he says.

"Why? Because you love hating life?"

"I make over half a million dollars a year," he says quietly. Almost menacingly. "I can't walk away from that."

The number is a gut punch. A tidy sum, to be sure. But at what cost?

"You might make a lot of money, but you're spending every ounce of your life to earn it," I remark before sipping at my coffee again. I want to keep this casual, friendly even, but my heart is pounding as I speak. This conversation won't remain lighthearted for long. "You didn't get off until nine last night, and that was 'early.'"

Gray's jaw flexes. "It won't be like this always. As soon as I get promoted to Managing Director—"

"When will that be?"

He shakes his head. "It could be a few more years."

"And when will you know?"

"The promotions are sporadic. I climbed early and fast, but it depends on redundancy and vacancies."

I chew on the inside of my lip. "So you could have multiple years of this ahead of you still." My stomach sinks faster than a boulder in Lake Erie. I knew he worked a lot, but I thought it had been more of a passion thing. Like how I work from dawn till dusk some days.

But the difference is, I love what I do. I don't go home at night and chuck my phone into the sofa and swear enough to rouse the devil.

"I get off by eight most nights," he offers, like this is somehow a consolation. "But this fucking issue we're having has—" He grimaces. "No. I'm done talking about it. I'm not at work right now."

I fiddle with the handle of my mug, suddenly uncertain what to say next. A tornado of doubts swirls through me, ripping roofs off my sanity, overturning the cars parked in my alley of stability. Grayson doesn't want to give up the lifestyle, even though he hates it.

"It doesn't seem like you love your job."

He scoffs. Bitterly. "I don't most days."

"Then why don't you find something else?"

"Didn't you hear me? I can't walk away from what I'm earning. I'm setting myself up for the rest of my life. I've got investments going in some big things right now. The money from the Bayshore house is going to a new start-up out in Silicon Valley, and I need to have the capital to invest." He's heated now, raking his hand through his hair as he paces the width of the living room. "It's not ideal—I see that. But it's a sacrifice I'm willing to make because I believe in what I'm striving for."

"And what is that?" I ask, keeping my voice calm. *Please don't say become a billionaire.*

He laughs a little, as if the question is ridiculous. "Seriously?"

"Yes. Tell me what it is you're striving for." I cross my arms. "I want to hear you say it. Just so we're on the same page."

He watches me, hands on his hips, the sunlight spilling in from the windows all around him. He's like some sort of magazine ad come to life. Except the tension in the room is so thick I'm close to choking.

"I want to be at the top."

I nod. "Right. You want to be the best. Like always."

"Like you don't?"

I pour more coffee into my mug, even though it's not empty. I need something to occupy my hands. To lessen the tension thrumming through me. "This isn't about me."

He scoffs. Now we're fighting. That noise signaled the starting gun. "Sure. When I aspire to be the best at my career, it's wrong. But when you do it, it's noble. I get it."

I shoot him a look. "What the fuck are you talking about?"

"Why are you acting like there's something wrong with what I'm gunning for?"

I clench my teeth and force myself to take a breath before responding. This could spiral into dangerous territory. Maybe it already has. "I never said there was anything wrong with what you wanted. I'm trying to help you feel better about life. You hate what you do, and I want you to love what you do. Is that so wrong?"

"Right. Well I didn't *Ask Hazel*, now, did I? You can save your advice for somebody who needs it." He sends me a dark look and storms out of the living room. The bedroom door shuts behind him, and I'm left gaping in the kitchen.

I replay our heated exchange in my head, feeling both defensive and regretful. I didn't want to attack him—but I do want him to do something he likes more. I want the relaxed, happy Grayson I knew in Bayshore. I want the man who can take me out to dinner before eight p.m., who can actually leave the workplace behind. I curl up on the couch, heart pounding as I wait for some sign of life from him.

When he finally comes out of the bedroom, he sits on the couch across from me. He's put on a T-shirt and running shoes. He doesn't meet my gaze.

"Better now?" I ask.

"I need to go for a run."

"Good. Do it." I sniff, coming to standing. "I'll go wander the neighborhood."

"Do you want to come with me?"

"No. I'm fine." I squeeze his shoulder as I walk past him. We should let the conversation lie for now...and he needs a chance to get his head straight. Before we entirely ruin these precious few hours he has away from work. "Get your run in, and then we'll go get breakfast."

Before I disappear into the bedroom, he grabs my wrist and brings me against him for a hard but brief kiss. There's anger there, as well as heartbreaking love. I watch him go, and when it's just me in the apartment, I'm sadder than ever.

But still, I rally. I try not to dwell on our unfinished conversation while he's gone, nor while we head out for a delicious brunch and occupy ourselves with a trip to Manhattan to visit museums. We end up having a great day and a sexy night. The tension that edged our morning dissolves.

Until Sunday, that is.

Gray wakes up to a phone call at eight a.m. Of course, it's work.

"Jesus fucking Christ, I told you, Ian," he spits, tearing the covers off him. We'd been spooning a half-second ago, and the second his phone went off, his entire body went rigid and tense. "You need to figure this out."

Ian must have got a word in edgewise, because Grayson is quiet for a moment. Then he groans, his head falling into his hands.

"So he quit?" Gray sounds resigned. More silence.

"I'll be in at seven," Gray says. I've never heard him so dejected. My flight leaves at six. I frown as he hangs up the phone. He sits at the edge of the bed, rubbing his forehead.

"You should quit too," I say, trying to lighten the mood. Gray throws his phone onto the floor, hard enough to make me wince, and storms into the bathroom.

Our morning is quiet. Brimming with unspoken sentiments. I know he's pissed about work, but no matter what I do to distract him or make him feel better, he bats it away. It's lose-lose with Grayson today. I flew five hundred miles to watch him hate his job and almost break his phone twice.

Great.

We manage to catch breakfast at a spot nearby and then spend some time walking in the park and window shopping. He loosens slightly during the day. I even coax a smile out of him a few times. But once we're in his car heading for the airport, that black cloud consumes him again.

"You know," I say, as we enter the gridlock of Sunday traffic heading toward the airport. "Maybe you should come to Bayshore next."

"That defeats the purpose," he says in a low voice, the *duh* tone more than clear. "This is about you moving out here, not the other way around."

Frustration kicks up to a boil. I can't keep the snark at bay anymore. "Sure seems like it would do you good to get out of the city again."

"New York is not the problem," he mutters, and then he swears under his breath. "What is this asshole doing?" He gestures toward the Corolla in front of us, hogging two lanes, not moving. He rolls down his window and sticks his head out. "Move your ass!"

"Grayson," I hiss, swatting at his arm.

"How are we supposed to move if you're fucking stopped?" he shouts. Honks swell around us. I cover my mouth. Unbelievable. But this is New York traffic, I guess. Everybody is impatient and stressed and stuck in traffic. Just like us.

He rolls the window up once the car jerks forward. A middle finger flies and his nostrils flare.

"That motherfucker—"

"Gray." I grab his arm. "Come back to me. Let that shit go."

A heated sigh escapes him. "What?" he snaps.

My eyes flutter shut. I'm counting to five. He's roped me into his stress bubble, and I do not want to be here on my purported vacay weekend.

Except nothing about this visit has felt like a vacation. Not like the first time. And I don't think there's much chance of Grayson's work life improving.

"You know," I start, once I've retrieved an ounce of calm. "New York *is* lovely."

"See?" He slaps the steering wheel, like I finally get it. "I've been telling you. You'll fall in love."

"It's the kind of place I love to *visit*."

He's quiet then, like he's mulling over the information. When he glances my way, there's suspicion in his gaze. "What are you trying to say?"

"It's a stressful place," I say. "I mean, look at you. I've never seen you act like this—"

"Everyone in the city drives like this—it's part of life here."

"And sure, there are lots of awesome things. I love where you live; I love your neighborhood. But is all the awesomeness worth...*this*?" I gesture around us at the sea of cars packed in. The highway stretches for miles, and there's no end in sight. "I mean, we plan getting to the airport like I'm taking a flight to Denmark, not to Ohio. Don't get me wrong. I like the hustle and bustle, but I—" My words bottom out suddenly. The truth is quivering on the edge—I just need the strength to speak it. "I don't know why I would join you in a place that doesn't make you *happy*."

His jaw flexes. He's white-knuckling the steering wheel again. He takes a long time to respond. "I love New York. And I'll admit, there is something missing here." When he glances at me, his blue eyes are swimming with sincerity. "But that something is you."

My eyes drift closed. The weight of this request isn't a good one. It isn't comforting or relieving. And that's when it hits me. If moving to New York to be with Grayson was the right thing to do, I wouldn't be fighting to convince myself. I wouldn't be scraping up willpower to imagine my career here.

I want to be a tourist in New York. Not a resident.

I can't do this. Not even for Gray.

"Then you know where to find me," I finally say, my voice a whisper. Tears are in my eyes already. This breaking-up shit sucks. But I can't force myself into a hole that isn't made for me. And if Grayson can't fit into the Bayshore-sized hole, then there's nowhere left to go.

Gray looks over at me, hurt creasing his face. *"Hazel."*

I swallow the knot in my throat, unable to say anything else right now.

"Come on," he says, desperation making his voice harsh. "Quit fucking around."

"This isn't going to work," I say, picking at my cuticles. "This isn't....it doesn't *feel good*. Maybe you like being stressed out and hating life. But that's not what I signed up for. I don't want to abandon what I worked for. And neither do you. So let's accept the facts and move on."

My own words hurt to say, but I need to stick with logic here. If I went with my emotions only, I'd be visiting Brooklyn once a month until I was ninety. But that's not what I'm looking for. Not a once-or-twice-a-month boyfriend.

And I know this.

I knew better.

The rest of the ride to the airport is taut. I blink away tears, wipe away a few that dare to spill, and when he pulls into the departures area, I'm halfway out the door before he's put the car in park.

I'm waiting at the trunk for him to open it, but he doesn't. He gets out of the car and walks toward me, anger and hurt mingling in his expression. The look on his face is a punch to the heart. It's hard to keep his gaze. But this is the last time. It needs to be done.

"Don't fucking do this," he pleads.

"Open the trunk," I say, finally yanking my eyes off him. If I look at him a second longer, I'm going to crumble. I'll take back everything and do the once-a-month thing until my death bed. That arrangement would be slightly less painful than not having him at all.

"Hazel," he says, stepping closer. "We need to be together. We're fucking—" He draws a terse breath. "We're fucking soul mates. You know that, right?"

I pinch my eyes shut, jiggling like I have to pee. "Open the trunk. I need to go check my bag. I'm late because you almost road-raged that Corolla. Come on, Grayson."

He watches me for another moment, and then the trunk clicks open. I tug out my luggage in a flash, and before I can turn away, he's got me by the wrist.

"Babe," he says, softer this time, the plea so intense it nearly sends me to my knees.

"This isn't gonna work," I say, my voice thick with tears. A few spill out now that I'm looking him in the eye, and I fight the sob that threatens to hitch out of me. "But don't worry. I'll be in love with you forever, so you can at least rest easy that you've ruined my love life."

I try to walk away, but he pulls me into him. The temptation is too great. I melt into his hug, clinging to him like he's the last piece of driftwood in the ocean. My tears dampen his T-shirt, but I can't stay here long. Because if stay here, I'll never leave.

"Goodbye, Grayson." I finally rip myself away and hurry toward the door.

I can feel his stormy blues cutting through me.

I don't look back.

CHAPTER TWENTY-EIGHT

GRAYSON

Once, back when I first moved into the city, I was taking the subway into Brooklyn. In the far-flung stop where I'd gotten off, a weird smell filled the underground cavern. It smelled like burning trash, the thick scent of rot and chemicals filling the air.

When I got to the exit, I found out that it really was trash burning.

And right now, that dumpster fire is appealing compared to the reality of my waking life.

If only I could stumble upon a flaming pile of actual shit, I'd feel like I'd hit the lottery.

I'm back to the grindstone at work, and now that I don't have the bright spot of Hazel in my life, it's one thousand percent worse.

I have nothing to look forward to, except the eventual zeros trailing behind my bank account total. But that's a someday thing. I don't have a now-day thing.

I have nothing.

The first few days after Hazel dumped me are full of work but laced with a sadness so profound I can barely eat a full meal. It feels like we've ended a twenty-year relationship. Like everything that grounded me has been torn up and thrown away.

We dated for roughly two months. Not a year. Not five years. Not even a full fiscal quarter. How could I miss someone who made up so little of my waking life?

I know how. It's because Hazel and I defy the rules. We've always been out to surpass the norm. Finally tapping into the deep well of emotion between us could only lead to this level of intensity. Even after two months.

But now? I've got to pick up the pieces, but I don't know where she threw them.

After a week of haunting dreams, I realize she didn't throw the pieces away—she took them with her.

Bayshore invades my subconscious. When I cross the Brooklyn Bridge each morning, I can only see the lake. One morning I have a dream about taking the Jet Ski to the sand bar and finding Luke there, and suddenly I have a six pack of beers underneath the seat of the Jet Ski—and then Hazel swims up. She's naked, but once I notice, Luke is gone. It's no wonder I woke up rock hard after that dream.

But that's not the only dream. In no particular order, I dream about: not being able to find a good wine at The Daily Shop and buying sparkling water—*the horror!*—instead; running into my mom in the middle of the old car wash that closed in the late 90s, where one drug deal took place and the local newspaper had a field day about it; and of course, Hazel.

I dream about her in ways that defy reason. In one dream, she's herself. In another, she's blonde and pregnant, but I never got the sense if the baby was mine or—God forbid—some other man's. In a different dream, she's a house I walk into.

I last four days without texting her. And then I send her one emoji, because apparently I'm a teenager. It's the emoji with the two hearts, in case you're wondering. It represents the throbbing that's going on in my chest cavity on a daily basis.

She takes a few days to write back. And when she does, it's with a broken heart.

So there's that.

It's easy for the days to melt by, despite heartbreak, because of the punishing pace of my work schedule. And the more I lose myself in the mess, the harder it becomes to tolerate. At least pre-Hazel, work was somehow a solace, if one I only begrudgingly accepted.

But now? I can't stop thinking about being back home. About being *literally anywhere* but at work. And more and more, I'm entertaining ideas about what might come after.

To be clear, I've *always* entertained ideas about what comes after investment banking. My plan was to retire by age forty-five, so that I could have a decent run at trying something else. It also occurred to me, during my month in Bayshore, that I might try turning to renovation work full time as my next gig.

But I'm thinking about it *now*. I can't stop imagining how I still want to finish that trim around the back door and lift the raggedy ass tile in the laundry room. Sometimes I still laugh to myself about all the hilarious conversations Weston, Mav and I had while we laid flooring. The morning rhythms of working on the house—thermos of coffee, sawdust everywhere, tools stacked up—are memories that plague me worse than locusts.

So when Mrs. Koch e-mails me a week after Hazel and I break up to finally talk about her son's potential schooling out here, I'm not surprised when our talk turns to Bayshore-related things. She mentions her husband's recent dental implants (very traumatizing), her son's graduation party (extremely windy, nobody could eat the cake), and the trouble she's had on the Bayshore Bicentennial Committee in their hunt for a renovation company to properly (and please, God, without price gouging) restore a building that Hazel purchased last year in the spirit of fostering community.

Hazel purchasing a downtown building? This is news to me. I'm almost offended that she never mentioned it. But I pursue all the necessary details through my nearly daily e-mails with Mrs. Koch. Progress is stalled because Bayshore's vision is to support local, and there aren't any local businesses that can do the job…and all the far-flung companies that placed bids want too much money to account for transportation and lodging expenses.

Mrs. Koch explains in great detail how they've only recently turned an eye toward renovating some of the flagging downtown buildings, and the vision they have is one that will be a sight to behold…if they can ever get there.

Each time I respond to her, pressing for more information, a weird heat in my chest spreads further. Like I'm wearing a winter coat in the middle of a sauna. Prickles and discomfort tinged with restlessness. Creativity is pulsing through me, even though I'm braindead and exhausted from work.

Within two days of learning all this about Mrs. Koch's issues, I have a business plan drawn up. I don't know what the fuck I'm doing. I'm simply passing time because I'm sad and heartbroken and physically wasting away in my office. I need something to do that doesn't involve assisting in mergers and acquisitions or advising clients about derivatives.

I want to use a fucking hammer again, and I'm bored despite being overworked. So in my meager down time, I create GrayWorks, LLC.

I use a template I found online. I've never started my own business before, so I could be doing this all wrong. I'd ask Hazel, but there isn't an emoji for it, and like she said all those years that were really just weeks ago—we're supposed to be weaning.

This is something to pass the time.

Before another two weeks go by, I run my idea by Mrs. Koch, and she's interested. I mean *deeply interested*. She asks me for my federal ID number so she can put together paperwork for my bid. My head spins when I read those words.

I can't possibly be bidding on this project. It would mean relocating to Bayshore for the duration of the project. Her e-mail forces me to research how to get the ID number, and long story short, I set up my LLC in the state of Ohio using my house as the address.

GrayWorks, LLC is a legal entity by the end of August.

And one of the most interesting things about my business plan?

I can finance the whole business myself. I run the numbers as a thought experiment. If I keep the house and ditch the investment in the west coast start-up, I have enough in my savings to cushion my first two years.

And as I finish out yet another ninety-hour work week at the bank I loathe to call home, I swing an idea past my boss.

A one-year sabbatical.

He can't guarantee me anything when I come back to work, but I'm eligible. And at this point, I don't fucking care if the entire company goes under while I'm gone.

The ink is dry before Labor Day.

CHAPTER TWENTY-NINE

HAZEL

Weeks trudge by without Gray. I can only hope that it'll get better, though I don't necessarily believe it.

See, he has a way of tainting everything. It started on the day we were born: September ninth. We have a pretty auspicious birthday, if you ask me. But this year, our birthday is going to be a little harder than usual. I always think of him on our shared day, but this Saturday? We're turning twenty-nine, and a few weeks ago we were still fucking, and *goddammit* why am I still considering showing up to his apartment in Brooklyn on the daily?

Everyone is relieved that I'm not moving. I gently informed my family friend that she couldn't buy my house. Hazel is staying in Bayshore.

At least until the grief drives me back to New York.

The other stupid thing about our birthday this year is that it falls on the same day as the Bicentennial Ball. So I can celebrate my birthday in style, drowning my sorrow in an evening gown while nursing martinis instead of cooped up in my house, alone and sad, in yoga pants.

Great.

The days leading up to our birthday turn into a sort of fever dream. I'm thinking about the double heart emoji he sent me three weeks ago like it's an epic love poem. He's sent one other emoji since—an owl. Which might as well be a new stanza in the texted love saga, because he knows how much I love owls.

One day at The Daily Shop, when I'm on the hunt for feta cheese, I swear I see him cross the end of the aisle. But it's got to be my broken heart, wanting him so badly that I'll conjure the sight of him anywhere.

I even fake-see him heading toward the lake the night before the Ball. But it can't be him, because he hates Bayshore, and he lives in Brooklyn and is happily engaged to his soul-draining job. Apparently my broken heart knows no bounds in imagining him *literally everywhere.*

The day of the ball arrives. Happy birthday to me. London shows up at my house after driving in from Columbus. We have brunch and mimosas planned, with a quick dip in the lake before we start officially preparing for the ball. I'm not taking my dad, but not for the reason you'd think. He's actually busy tonight. But yeah—I invited him.

"You seriously didn't get a date for the ball?" London looks genuinely disappointed as we begin laying out our makeup bags in my spacious master bath. "I thought I told you to put an ad on Craigslist."

I snort. "Well, I did just a little worse than soliciting a stand-in boyfriend on Craigslist. I actually snagged a real boyfriend long enough for us to *not* attend the ball together."

London sighs, her mouth rounding as she works on her mascara. "Men."

"Yeah. Specifically, *the Daly brothers.*"

I crank up some happy pop music to guide us through our make-up process and to help me keep my mind off Grayson. But it's useless. It always is. He's the stain at the back of my mind that won't lift, no matter how much baking soda or vinegar I use.

I wonder what he's doing *every day.* I imagine him shirtless in his apartment, looking out the tall windows. I imagine him barking at other drivers like the road-rage psycho he has apparently become. I imagine him groggy and just waking up, morning breath and all.

And then the doubts creep in. Maybe I'm the only one still smarting from the break-up. Even though I initiated it. Maybe he's had three girls into his apartment since I left. That thought pushes my lips into a frown, which makes me frown more. I almost mess up my eyeliner because of it.

The only way to beat back the jealousy is to tell myself he doesn't have the time—or energy—to take a lover. With his crazy work schedule, how could he? Inside my head, I'm nervous laughing and patting my own back. *Hazel, you're fine. Everything is fine.*

London and I are legitimate bombshells by the time we're done. Callie comes over at the tail end of our prep session, already in full regalia. She's meeting Anthony here, and then the four of us will head to the ball together. Callie and London hug and get caught up in my living room, sipping chardonnay, while I rush around tending to the final details.

I'm wearing a teal, satin, floor-length evening gown. It's got a V-neck that dips low enough to tease, and it's sleeveless, so I won't melt from the late-summer heat. The air is blasting in my house, but brief forays outside have my foundation threatening to slide off. It's okay—I'm a professional. I used the setting spray.

Together, the three of us gals looks like any man's wet dream. Tanned, dolled up, and voluptuous. My hair, which has been the color of dark mahogany for a few weeks now, is pulled half up with soft waves flowing down my back. Each time I catch a glimpse of myself in the mirror, I pause.

Hot damn.

Now if only Grayson cared enough to be here.

My fingers twitch with the thought of sending him a selfie, but no. He doesn't deserve this. Tonight, I'm a Bayshore exclusive. To be appreciated within the city limits. I've gotten pretty good at rationalizing my way out of texting him these past couple weeks. Even though I heavily consider doing it about three times a day.

When Anthony shows up in a black suit and shiny shoes, his hair as curly and wild as it is after an evening on the boat, he gives a low whistle. But his gaze settles—and stays—on Callie.

"Hooooly shit." He walks over to her slowly, his hands finding her waist. I have to look away. I'm still sensitive to overt displays of happy couples, being that I'm still mourning the loss of the love that seemed fated but wasn't.

The four of us trek to Anthony's SUV. As the maple and oak tree-lined streets blur past us, the scent of the lake in the air, I resolve to make this the best birthday yet. I might be sad about Grayson, but my future doesn't have to be sad. I've hit nearly every marker I've set for myself. So why not add a new love interest to the amazing possibilities of life?

I try to imagine someone else. Some other tall, dark, and handsome man. *Like a birthday gift to myself.* But my mind always jerks back to Grayson.

It might always be that way.

The parking lot outside the downtown convention center is packed. We hike our dresses and sweat out the walk toward the gilded double doors at the front. The building used to be a public ballroom back in the 1800s, and since 1960 it's been the Bayshore Convention Center.

Inside, cool air sweeps around us. Everything is glossy and fancy. I don't take three steps before someone offers me a cube of cheese with a toothpick in it. Thirty seconds later, champagne. A minute later, shrimp.

Already this is the best party ever.

Callie and London and I wander around, bright-eyed and mingling. Everyone is here. *Everyone.* It's like the social volcano of Bayshore erupted right into this building. I'm stopped nearly every ten feet by someone else I know. Compliments on my dress. Questions about real estate. Even a couple single guys striking up clearly manufactured conversation.

It's a gorgeous, gilded rosette blur. The parquet floors of the grand ballroom shine under the light of the glittering chandeliers. Elegant sconces line the walls, with the occasional white pillar shooting upward to the tall ceiling. Everyone in here is in awe and beaming.

And I'm trying to look as happy as the rest of them.

Dinner tables fill half of the ballroom. We have assigned seating, but I'll look for my spot later. For now, it's all about the hors d'oeuvres and champagne. A small stage where presentations will be made and speeches given faces the open part of the ballroom. There's a whole slew of programming, which I would know about if I actually read the program they'd handed me upon entering.

But instead, I drift around, smiling at people. Enjoying the jazz being provided by the live trio tucked into the corner. Trying to feel as put together and satisfied with life as the rest of the world sees me.

One of the organizers comes onto the stage to formally welcome everyone. Applause fills the ballroom, and I realize then that I've entirely lost Callie, London, and Anthony. I spot Bryce across the room, and I don't know whether to wave or slink away, so I just grimace and awkwardly turn toward the nearest plate of snacks. I reach for a canape, even though I've already had three.

A few announcements come and go. The chair of the Chamber of Commerce gives a speech, and I'm only half paying attention at this point. Mrs. Koch sweeps onto the stage a moment later, and as I'm admiring her dress, she begins talking about the work of her Bicentennial Committee. I tune in slightly, mostly concerned with getting another flute of champagne while the waiter is near. I snag one—and two panko-breaded shrimp. Score.

"...which is why we're incredibly proud to be partnering with Bayshore's newest local business, GrayWorks!"

Applause fills the ballroom once more. I pop the shrimp into my mouth, munching happily. At the stage, a swath of dark hair catches my eyes. Broad shoulders. The build of a soccer player turned businessman.

God, he looks like Grayson. *This* is how head over heels I am. Now I'm imagining *basically anyone* could be the love of my life. Still, I can't rip my eyes away from the back of this man as he jogs up the stairs. He takes the microphone from Mrs. Koch, squeezes her arm, and then faces the crowd.

Grayson Freakin' Daly is smiling out at the ballroom.

I go rigid, champagne flute paused halfway to my mouth. I can only stare as his sexy bass fills the ballroom.

"Thanks, Mrs. Koch, for that lovely introduction." He laughs a little, smoothing a palm over the side of his hair. The previously shorn sides are growing out, and the curls on top are glossy and neat. He's wearing a jet-black tuxedo, complete with leather oxfords. My mouth parts involuntarily. I cannot believe my eyes. London appears at my side a moment later, gripping my forearm.

"Is that Grayson?" she hisses.

I nod. Somehow, he makes black tie look easygoing and impossibly sexy. Questions form a logjam inside my body. I'm not sure I'm breathing.

"I'm extremely pleased to be back in Bayshore to announce the GrayWorks initiative," he says, a hand in his pocket as he addresses the crowd. "This is a pet project of mine that ballooned into...well...something much larger than I anticipated. But when I realized that my beloved hometown needed this service, the type of service I want to provide, I knew that I was the man for the job. I plan to renovate not only buildings, but also relationships while I'm in Bayshore."

Beloved hometown. I miss a full fourth of his speech as I mull over these words. This cannot be Grayson Daly. Unless he was abducted and lobotomized. I blink, looking around, trying to find any other Daly family member. Just to check that Gray's okay. That he hadn't suffered a major brain injury that erased the last fifteen years of his life.

But I know for a fact that Annette wasn't planning on coming, much less Weston and Maverick. Connor has been back on the west coast for weeks, and Dominic? Who knows? I'll have to talk to Grayson myself. Which still sounds surreal. Because he's here.

In Bayshore.

On the stage.

His speech winds down, and my palms begin to sweat. London turns to me, her glossy blonde hair shining under the lights.

"Wait. Did you know about this?"

I blink several times. My voice has completely disappeared.

"Don't worry. That's all the answer I need." She tuts, shaking her head. "Damn, Grayson looks good."

I agree with her—obviously—but still can't force a word past my lips as I struggle to keep track of Grayson now that he's stepped off the stage and started winding through the crowds. Announcements continue, but I don't hear a word of them. All I can see is that one curl of dark hair on the top of Grayson's head. It is my beacon as he gets lost in the crowd. Until—*poof.*

He's gone. And judging by how magically he appeared tonight, I'm not sure I'll see him again. I could have dreamed the whole thing and roped London into my fever sweat. I can be very persuasive while ill—I wouldn't put it past me.

My stomach shrinks to an acorn as I move around the ballroom, searching for Gray. I lose London in the mix. Familiar faces all around me light up with recognition as I flit around the room. Once I've circled back toward the buffet tables, which are being discretely prepped by the catering staff, I feel like I've finally faced the hard truth about tonight: I imagined that speech and Grayson is actually in Brooklyn.

But when I turn, I catch the assured stride of the one man I've ever cared to notice. Grayson's icy blues land on me, and my entire body feels electrified. Like I could burn to a crisp on the spot.

I stall. Like, deer-in-headlights style. Grayson stops, narrowing his eyes at me. He points at me.

"Hazel Matheson?" He tilts his head, perfecting that air of *haven't seen each other in decades.* "From high school?"

His joke breaks my spell. I laugh, cocking a hip. "The one and only."

He saunters my way, his hands shoved into his pockets. He's smirking like a man with secret knowledge. And boy, did he have plenty of it tonight. By the time he reaches me, my head is tipped back, and I'm gazing up at him. Still hesitant to believe that this is fully true. It could still be in a fever sweat. It could still be the best dream of my life.

"What are you doing here?" I murmur, unable to hide my smile.

"I covered all of that in my speech," he says, looking supremely satisfied. "I take it you didn't listen."

"I was too distracted by *this.*" I wave my fingers over the expanse of his tuxedo. "And too busy thinking that this entire night has been a hallucination."

His smile spreads wider. "Hallucination?"

"Yeah. Because you're supposed to be in Brooklyn shouting at the shitty drivers."

A laugh rockets out of him. "Let's just say I needed to come back for a very special event. Happy birthday, by the way."

"Yeah." My fingers curl, nails biting into palm, as I fight the urge to throw my arms around him. I want him naked and *mine* already, but I need to play it cool. At least take him to a storage closet or something. "Same to you."

"Twenty-nine." He clucks his tongue, looking around. "It's a pretty good age to shake things up. Take some leaps. Shit like that."

I blink rapidly, feeling tears bloom where there previously were none. "Yeah?"

His grin softens as he looks down at me again. He rocks back onto his heels. When he speaks next, his voice is tender. "Hazel, can I kiss you already?"

I nod, and he surges forward, capturing my head between his hands. We kiss indecently, pure tongue and panting and repressed moans. When we pull apart, his eyes are cloudy with arousal.

"You look fucking amazing," he whispers.

"Why did you come back?" I demand again, already feeling the sadness settling in. Emotion tightens my throat. "Gray, I can't handle losing this again. I won't be able to let you go now."

"You really didn't listen to my speech."

I shake my head, pouting. He's a blurry mess through the veil of tears.

"I'm not going anywhere, babe," he whispers before he presses his lips to mine. I clutch the lapel of his coat, needing him infinitely closer. Needing to hear those words a thousand more times before I'll believe them. "I started the business you said I should invest in. Because if Brooklyn doesn't work for you, then maybe Bayshore will work for me."

The tears spill out, inglorious and plentiful. My bottom lip is quivering like a newborn puppy. I don't have words. He's robbed me of my faculties, for the billionth time in my life.

"Are you serious?" I finally ask.

He nods, running his thumb over the line of my collarbone. Goosebumps flare under his touch. I want to sob into his chest and fuck him until sunrise. I could also throw in one good tennis match for good measure.

And whatever I get from him, I need more of it. I can't handle one night of it, or one week. I need Gray for a lifetime. Until the end of my days. That much is certain, as I hook my arms around his neck. His big hands push over my hips, fingers dancing at the top of my ass. My breath hitches, and then a sob escapes me, unbidden.

"I love you, Hazel Mae," he whispers hotly into my ear. "Will you be my girlfriend?"

I dissolve into laughter. The question is absurd.

"I already am, you doofus." I swat at his chest, and then dab at my eye. "I've been your girlfriend since the day we were born."

The smile that blooms on his lips is pure joy and warmth. "And I need you until the day we die."

I laugh again. Applause swells around us as another speaker comes or goes, but it sort of feels like they're clapping for us. I have no idea what's going on anymore. Just that Grayson is here, and he's all I need. Life is fine. Life is *perfect*.

"So you've already planned for us to die on the same day?" I tease.

"I know that's how it'll work." He's started swaying slightly. "I won't let you win. You'll try to make me lose. So we'll end up going on the same day. And that's all right. Because I'm not planning on spending a single day without you, babe."

More tears arrive. They're streaming down my face now, prompted mostly by the emotional onslaught but also a little by the early champagne.

Because he's right.

That's how we've always been.

And God help me, I hope that's how we always stay.

EPILOGUE

ONE YEAR LATER

HAZEL

It's another humid September ninth, except this year, we're not decked out and heading downtown for the ball. No, this year, Grayson and I are celebrating our birthdays *and* our one year-ish anniversary with a good old-fashioned tennis battle.

And believe me. I'm here to win.

We saunter up to the courts behind the high school with mischievous looks on our faces. I've brought his birthday gift with me to distract him and secure my birthday victory. He glances down at the blue and white striped box in my arms every so often.

"When can I open it?" he asks.

"After I beat you," I inform him.

"I wanted to open it *this year*," he says, a smile ghosting his lips.

"Ha ha," I intone. "You'll be opening it in a matter of *minutes*. And what about my gift? You didn't even bring it."

"No, it came along." He sniffs, looking toward the horizon. "You'll see it when it's time."

The cryptic answer drives me wild. I want to know *now*, but I've got to keep my head in the game. We've had a lovely birthday so far, starting with our usual weekend slow sex in the morning, followed by coffee, followed by a jog around the neighborhood, followed by pancakes.

We moved into Grayson's house about six months ago. After he came to live in Bayshore, we decided that my house made more sense while he finished renovating his. But once it was done, neither of us could ignore how much we wanted to live there. Besides, he's got the better view of the lake. And the balcony he rehabbed is too perfect. We spend almost every summer night up there, drinking wine or reading books.

Life has never been better.

Life finally feels *complete*.

The tennis courts are empty as we roll up. Before he struts over to his side, I hand over the gift. My heart is racing. "Open it now."

He pumps his arm and digs in. He removes the wrapping paper in one slick tug, and soon he's staring at the cardboard box I stuffed his gift in. He eyes me, carefully opening it. And then he slides the main feature out of its hiding spot.

He blinks, his gaze sliding over the piece. It's a cross-stitch I commissioned. Slowly, the smile blossoms on his face.

It says, "My love for you is like a cockroach." And there's a cross-stitched cartoon rendition of the insect. Much cuter than in real life. That was my input.

He laughs once and then again. Pretty soon he's cracking up.

"Do you like it?" I bound over to look at it beside him. "My love for you will survive anything. Ten years of absence. Complete neglect. Even wild misunderstandings from high school."

Grayson is beaming. He leans in to kiss me, and we make out a little in the middle of the tennis courts. When I feel the sun prickling at the tops of my shoulders, I realize we need to get this show on the road. Besides, I want to see when my gift will appear. I've been curious for weeks.

Once the cockroach cross-stitch is safely tucked away, we launch into a brutal game. Any goodwill I might have accumulated with my perfect gift dissolves under the intensity of our competition. We dart back and forth, grunting like animals, the only sound the scuffing of our shoes and the *thwunk* of the ball volleying back and forth.

He wins the first set. I win the second. Of course, we're tied. Like always. But toward the end of the third set, something changes. Grayson taps out. The wind goes out of him, and he drops his racket. The ball soars past him and out of bounds. He rests his palms behind his head and stares at me, chest heaving.

I blink, instantly miffed. "What the hell was that?"

He grins a little, walking toward the net in the center of the court.

"You dropped your racket and *stopped playing*," I explain. "I win by default, but that—" I point at the ball in the far-left corner of the court. "That was not an earned win."

Grayson still hasn't said anything. He stops at the net.

"What is wrong with you?" I demand, storming up to him. As soon as I arrive, he drops to one knee. It takes me a minute to understand what's happening. He rummages in the pocket of his mesh shorts and then produces a mystifyingly tiny black box. When he looks up at me, shiny faced and smiling, it still doesn't click.

"Hazel," he starts, and that's when I realize what's going on here. My eyes turn to saucers. He pops open the box.

A diamond the size of a molar stares back at me, and I clamp a hand over my mouth, stumbling backward.

"Hazel, you and I both know that we are the perfect match for each other. And this tennis game is the last one you'll ever win by default. Because I promise to never go easy on you. As long as you promise me the same. I want to spend the rest of my life with you, babe. Matching you. Growing with you. Loving you." His grin widens, and that's when I notice the tears in his eyes. "Will you marry me?"

My mouth parts, and all the air in my body has vanished. Somehow, though, I find the sense to answer him.

"Yes," I whisper, my voice raw. "Are you fucking kidding me? Of course!" He captures me in a hug and whoops. I cling to him, the tennis net caught between us. But it doesn't matter. It deserves a spot in this as much as we do. Tears stream down my cheeks, and it will be a while before I can find words.

All I know is that this man in my arms is the only one for me. And we're about to continue the adventure that we started thirty years ago. The one that everyone knew we were destined for. Everyone except us.

Life has never been better.

But we'll keep trying to see how much better it can get.

THE END

Ready for MORE Daly Brothers? Don't worry, there are still four brothers left. Next up? *Make Me Fall (http://books2read.com/mak e-me-fall)*, Connor's story, a fake romance with the daughter of the rival Cabana family.

Want even MORE brothers? Get to know the Fairchild brothers in an intense and steamy billionaire romance series, *The Bad Boys of Wall Street.* Start with the first book, *The Price of Revenge (htt p://books2read.com/price-of-revenge),* as Axel Fairchild reunites with his first—and only—love, Cora Margulis, 8 years after she broke his heart and married someone else.

DON'T MISS 'MAKE ME FALL' (BAYSHORE #2)

CHAPTER ONE

KINSLEY

"Are you kidding me? I'm gonna need to see some ID."

The warning bark of the bartender makes me grit my teeth. He's acting like I'm a sixteen-year-old sneaking into the bar to inhale shots of RumChata.

But he's got it all wrong. I'm a twenty-five-year-old who is legally seeking shots of RumChata, because I've earned it after my work week.

"Here, hang on." I fumble with my purse, which also looks like something a sixteen-year-old might buy while posing as an adult. It was from a thrift store near my apartment, which specializes in forgotten goods from the eighties. The overly large pearl snap pops free and shoots across the bar like a fifty-cent firework.

I get carded a lot, so you'd think I'd be used to having to prove my baby face. But no. Today, I'm fucking over it.

My license won't come out of the hardened plastic cover of my snap wallet, which also has an entire section available for checks. I don't carry checks, so instead I shove interesting business cards in the flap. One flutters out—a funny sex shop I stumbled across recently, *Spankin' Trails*. I look like a total mess, and I know it.

"Look." I shove the whole wallet his way, and he peers at it like he's never seen a license in his life.

"Fakes are getting pretty good these days," he mumbles, then pushes it back my way. "You don't look a day over twelve."

I huff and roll my eyes. "Come on. I might look young, but I'm not prepubescent, for God's sake. So come on. RumChata, buddy."

He side-eyes me while he stomps off to prepare my drink, like he's trying to figure out my game. This is no game. This is one hundred percent Kinsley: stumbling, gangly, baby-faced Kinsley.

I sigh and relax into the high-backed barstool. I came here for one express purpose—to forget the hell that is my job—but now, I can't get past the hell that is my life outside of work.

I've been on the west coast for almost eight years. Since I left Bayshore at age eighteen to study at UCLA, I've been cultivating the Californian side of my Ohio-based DNA. And really, things started out great. College was wild and fun. I got a degree. I found an amazing job. But then…things went south. Like all the way down to Antarctica south.

My dream job turned into professional purgatory. My apartment rent skyrocketed, because #SanDiego. And then I realized that all my peers were maturing in some other universe. My contoured contemporaries look like gorgeous aliens compared to my plain, un-mascara'd Midwestern features. I don't know how to catch up, and more importantly, I'm not sure if I want to. And more than that, the only man I ever dared to date turned out to be only a touch more stable than the type of men you might see on those true crime shows.

How can I be twenty-five and already as lost as an octogenarian with an iPhone? All the inspirational memes imploring me to *Live Truthfully* and *Be Your Authentic Self* just piss me off. How can I be truthful and authentic *and* make my rent?

I guess this is what they call the quarter-life crisis.

Great.

Voices murmur quietly around me in this lounge. It's the closest bar to my workplace, and I've been here a few times before. Never with Burly the Bartender though. He must be new. This is the type of fancy place which has wood floors and mirrors along the walls. So everyone can see how rich and powerful they are while sipping the sweet nectars that distract us from our terrible jobs.

If this isn't the definition of #adulting, I don't know what is.

Burly finally comes back with my RumChata—*thankyouverymuch*—and I sip quietly, finally feeling some of the tension leaving my shoulders. Ahh, this is the life. Coaxing myself into forgetfulness about my stifling boss before I go home, alone, to my overpriced apartment and lack of social life.

One of the nearby tables, a cluster of businessmen, breaks up with a flurry of platitudes and good-natured shoulder clapping. They were here when I came in, and as they disperse, one of the biz bros catches my eye.

He's broad-shouldered, and even his gray button-down can't hide the fact that he's built beneath his clothes. A dimpled grin steals my breath as he turns my way.

I know this face.

He's Connor Daly. That blond and toned hunk who works at the same company as me. One of the infamous Daly brothers from back home. The man who the sixteen-year-old drinking RumChata inside of me is suddenly squealing over.

Instead of leaving with the rest of his business squad, Connor heads for the bar. The smile drops from his chiseled jaw, and something raw pours out of him. He probably doesn't notice me spying. I blend into anything eighties themed, as well as most lounge spaces. I can't pry my gaze off him as he slides onto a barstool about five seats down from me. The bartender serves him immediately, no crap given about his age, and pretty soon, Connor has three shots lined up in front of him.

Now, I'm really curious. Connor has always been the golden boy, even back in our school days. I didn't see him all the time, since he was a grade ahead of me, but it's as true now as it was then. Back in the days when I fawned over him, it was because he delivered good-natured lectures about not drinking and driving. And now, I fawn over him because he's one of the top developers at our company.

He tosses back a shot. And then another. After the third one is downed, I can't resist the urge to know more. I pick up my hard-sided purse and shuffle his way.

He doesn't seem to notice me. Which is whatever. Nobody really does anymore. Not since college. It's the theme of my adulthood—no longer a girl, but somehow not a woman. I don't know what the secret code is that all females received, but the package never showed up at my door, despite being promised two-day delivery.

I clear my throat as I settle into my spot and flag down the bartender. He shows up a moment later.

"Another RumChata, please." I pause, glancing over at Connor. "And whatever he had there, two more of those."

Connor snorts, and his unfocused gaze swings my way. He has the same electric blue eyes as the rest of his brothers, which is the sort of blue that will land most people a modeling deal in these parts. It's almost painful to meet his gaze. His handsomeness is foreboding.

Like he's going to break my heart, and I don't know it yet. Even though that's impossible.

Connor would never be with someone like me.

How do I know this? Because he's with my boss. And that evil witch is my opposite. So, thanks to math, we know scientifically, he is incapable of being with someone like me.

"Are you buying me another shot?" he asks, and the tang of rum reaches me. I shrug.

"Seems like you're lamenting something. I am too. Why not lament together?"

My heart is racing. God, it's hard work to sound casual. But maybe this is the start of my new journey as a real woman. Striking up conversations at the bar with my disgruntled colleague and former heartthrob. I'm pretty sure Connor and I haven't exchanged more than thirty words in our lifetime, but that doesn't matter. I'm here to push that count up to forty.

Connor heaves a long, drawn out sigh. "My grandma died."

I wince. "Oh, shit. I'm really sorry to hear that." I pinch the bridge of my nose, trying to search out her name in my memory banks. I don't know much about the Dalys, other than the following: all of the brothers are stupidly hot; and all of the brothers are stupidly off-limits.

My parents got into it with Connor's parents a billion years ago, and nobody has gotten over it. I grew up knowing the Dalys were a bad bunch without ever really knowing why. But that doesn't matter to me. We're in San Diego. My parents won't see me unless I accidentally FaceTime, which I've actually done during a make-out session before. I'll fraternize with the devil if I want to. Especially if he's built like an Abercrombie model turned software nerd.

"She had dementia really bad," Connor says, and he sounds choked, fighting emotion. I frown, scooting closer to him. I resist the urge to sling my arm over his shoulders.

"That's the worst," I offer. "Did you just find out?"

He shakes his head. "At work earlier, but I had this meeting right after."

"Ah. So it's still...fresh."

Burly returns with our shots, and I push one immediately over to Connor. I lift mine in the air, gesturing it toward him as if to ask, *Ready?* He nods and picks it up.

Then his gaze swings up to meet mine. Electricity doesn't just spark, it damn near fries my bones to dust. My forearms go hot, and I wonder if he felt that too. Or maybe this is my teenaged unrequited love acting up again.

We take the shots with a grimace. Once he slams the glass to the bar top, he clutches at the front of his hair.

"I have to go back to Bayshore."

I nod, studying the dark blond hairs at his neckline. "I haven't been there in ages," I say.

What does the man look like under this business-casual attire? I've caught his shirt unbuttoned down to the third button on two occasions, but usually it's unbuttoned two down. Not that I keep track of this in a spreadsheet. *Anymore*, I mean.

He blinks a few times, and then, he's watching me again. Something churns behind those eyes, but I can't meet his gaze long enough to figure it out.

He snorts, and then he reaches out, wrapping an arm around my shoulders. He brings me into him, like a side hug.

"My Bayshore buddy," he croons. He squeezes my shoulder again, which sends heat tiptoeing between my legs. I want to pretend this is a romantic grab, but it's not. He's jostling me like he's greeting a frat brother after years apart.

I laugh nervously, and he leans in, his eyes sparkling.

When he opens his mouth to speak, the blunt rum force reaches me before his words. "You should come with me."

KEEP READING at
http://books2read.com/make-me-fall

AUTHOR'S NOTE

The choppy waters of Lake Erie in the summertime are a special sort of haven, shrieking sea gulls and all. This series is set in a fictionalized mixture of my hometown and a neighboring town in northern Ohio. Writing this series has become a love song to my homeland.

Even though I grew up mostly critical of my little slice of the world (like most moody, dissatisfied teens—HA!), I now recognize it for what it is: a gorgeous spot in the Midwestern landscape, one that is capable of producing all the love and emotion and depth that a romance author could hope for.

I sincerely hope you enjoy this visit to Bayshore...and I hope you'll continue this journey with the brothers of the Daly family!

STAY CONNECTED

Stay connected with me via my newsletter (http://bit.ly/EL-news letter), where I share teasers, sales, and other exciting news. (Plus, if you haven't heard, I have an MMA romance series available, and **you'll get the prequel novella FOR FREE** when you sign up to my newsletter).

Or join my reader group, EMBER'S BLOSSOMS, to hang out up-close and personal! Early looks at new covers, exclusive access to ARC sign-ups, and more.

FACEBOOK

INSTAGRAM

GOODREADS

BOOKBUB

http://www.emberleighromance.com/

***

And before you go...

Please consider leaving an honest review about this book! Even just a few words or a line mean so much to us authors.

ALSO BY EMBER LEIGH

THE BAD BOYS OF WALL STREET
The Price of Revenge
The Price of Passion
The Price of Infamy
The Price of Forever

WINTER HARBOR
(co-written with Whitley Cox)
The Bastard Heir
The Asshole Heir
The Rebel Heir
The Matchmaking Heirs

THE BAYSHORE SERIES
Make Me Lose
Make Me Fall
Make Me Yours
Make Me Choose
Make Me Hot

Make Me Smile

THE BREAKING SERIES
Breaking the Rules
Changing the Game
Breaking the Sinner
Breaking the Habit
Breaking the Fall

www.ingramcontent.com/pod-product-compliance
Lightning Source LLC
Chambersburg PA
CBHW032242310726
48973CB00008B/2249